Goodbye to Yesterday

By

Alfred Brady Moore

To:
Esther Brace,
Thanks for your
support. Best Wishes
to you.

Alfred Moore
"Al"

7-18-03

This book is a work of fiction. Places, events, and situations in this story are purely fictional. Any resemblance to actual persons, living or dead, is coincidental.

ISBN: 1-4033-5757-9 (e-book)
ISBN: 1-4033-5758-7 (Paperback)

Library of Congress Control Number: 2002093527

This book is printed on acid free paper.

Printed in the United States of America
Bloomington, IN

1st Books - rev. 02/28/03

Acknowledgements

I thank God for giving me the vision, will power, and strength to complete this book. Special thanks to my mother, Katie Bertha Moore, for teaching me common sense and humility. To my father, the late James Moore, for teaching me good work ethics. Thanks to my brothers and sister, who supported me over the years: Dorothy, Benjamin, Elwood, Linwood, and Lutis. To my wife Connie for believing in me.

Many thanks to Leslie Johnson, my typist, proofreader, and chief advocate. To H. Michael Harvey for the reminiscences; to writer Angela Benson, who acquainted me with the late Nora Deloach, who in turn advised me to attend a writers' conference. I'm thankful for the joy of our children: Malcolm, Marcus, Liva and Iman.

To my first readers, thank you all: Arthur Anderson, Phyllis Banks, Fred Cleveland, Richard Conley, Kim Prillerman and Maxine Walker.

Thanks to the many teachers who encouraged me or had a positive influence on me (some are no longer with us): the late Corine Mahogany, elementary school; Mrs. Agnes Lowe and Mr. Lester Mason, high school; in college, Ms. Glynn Agnes Barr, Dr. Joan LaFontaine, Dr. Robert L. Judkins, and Dr. H. Frank Leftwitch. Also, my grandfather, the late Brady Moore taught me a few things about life. I would be remiss not to mention the late Reverend Marion Wiggins, Jr., Team owner and manager, who brought organized baseball to our little country community. To all my friends, I love you all.

Dedication

This book is dedicated to my wife, Constance Pearce
Johnson Moore.

Part 1

To Follow a Trail

Prologue

A young black man, wearing a navy blue skullcap and a beige trench coat, paced back and forth outside a glass-enclosed phone booth. The door of the phone booth opened and closed like a school bus door. Inside, an elderly white woman in a long black coat, held provisions in a brown shopping bag and talked into the phone. It was a windy afternoon in February, during the days of the early 70's.

Out beyond the parking meters, in the center of the town square, stood a bronze statue of a Confederate General, a man on a horse. The previous Spring, black student demonstrators spray painted the statue black. When the woman exited the phone booth, she avoided eye contact with the impatient stranger.

The young man closed the booth door, dialed a number, and talked low. "Hey man, it's me. Don't say my name out."

"What's going on, Ja—?"

"I said don't say my name out loud. I don't want nobody to know it's me. These telephone people—you know what I mean? I'm calling you from Alabama."

"I thought you was playing ball down there. What's going on?"

"I got a job I need you to handle. You need to get here in two days. I'm gone pay you for your time and travel."

"Man, I ain't lost nothing in Alabama."

"Look, this is important. Remember how I saved your ass down on the south side? Well, you owe me, man. I need you here. I've been kicked out of school. Ain't playing ball no more, and my weed business been interfered with. Some dude sold me out and I want you to take care of him."

"Damn, how bad can it be on a college campus? You said take care of him. How much? Rough him up a little bit, break his legs, or 'off' him?"

"I want you to 'off' the bastard! Now, get a pencil and I'll tell you what do."

Chapter 1
A Good Send Off

I really wanted to put it all behind me. The second half of my senior year was a bust. An off-campus mishap had left me wounded and scarred, and I wished I could've summoned up a mental lapse to forget about it. If a memory lapse failed me, then a case of amnesia would've served me well. Of course I've never heard of a real person suffering from amnesia. Don't get me wrong, a college campus in a small town out in the middle of nowhere, is probably the safest, most crime-free place you can live. My troubles happened off campus—trespassing on private property and carrying on a complicated affair.

It was a given that I make good grades, graduate on time, and find a good job. Other than that, all I wanted to do was have a good season on the baseball team and keep things going good with my girlfriend. But that was not to be. Maybe that's the mistake I made—only wanting everything to be *good*. The concept of great or excellent never entered into my mind.

With graduation out of the way and the summer gone, I chose to put some distance and time between me and Waukeegan, Alabama. Within a week, I would be a Peace Corps volunteer in West Africa. I almost succeeded in saying goodbye senior year, goodbye early 70's. Then came a phone call, and now this re-visit.

My former roommate, Leonardo, prevailed upon me, rather he put me on a guilt trip. Destination—right back on campus to the first football game of the season. The music department had planned a memorial

1

tribute for the half-time show in honor of a friend of ours who had recently passed. His folks at home had called him "Junior" and he was the Band announcer and narrator last year.

"Porch, it's your duty to be there, man. He was our friend," Leonardo reminded me. "I know you were out of town visiting your kinfolks and missed the funeral and everything, but this is your opportunity to make things right. Get past all that stuff you went through. You came out alright in the end, didn't you? So, I can count on you to be there, right?" He said it a second time. "Right?"

After much tension, sweating palms, rapid heartbeats, and just plain old scaredness, I approached the ticket booth in the midst of the Saturday afternoon crowd. The attendant gave me a ticket and asked if I received the correct change. "Right," I answered.

I only returned to campus because Leonardo asked me, and our friendship of the past two years carried some weight. We'd helped each other out of a few jams. Loyalty, at least counted for something.

My apprehension to return to Waukeegan had nothing to do with the guilt I felt over Junior's demise. My greatest fear was that if I didn't leave Alabama now, something might happen to trap me here forever—a job, a wife and family, a whole lot of debt, or just any one thing that might tie me down. I was free and broke and had no debt. A voice inside my head warned me: "Calvin Porch, you better get out while you can." If I was ever going to see any other part of the world, I'd better do it now, or forever hold my peace. I didn't want to be like Lot's wife from Sodom and Gomorrah, who looked back and turned into a pillar of salt, frozen in time. I was running hard, remembering the old saying by the baseball legend, Satchel Paige: "Don't look back. Somebody may be gaining on you."

I remember vividly how Junior used to set the mood for the band's performance. He invited me up once and I watched him as he sat at the press box table in front of a microphone, wearing an earphone headset. He took on the personality of an R&B radio disc jockey: "Alright, my fellow Tigers, this is just what you've been waiting for. Come go with us on a magical trip to Loveland! Watch the precision, the steps, and the dance movements—guaranteed to get you moving and grooving. And, if you think that's something, you ain't seen nothing yet. Come on, Marching 100's, do your thang! Show 'em what you can do!"

Lately, I've found out a lot of things about him that I didn't know before—his favorite song, some of his hobbies, the family nickname "Junior." These facts were printed in the game souvenir program. Sorry, Buddy, I didn't know all of that before, I said to myself. Wish I had asked you more questions.

The Summer warmth still clung to the air. Green leaves on the trees and shrubbery in front of campus buildings gave no hint of Autumn. Our stadium stood in a gulch on the south corner of campus, down the hill from the gymnasium, where on three sides, the bleachers blended into the hillside. Big time colleges with giant bowl stadiums had to work at creating anything similar. This stadium, seating less than six thousand fans, is the home of the Waukeegan Tigers, a team with a history of more wins than losses within a mediocre football conference, a big fish in a small pond.

As I walked among the football fans, it came back to my mind that I still had the pistol locked in the car. Earlier during the morning, I greased and oiled the gun, wiped it off with a soft white cloth, and rubbed the smooth surfaces and indentations of the brown-handled, blue-black metal handiwork, and I weighed and balanced it in my hand just to enjoy the feel of it. I put it in a brown paper bag and laid it under the seat on the driver's side of my borrowed car. During the Spring, I had planned to use the gun, but never got the opportunity. You see, I got shot while hanging out with some friends at a Mansion. I sustained two bullet wounds—one on the left shoulder and another one on the left cheek of my butt. The police concluded that it all happened under mysterious circumstances, but I wasn't too sure of that.

My thinking was quite clear, now. After the half-time show I'll leave the stadium and dispose of the gun. I didn't need it any more. Haven't for quite some time. But back in February when I was lying in a hospital bed, I had vowed in front of my parents and my little bother, that if the police failed to capture the man who shot me, I'd find him myself. In retrospect, it was such a ridiculous notion. Even my twelve-year old kid brother had quipped that it sounded like something out of the movies.

Unlike my undergraduate days when I sat on the home side of the stadium, for today's game, I sat on the opposing team's side of the field. In some distant way I felt I didn't belong here any more. The events of the last semester put an end to those collegian-devil-may-care days.

Then, I focused on the band down on the field. The musicians dressed in maroon-colored uniforms, with gold stripes down their outer pants legs and gold embroidery on the cuffs of their sleeves and across their chests. They created a flashy sight every time they turned or made a sharp dip. Some of them had golden horns, while others had silver ones. There had been times when the band's well-rehearsed formations, coupled with the right song, and the narrator's voice, made us believe we had the best band in the land.

The band formed the human outline of two shoes, and tap-danced to the tune of "Mr. Bo Jangles," Junior's favorite song. The dancing shoes looked like the old wooden shoes made in Holland.

Though I sat among four thousand fans, I felt that the gun had linked me to Junior forever; even though several months and hundreds of miles had passed between us by the time he met his end. Because the gun had passed through a few hands like a baton in a relay race, I felt that everyone who had touched it, contributed to Junior's demise. Me, even more so, because I possessed the weapon early in the relay and ended up holding it for safekeeping, long after the event was over. If a judge in a black robe, armed with a gavel heard the extent of my involvement, he would shout guilty and slam the wooden hammer hard on my fingers. I knew even before I got to the game that I would bury the gun after the half-time tribute. It was about time to drop this hot potato out of my hands.

When the band in concert formation played the spiritual song "Deep River," I felt a soothing, warm peace in my chest, even a quiet sigh of relief. Then a surge of emotion wailed up inside of my chest. I swallowed hard in a speechless gulp. I felt my eyes moisten. It was time to fight back the tears before the floodgate opened. Looking straight ahead, I was able to keep the tide at bay. Who said 'a man ain't supposed to cry?' I took a handkerchief and dabbed both eyes, never looking to the right or left. Why was I feeling ashamed of crying? Sorry to disappoint you, Junior, I said to myself. You were more expressive than I am.

To envision the words and meaning of that song, *Deep River*, was like imagining escaped slaves crossing a deep river to safety and finding joy and happiness among their loved ones who waited at a campground on the other side. This song from its inception impressed upon our ancestors—Negro slaves, and our present souls—a journey like crossing over the Jordan River to the promised land, a land of milk and honey, where everyday is Sunday, a place to rest, to study war no more, hallelujah! In essence, it was like crossing over to heaven. I inhaled and exhaled, sucking in and releasing air in a full sigh. Well, Junior, they gave you a good send-off.

The horn players, with their instruments tilted upward and straight ahead, bent backwards and played to the skies. Then the men and women in the maroon uniforms marched off the field in an upbeat tempo, playing a John Phillip Sousa March, hinting that the moment and the mood sought, had been reached and was now over. With that, the band transitioned into a quick drum cadence and dashed off the field, returning us back to the present, where the football game was again the matter at hand.

The coaches stood on the sideline. Coach John Benson, assistant football coach and head baseball coach, was absent. Maybe he no longer worked here. I wondered what happened to him. I'd played Baseball under him for the past three seasons. Why in the hell was I thinking about him? I was probably one of the last persons he would rather see right now. To make a long story short, I scored a big play that worked out well for me, but it made him look bad and bruised his ego. So he held a grudge against me, benched me and limited my playing time in an attempt to run me off.

As the Football game resumed, I thought to myself, let me get out of here now. I don't need to get delayed by someone I know who might want to carry on a lengthy conversation. It's going to be time consuming enough with the small talk and greetings I'm going to have to make, just to get from this seat back to my car. But there were other things I still had to do before leaving Waukeegan, Alabama. First, I'd cruise around campus while it was still quiet and look over the old buildings one last time to permanently etch them in my mind. I may never pass this way again. Second, I needed to hurl the gun into the deep, nearby Tallapoosa River.

Chapter 2
Gone With the Wind

As I look back on the day I got shot, I remember it as a day that started out with a lot of promise. It happened on a Saturday afternoon after Baseball practice ended abruptly for me and Aaron Aldrich. We collided on the field chasing after a fly ball and were both knocked in a daze. Coach Benson sent us up to the gym to be rubbed with ice packs. He released us from practice with instructions to take aspirins if the pain kept up. "Hell, if Aaron had stayed on his side of the damn field, none of this would've happened."

It wasn't all bad that I got shot. I learned a few things. Never mind that I had a disappointing season on the baseball team. The feud I had with Coach Benson pretty much consumed the whole season. It didn't even have to be that way. I didn't feel that I had done anything wrong. He just wanted to use his power and authority to keep me in check. Along with that, my attempt to rekindle the flames with an old girlfriend fizzled as well. In the end, I learned something about the fairness of 'love and war.' I learned that in the real adult world, each individual player in a scenario is responsible for his or her own part, and cannot claim innocence if the outcome turns out ugly.

When entering campus from the east, the first building in sight is Parkersburg Hall, an old brick, windowless, one-story cottage on the right side of the road. But the Mansion, the place where I got shot, stands on the opposite side of the road, less than a quarter of a mile east of Parkersburg Hall.

In front of the Mansion, a stretch of ground, approximately sixty-five yards wide and a hundred and fifty yards deep, lay between woods on the right and left sides. The lawn, when not maintained, looked like an overgrown crop field after the harvest.

An asphalt track, barely large enough for one car to pass, snaked its way from the main road to a battleship-gray painted mansion that stood partially visible behind the shaded oak trees aligning the front of the building. The roof of this antebellum home had a slate roof the color and texture of red brick.

It was precisely on this property—posted "No Trespassing"—that I experienced something I'll never forget. How did I go from a Saturday morning baseball practice to a crime scene on the grounds of a Mansion? Simple, according to the police—"you three were trespassing in the wrong place at the wrong time." You three meant me, a girl named Hollie and a guy named Bakarie.

I'd earned some idle time—combat R&R for taking part in that collision with Aaron on the ball field. Once released by the team trainer, I left the gym. Still not quite myself, I had given the ice packs and aspirins enough time to give me some relief.

The collision: I hadn't been on the field twenty minutes when it happened. Shortly after the warm-up laps and stretching exercises, batting practice started. The pitchers ran laps in the outfield near the homerun fence. When I was not warming up pitchers or catching batting practice, I went into the outfield to shag balls with the other players, while waiting my turn to bat. While most of the veteran players wore a combination of the school's maroon and gold colors, this morning I

9

was unable to wash and dry my standard outfit in time for practice, and had dressed out in a navy blue sweat suit with a white short-sleeved T-shirt worn over the blue long-sleeved sweatshirt. Aaron Aldrich, always one to wear his own choice of colors, had dressed similarly in navy blue sweatpants and a white Baseball undershirt that had long navy blue sleeves, so our torsos were clothed in white and out legs and arms in blue. Both of us had on our Waukeegan-issued maroon caps.

On a particularly hard hit line drive ball in the air to right center field, there was no time to yell out "I got it" or "You take it!" Aaron and I dashed into a head-on collision. Aaron was a skinny, brown-skinned athlete, who wore black-framed, tinted lens eyeglasses. Because he didn't eat meat, someone on the team nicked-named him "Streak-o-lean." He didn't like the nickname, but it stuck. The more he got upset with the teasing, the more the nickname flourished. Aaron couldn't beat up everybody, so he had to accept the acquired label.

My forehead banged into Aaron's forehead on his left side above his eyeglasses. After the fray of glasses, caps, gloves, and arms in all directions, the recoil and thump of the blow landed us both on the ground, dazed and momentarily disoriented.

The whole baseball team dropped everything and rushed to the outfield. Their questions added to my already groggy state of being: "Are you alright?" "Can you get up?" "Can you see my hand?" "Do you feel any pain?" "Move your hands. Move your legs. Can you walk?" "What's my name?" "What's your name?" "How many fingers do you see?"

The guys helped us both to our feet and carried us off the field.

Wesley Knuckles was one of the team captains. We called him "Deacon West," because he had the demeanor of a Baptist preacher in a church prayer meeting. Sometimes we called him "Brer Deek." Other times we called him just plain "Deek." We couldn't call him Rev or Reb, because we already had a real preacher on the team—a young kid that transferred to Waukeegan a year before. When Deacon West led us in the team cheer in the huddle before we ran on the field to start a game, he always used his trademark speech to fire us up. Married, with a toddler son, Deacon West, an Army veteran, was a few years older than the seniors on the team.

Coach Benson instructed Deacon West and R. P. Willingham, the team Trainer, to take us two hard heads up to the gym. R. P. put ice packs on our heads and gave us some aspirins.

Deacon West had a car, and he drove it to the field to practice everyday. He drove the car calmly and deliberately slow. The gym was about a block and a half from the baseball diamond.

"Give us the speech, Deek," I said. "I feel like charging onto the field. I feel like playing a game."

"You ain't in no shape to play nobody," he said. "You sound like you're out of your head. Boy, I'll tell you, y'all looked like the Doublemint Chewing Gum twins on a T.V. commercial, out there laying on the ground."

"I don't feel like playing at all," Aaron said.

"Give us the speech, Deek, come on!"

"Brer Deek, you might as well give him the speech," R. P. advised. "Porch might talk himself sicker if you don't."

"Alright. Here goes: Calvin Coolidge once said— 'Nothing in the world can take the place of persistence. Talent will not; nothing is more common than unsuccessful men with talent. Genius will not; unrewarded genius is almost a proverb. Education will not; the world is full of educated derelicts. Persistence and determination alone are omnipotent.'"

"But the slogan Press on," Deacon West preached, "has solved, and always will solve, the problems of mankind. All For One!" he cheered. "One For All. God For Us All! Yea-ea-yeah!"

When he gave this spirited, pre-game speech, I felt that we could win any game we played. It was better than anything the coach had come up with.

Once I received the ice pack and the aspirins from the trainer, I felt better. I headed up to the Library to tell my friend Bakarie that it was no need for him to come over to the ball field, since I had been dismissed from practice early.

I met Hollie Drummond on the steps of the library. She had a varnish brown skin tone and was fond of wearing bell-bottom jeans and assorted sweatshirts to go with her long Afro hair-do. This was one consistency she had maintained since our freshman year. A social activist, she had participated in a number of student protests. Last Spring she was involved with a group that spray painted the Waukeegan Confederate statue on the town square with black paint. She was proud that she got arrested. Of course, her parents got her out of jail without it going on her record.

Now, we were seniors. I hadn't had an extended conversation with her in three years. I had only greeted her in passing. Sometimes she was with the small clique of girls she associated with and other times, she hung out with the boyfriend that was current at the time.

"Hey, Hollie, what's happening?"

"Oh, Hi Calvin. How have you been?"

"I could say I'm alright, but that would be a lie. I'm okay, though."

"What's the matter?" Hollie asked with the same old smile and concern she used to show.

"I'll be alright. It's nothing. Well, my head is throbbing. But not as much as it was." I took off the maroon baseball cap and showed her the tender spot above my forehead.

We stood on the lawn, just off the sidewalk to allow passers by to go in and out of the library. We remained within two feet of the hedges that aligned the three-story, red brick building. It was like a visit among two old friends who hadn't seen each other for awhile, as if time and distance had separated us, when in reality, we could've seen each other every day if both of us had deemed it so. I would've spoken, if there had been anything more to say. I held both of her hands in mine, and we both felt comfortable, grinning and chatting like three years hadn't passed at all.

"About an hour ago, I collided with a teammate while chasing after a fly ball. It almost knocked us both unconscious. Aaron Aldrich got it worse because it broke his glasses. Before I came by here, I had been in the locker room holding an ice pack to my head. It's no big deal, though." I changed the subject. "So when are you going to loan me your car?"

"Anytime you need it, Calvin. Just ask me."

Hollie drove a Volkswagen that her parents had given her the previous semester. I had seen her boyfriend driving the canary yellow car a couple of weeks before, and I had heard it through the grapevine that Hollie had broken up with the guy. But I wouldn't be the one to bring it up.

"You would do that?"

"Sure, why not? You're my 'homeboy.' We have to look out for each other. It's just so comforting to talk to you. I don't know why I haven't talked to you more."

"Really?" my question went unanswered. She kept talking.

"My parents have moved again. That's two times since our freshman year. That's the military for you. So my dad gave me this yellow beetle last semester. He was in no position to move two cars at the time. So I've been through a lot of changes lately. Enough about me. How are you? How are you really, Calvin?"

Before I could answer, Hollie spoke again. "Oh, it's swollen. There's a little red knot there. You poor baby. Is there anything I can do?"

"You could kiss me and make it better," I said. What had gotten into me? That off-the-cuff remark might get me slapped, instead of kissed, relying on sympathy for my misfortune.

"Alright." Surprisingly she kissed me on the center of my forehead, in the spot away from the injured place.

"That was nice."

"There's more," she added. Then she gave me a quick, pecking kiss on the mouth.

"Maybe I should get hit in the head more often."

"You don't have to do that," Hollie said.

"Very nice, very nice! What a cute couple you make." Bakarie Seesay, a West African student, greeted us as he came out of the library. "Hello, Porch. And, how are you today, Hollie?"

"I'm alright. How are you, Professor?"

"Professor? You two know each other?"

"Of course. I met Hollie at a party one Saturday night. She thought I was a college professor."

"Because of his accent and the way he dresses," Hollie added.

"Don't let those tweed sport coats and dress shirts fool you," I assured her. "He's just an old man, that's all."

Like many students from developing countries at that time, the convoluted and disjointed path of secondary education, coupled with the cost and clearance of getting a passport, and waiting to travel, caused for Bakarie, a delay that aged him five years beyond the average age of the typical U.S. citizen beginning college.

"Rather than call it old age, call it wisdom," Bakarie said. True to his image at other times, today, he wore a gray tweed sports coat, a white dress shirt with no necktie, black trousers, and black shoes.

How's Adelaide doing?"

"Oh, she's doing great, Hollie."

"I'm sorry about that incident."

"What incident?" I asked.

"Oh, it's a long story," Bakarie said. "Professor Mansaray and I almost came to blows. He didn't want me to have anything to do with his daughter, Adelaide. Our two tribes back home are fighting a civil war against each other. He's more accepting now that he sees I'm not going to stop seeing her. It's touch and go. His mood changes from one moment to another. I'm sure he's not finished with me yet."

"It sounds like the feud between the Capulets' and the Montagues'," I said.

"What's that?"

"You know, the families in Romeo and Juliet!"

"Oh, yes. Similar, but Adelaide and I are nowhere near the point of committing suicide. We would never do that. That's where the similarities end." Then he changed the subject. "I was just heading over to the field to watch the baseball team practice. So you finished early?"

"This is another long story," I said. "I'm trying to get my 'home girl' here to take me for a ride in her car."

"Where do you want to go?" Hollie asked.

"How about we go over to the old Mansion and look around. Even though it's posted 'no trespassing,' I've heard it's a good place to sneak around and check out while they're closed for renovations. Then after that, we could go and hang out at the Dairy Bar."

"Yeah, okay. That sounds alright. Professor, do you want to come along with us?"

"I won't be in the way, will I?"

"Of course not," Hollie said.

So we were off to a sightseeing excursion that would end with us dining on milk shakes and hamburgers.

Chapter 3
I'll Be There, I'll Be Around

The old Mansion stood just east of campus. A wooded area, about a quarter of a mile wide, acted as a buffer zone between campus and the Mansion property. The three of us rode down the narrow, winding asphalt track, approaching the old battleship gray painted relic that was capped with a brick red colored, slate roof.

On an oak tree in front of the Mansion, was posted a sign that said 'No Trespassing.' On the front door, another sign read 'Closed Due to Renovations.' White paper sheets hung inside, covered all the windows, but left a few inches of clearance between the shades and the bottom of the windowsills. Peering through the opening, we saw the hardwood floors inside and the bottom of table legs and shelves, everything a varnished brown. Hollie parked the car in the parking space in the back of the Mansion. On the back porch in the rear of this former slave owner's home, stood two carpenter's saw horses beside a long metal ladder laying on the top of fresh cut planks and plywood boards, arranged on the floor.

Approximately twenty-five feet out beyond the house, a small patch of lawn between the two, lay a rectangular swimming pool that ran in a line parallel to the back of the Mansion. No doubt the pre-Civil War occupants never envisioned a modern day swimming pool on their property. A mildewy, blue tarpaulin covered the pool, whereby on a half dozen spots, puddles of standing water remained from the previous night's rain. Matching blue tarpaulin sand snakes anchored the covering all around the pool. In four places, balanced on all sides, were ropes fitted through the metal, washer-ringed holds in the tarpaulin, and tied to turnbuckle hooks fastened to iron stakes in the ground beside the pool deck. Beyond the unkempt, terraced lawn past the swimming pool, on the left side of the house, stood a gazebo. A recent coat of white paint gave it a new look, even though it dated back to the past.

On the right rear of the grounds, lay a parking lot, walled in on the front side of the property by a gathering of heavy leafed trees, that hid the parking lot from view from the main road to campus.

A gravel road led from the parking lot and trailed past a concrete block shed-workshop, the size of a small house that stood out in a field. Beyond the gravel road past the shed, stood a wrought iron bench beside a concrete goldfish fountain and pond. Murky water remained in the pond, but no goldfish resided there. Another bench stood under overhanging shade trees farther along the curve of the gravel road, behind the shed and out of sight of the backyard.

On this second wrought iron bench leading to the old plantation grounds, is where Hollie and I sat. A few minutes earlier, Bakarie had said: "I'm going over to check out the gazebo."

We walked along the gravel road beyond the concrete block shed that stood on the field. Then we stood on ground that was less than a quarter of a mile from the baseball diamond on the southeast corner of campus. In the winter time, when there were no leaves on the trees, the Mansion was visible from the ball field if you stood out by the scoreboard along the left field fence.

"But, you knew I liked you. That I cared for you," I said, rehashing a conversation that should have happened three years ago.

"I had a boyfriend back home," Hollie said. "And, I kept telling you that. The only thing was I found out much too late that he didn't care for me."

"The way I remember it, for the first few months of our freshman year, I used to come by your dorm three or four times a week, and sometimes I'd walk with you from the library in the evenings, and we'd go to dances at the gym, and we'd be together after football games."

"I know. And, you were so nice. Then you stopped coming around. It was probably for the better, because I've always thought we were not compatible."

"Not compatible? I thought we got along fine," I said. "I stopped coming around because I felt you owed me an explanation."

"An explanation? For what?"

"You know how you kept beating me over the head with the fact that you had a boyfriend back home, even after I had told you to drop him and think of me. And, I couldn't push you too hard, 'cause I thought you might get away from me and not want me around. Maybe that's why you never considered me to be anything more than a friend.

"During the week of the final exams, I didn't see you at all. Then, the Christmas holidays came and went, and I didn't have your home phone number or address. By the time the second semester started, I saw you talking with another guy in the lobby of your dorm, and I left and came back an hour later, and your roommate said you were out. I came by the next day, and you were out again, Hollie.

"Then, a few evenings later, I saw you two holding hands and all lovey-dovey at a basketball game. So, I stopped coming around, 'cause I felt you owed me an explanation. I thought you would've found out why I stopped coming to see you. But you never considered that I even existed. I was hurt. Still am."

"You just don't understand," Hollie said. "We were young then, just freshmen. So much happened over the holidays back then, that by the time I came back on campus, I got so wrapped up in making a new start, that I just kinda' associated you with the past that I was trying to make a break from."

While she talked, I was thinking to myself. Why does she make me feel like the guy in that song by the Spinners? I'll Be Around. It had a few clichés about a fork in the road and bowing out with grace.

Suddenly, we heard someone yell out, "NO-NO! What are you doing?" It was Bakarie's voice. Two gunshots followed.

I left Hollie and ran up the gravel road around the bend in view of the swimming pool. A tall black man wearing a gray, Big Apple hat, a khaki windbreaker jacket and blue jeans, wheeled around and fired four shots at me. I turned and ran. The pop and whistling of the shots happened in what seemed like less than a second. Yet the sounds, now gone, seemed frozen in time, distinct and permanently stored in my mind.

I was hit, but I didn't know where. The contact had been like a hornet's sting, a buzzing sledgehammer of a blow that sent pain all over my body, even though the initial shot had a pinpoint entry. Blood ran down the back of my left thigh under my sweatpants and down my left arm and side, wetting my clothes. Nauseously, hobbling down the gravel pathway, I yelled, "Run, Hollie, Run!"

Instead of running away, she ran to me. "Calvin, you're hurt. Come on."

She helped me to a thicket of trees out from the field near the wrought iron bench off the road. The man pursued. "Come back here, motherfucker!" he called out.

Walking up to us quickly, he started to empty the cartridges to reload his pistol. But when he saw Hollie, he stopped. By then, Hollie was screaming helplessly. Unexpectedly startled, the gunman turned and ran, as if his killing time had expired.

"That's okay, just leave me here," I said, panting. "Go through the woods, pass the ball field and get help at the gym. Don't try to get your car. He may come back."

"But should I leave you here alone?"

"Yeah, go on. I'll be alright."

Hollie found help at the ball field. Deacon West, Nehemiah Luckie, and a few other teammates had stayed after practice for extra batting practice. By the time Hollie returned with help, I was dizzy and faint, weak and cold.

Deacon West was a few years older than the rest of the guys standing around in assorted sweat suits and maroon baseball caps. He had been in the Army three years before entering college. Even in my blurred state of mind, it seemed providential that the stocky-built ex-Sergeant was there to take charge.

"Ga-ar-rr-lee!" Deacon West said calmly, shaking his head. "What happened to you, Porch?"

The last thing I remembered saying was 'go see what happened to Bakarie.'

"Who's Bakarie?"

"Professor Bakarie," Hollie shouted. "We left him over by the gazebo."

The next time I woke up, I was in the hospital and had no idea of how long I had been there. I learned that I had received a flesh wound on my back under my left shoulder, and had incurred a deeper gunshot wound to the left cheek of my behind.

It was R. P., the athletic trainer, who was fond of wearing his baseball cap on backwards, that later informed me of what had happened.

"Man, you were bleeding like a dog," he said. "All of us left on the field ran over there. Deacon West handled it like a champ!"

"'Hollie, you ain't in no shape to drive,' Deek said. 'Give me your keys. Porch, we're gonna load you into Hollie's car and get you to the hospital.'

"Then he told Wiley Jakes, 'Jakes, you drive the car. McCoy, you run over to the gym and call the police. Looka here, Luckie, you walk back with Hollie. Y'all take it easy, don't run. Just calm her down. Here are my keys. And, Luckie, when y'all get everything taken care of, bring my car down here. R. P., you and I are gonna look for Bakarie and wait for the police.'"

By evening time, most of the visitors had come and gone. I remember drifting off to sleep, seeing one group of visitors fade, then suddenly seeing different persons, as if it had happened at the blinking of an eye, when actually, scattered minutes, even hours had passed. Someone had said it was the medication that caused me to drift in and out of sleep and awareness. My roommate, the guys on our floor at the dorm, and my teammates on the baseball team, had each put in an appearance and left.

Then it was evening, and I was awake and alert. I knew that my parents would arrive soon. The radio on the portable table top near my bed, was playing pop music, turned down low. I had to endure some song about Colorado, "Rocky Mountain High, Colorado," another one hollering about "Your mama don't dance and your daddy don't rock and roll," and others.

Beside the radio was a piece of writing paper folded into what looked like a letter. Among the bandages, I felt pain in my arm as I reached over to look at the note. "Whew! That hurt. I'd better take it easy." In the background, a familiar song came on the radio and was now towards its middle. That's the song I was thinking about at the Mansion with Hollie. I'll Be Around.

I read the note:

> Dear Calvin,
>
> I sat by your bed for quite a while. You were sleeping so peacefully. It would have been a shame to wake you up. The nurse said it would only be a matter of days before you would be "up and at 'em again."
>
> You were so brave today. And, you were sweet, too. I'll get back up here before you're released.
>
> Love,
> Hollie

Chapter 4
Vengeance Is Mine

By sundown, a parade of people had come to see me. The Waukeegan Police Department's position on the shooting was that they had documented everything reported by the guy's at the Mansion scene, and would keep everything under observation.

Roland Trotter, the chief of campus security, was present at the time the two policemen came to my hospital room. He acted as a liaison between campus security and the downtown police department, as technically, we had been trespassing on the Mansion property. Trotter, a former Dormitory Residence Manager, was there in the interest of the College.

This reddish, light-skinned man with a big hawk-billed nose and neatly trimmed mustache, was now given to wearing dress suits on campus. He was tall and bow-legged in addition to the big nose, and someone had tagged him with the nickname "Big Bird" after the puppet character on the children's TV program *Sesame Street*. If you called him Big Bird, you had better be ready to run. Roland Trotter didn't like the nickname. The old security guards respected him and called him "chief," because he had attained an M.B.A. degree, a level of education far advanced than theirs. Plus, he occasionally moonlighted with the police department downtown.

I vaguely remembered the questions asked by the officers. I had been groggy from the medication. The Black officer, the detective in charge, had on a dark suit, and he asked all the questions. The White officer, the younger of the two, wore a regular navy blue policeman's uniform, and he wrote down the details of the conversation in a small wire tablet note pad. After asking all the necessary questions, they left. "Big Bird" Trotter went out of the room with them, but returned after a few minutes.

"So, what did they figure out?" I asked, feeling somewhat revived.

"Their position on the matter—if you follow one theory—is that a gunman followed you from campus. It's no telling how long he would've been trailing you—an hour, a day, a week—who knows? Given your good conduct, and the typical student life on campus, that theory is real weak. Their other theory, which they think more likely happened, is that one isolated man was chasing after another isolated man, who might have been dressed like you. The hunter and the hunted got away, leaving you shot in the butt. How do you explain that neither Bakarie nor Hollie was shot, and that in the end, the gunman turned and ran, when he could've killed you?"

"I haven't done anything to anybody. I don't have any enemies. I told them that."

"I heard what you told them, Porch. But just in case that weak, remote theory comes into play, you need to be concerned. It could be related to a friend of yours, or a friend of a friend. Lord knows who that could be. That's why they're limited in what they can do."

"So nothing may not get done at all?"

"Well, the last thing the detective said was "'If it was me, I'd go back six months and write down the names of everybody I had an argument with, or had a serious disagreement with. And, I'd see how they fit into the picture.'"

"Roland, ain't nothing exciting happened to me lately."

"We're going to have to just leave it at that then."

"You know, I haven't even thought about Bakarie Seesay," I remembered. "What happened with him?"

"Oh, yeah. Phillip Bakarr, the African exchange student."

"No. I'm talking about Bakarie Seesay."

"Phillip Bakarr-Seesay Momodu is his full name on his driver's license," he revealed. "They had to rush him to County General Hospital, where they've got a good Cardio-Respiratory Department. You see, they had to pull him out of the swimming pool at the Mansion. He had been trapped in the water under the canvas cover for a while before anybody noticed the skid marks of his shoe prints on the deck.

"The gunman struck him on the head behind the ear before he pushed Bakarie in the water, just before he came after you. The only thing that saved Bakarie was his will to live. He was conscious and flailing around in the dark under that canvas for a long time, before he got weak and gave out of breath. But nobody noticed him while they were taking care of you.

Shortly after that, the guys on the team found him and gave him artificial respiration. From what I understand, he's recovering fairly well, but his condition is still listed as serious. He didn't get shot. The hit man saved all the bullets for you."

"That's good to know," I said, trying to be sarcastic. "There's something else I found out— Bakarie has had run-ins with his girlfriend's dad.

Maybe he was out to get Bakarie." I told him about the tribal civil war going on in Africa.

"We'll look into it. I've got to go now. Can I get you anything? Do you need anything?"

"No, I'm alright. Thanks for coming by Roland."

"Alright, take it easy," he said on his way out.

It wasn't long after Roland Trotter left that Coach Benson paid me a visit. He greeted me while I lay on my side on the propped-up bed that the nurse had not long ago adjusted.

John Benson was no more than six or seven years older than me. As long as I could remember, the dark-brown skinned man always carried himself as a man older in years than his actual age. "Who shot you, son?"

"I don't know." I must have repeated those words over a dozen times since I woke up in that hospital bed.

"What did the police have to say?"

"Roland Trotter said it wasn't a case of us just trespassing. Because the guy fired most of the shots at me, he knew what he was there for. He'd probably followed me from campus?"

"Roland is just a Keystone cop—that's Campus Security. What did the real police have to say?"

"Pretty much the same thing."

"How long you think you'll be here? Can I get you anything? Have you called your parents yet?" Coach spoke all these questions in one breath.

"I'm alright! My folks are coming over this evening. The Doctor said I'm gonna need four to six weeks of physical therapy and rehabilitation to regain full use of my limbs. It's gonna require a couple of hours a day, three days a week. But if I go home to Venetian Creek or over to Montgomery, I'll have to miss a lot of classes and days off campus."

"Maybe you won't. I know someone over at the V.A. Hospital who owes me a favor. I'll see what I can do."

That was reassuring coming from Coach Benson. In my mind, as a "walk-on," non-scholarship player, I had always felt that Coach had little or no concern for the "walk-on" athletes, only focusing his attention on the prized, athletic scholarship players.

Just before he left, he reminded me, "One thing I have to tell you now, so that you won't get your hopes too high. You were in line to compete for the starting job, come opening day. We'll be about halfway through the season before you can do us any good now. Even then, you may have to work from third string and never get pass the second string position. I don't know how you feel about that, being a senior, you know?"

"I know, Coach."

"Just thought I'd tell you." He told me to take it easy, and he would see me later. Then he left.

Now with all my bandages and patches, I had a new pain to go with the bullet wounds—a wound to my pride. Coach Benson had just given me the hint that I should consider quitting the team, since it might not look too good for a senior to be a bench warmer, sitting on the pine, not getting an opportunity to play.

So Coach Benson doesn't have any faith in me now, huh?" I reasoned. Just the other day he was telling us seniors how he expected a lot out of us. That's alright. Kick a man when he's down. I'll be alright. I tried to reassure myself. But deep down inside, the wound to my pride hurt even more than the gunshot wounds that brought me to the hospital.

I didn't have much time to dwell on this new, unforeseen possibility, before I heard my little brother's voice just outside the door that was left ajar.

"He's in here. I see his name on the door." My twelve-year old brother, Nathaniel, had an Afro hair-do that was three times the length of mine, and he wore a denim jacket and jeans, with white high-top tennis shoes.

"How you doing, Calvin? I hope you're feeling better. Mother and Daddy are here."

"Hey, Dude! Come on over here."

Outside the door, we heard our parents talking, Alfred James and Francine Porch. "I told that boy to wait for us," he said.

"Don't worry about him, A.J. He's just like you and his brother—always rushing off to do something."

They entered the room. Mother, a tall, brown-skinned woman in her mid-forties, had her hair straightened and combed back behind her ears, and it draped down to the edge of her neck. Stately and competent in her eyeglasses, she wore a beige sweater over a long, dark green dress.

"We got here as soon as we could," she said, moving over to the bed to hug me. "How you doing, Calvin? Are they treating you alright here?"

"Yes, mother. I'm fine. I should be getting out of here in a day or two. Hi, Dad! How you doing?"

"I'm alright. The question is—how are you doing? I'm glad it's not as bad as I thought it was. Until we talked to the nurse down the hall, we were expecting you to be worse off than you are."

Dad stood by my bed and shook my hand. He was among the quiet, reserved men of his day who found it hard to show affection. There was no hug between us. He is a dark-skinned, middle-aged man, and he wore a navy blue windbreaker jacket with brown pants and a plaid shirt. His favorite hat rest on his head. The black dress hat had a small rim around it, like the ones Frank Sinatra wore in his movies and on the pictures of his album covers. After the greetings and small talk ended, he bore in: "Son, you ain't tied up with no crooks now, are you?"

"No, Dad, I'm not. All I know is I got shot. But if the police don't catch him, I'm gonna do it. I'll get 'em."

"Boy! This sounds just like the movies," my kid brother offered.

"This ain't no picture show, child," Mother said. "Bless his heart. He don't know how serious this is. But Calvin, I have to tell you. It ain't your job to catch the one who did it."

I sensed a sermon coming.

"Better yet," she assured me, "even if the police don't catch the man, God will deal with him. For it is written, 'vengeance is mine; I will repay, saith the Lord.' Let the Lord handle it. You just get well, and study your books so you can graduate and get a good job."

I had learned a long time ago how to deal with Mother. Agree with her, lest she comes back with more scriptures. I acquiesced in words, but in my heart, my plan remained the same. "Okay, Mother, you're right. I don't know what got into me. I got enough to do just to finish college."

As the last visitation hour concluded, my folks left the hospital and took the car ride back to Venetian Creek.

Chapter 5
Wild-Ass Guesses

The night was long, and I couldn't sleep. Then some things from the past came to my mind that I wished I could redesign—asking myself "what if," "had I known this," "if only I had done this," "why couldn't he or she have just done that," etc., etc. All the king's horses and all the king's men couldn't put him back together again.

I replayed one event after another in my head like a tape recorder, until sleep finally came around daybreak. What sense could I make of the passing day? The only thing that gave me a sense of order, a logical starting point, was to think about what the police detective had said earlier: "If it was me, I'd go back six months and write down the names of everybody I had an argument with, or had a serious disagreement with. And, I'd see how they fit into the picture."

I had a distant thought in my mind that seemed like a dream. It occurred to me that Professor Mansaray hired someone to kill Bakarie. The gunman did hit Bakarie over the head with the gun before shoving him into the pool. That was enough to kill the average person. And, maybe the bad guy fired on me because he thought I was a witness. I'm going to check out Bakarie myself. Remember, it could be a friend of a friend.

I considered what the cop had said. Six months, huh? Every squabble, argument, serious disagreement, huh? Now it was the end of February, so that would take me back to August, a month before school started.

In August, just outside of my hometown, a jealous moonshine bootlegger tried to cut me with a hawk-bill knife, because someone had flirted with his girlfriend, and I got caught in the middle of it.

In October, local toughs from a nightclub off campus fingered my friend, Wiley Jakes, as a stool pigeon. They linked my association with him to a police raid. Nothing became of it.

In November, two things happened. First, I lied to a nun, Sister Margaret DuMaine, about a book report. Even though I was certain that she hadn't ordered it, maybe it was God's way of punishing me by having me shot.

Secondly, one night during one of the late night 'cook-ins' foreign students were known to hold in the dorm, I ticked off a West African student named Kojo Tarawallie. We talked about politics, history, and economics, and I said something about West Africa being 'backwards.'

Kojo lit into me, "You Negroes are just like the white man. You're a puppet. You're an ass!"

"Who are you calling an ass?"

The dark man with the British-African accent walked up to me and shook his index finger in my face. "I'm calling you a puppet, an ass, and a tool of the white man."

I could take the words, but I couldn't take that finger waving in my face. I put both hands up, like a traffic police yelling out STOP! Then, I pushed Kojo back hard, causing him to fall helplessly onto two other students sitting on his roommate's bed. The force of the shove frightened me, because I knew I would be in for a fight if his head had hit the concrete wall against the bed.

"Don't put your hands in my face," I warned him. "You hear me?"

Bakarie, a West African, and Neville, the Jamaican, parted us. We both apologized, and the matter was settled. Once I calmed down, they informed me that Africans did not consider it offensive to point at someone or shake an index finger in their face. Whereas with us born and raised in the States, we had been taught from our youth that this same gesture was a gross insult. Kojo was basically a good guy. Though I was cautious around Kojo from then on, who knows what he was thinking deep down inside. This was mindless rambling because I couldn't go to sleep.

The night was long after everyone left, and I lay alone, sleepless, in a cold and silent semi-private hospital room, with the other bed vacant, and only the sound of a distant, intermittent voice in the hallway. It had been an hour since the nurse gave me medicine for the pain. She reminded me of the stages of pain I could expect to have. The ache I presently experienced did not rate a call for assistance.

They had put a long, white gown on me. The back of it was opened vertically down the center, tied together by two small apron strings on the middle of the garment. My butt was embarrassingly exposed when the nurses examined me or checked my wounds. You are stripped of all of your dignity when lying there at the mercy of those who examine and prod you, turn and twist your resting positions, assist you when you throw up, gag, or have a bowel movement. The whole business of doing 'number one or number two' was at the mercy of a nurse's assistance. One thing I learned, though—when the pain got unbearable and my state of consciousness wavered, all dignity was 'thrown out the window.' I just wanted relief!

Back in August, before school started, I played Summer league, weekend baseball in a small rural community, just outside of my hometown. The teams consisted of laborer-type athletes who played in these leagues until they couldn't play anymore. You might see a forty-year old man still trying to play. They had good talent, and the level of play was called semi-pro. No team had a formal budget. One team might don jeans, T-shirts, assorted shoes, with their caps as the only thing similar. Another team might be fully uniformed like a professional team.

One of my teammates, a guy named Noland, was in the on-deck circle, waiting to bat. The good-natured cotton mill worker that he was, he flirted with a bootlegger's girlfriend. "Hey baby, can I go with you? You sho' is looking good!" The woman wore tight fitting, short jeans and a dark blue and white tabletop patterned plaid blouse that featured her prominent breasts. She carried herself like she was on display, never even noticing Noland as she went around the playing area to the parked cars off the field.

The bootlegger, a common fixture at these ball games, was a dark-skinned man who wore blue denim, bibbed overalls, a white T-shirt, and a red cap. He sold soft drinks, barbecue and ice cream, in addition to the corn liquor, which was what he really came out to sell. The other stuff was just a front for the liquor business. He sold these items from a makeshift snack stand.

In a jealous rage, the bootlegger pulled out a hawk-bill pocketknife to cut Noland in response to the ball player's remark to his woman as he stood in the on-deck circle. I was the next batter behind Noland, who hadn't seen the attacker approach. I slammed my baseball bat hard into the arm of the bootlegger. Now, even more pissed off at me than he was Noland, the bootlegger swore: "I'll kill you! I'll kill you!" He picked up his knife in his other hand and chased after me, but he couldn't catch me. He chased me to the parking grounds out of the playing area, cussing all the way. The game was over then for me. I had more important things to worry about.

The very woman Noland had flirted with, saw me running and also saw her boyfriend, the bootlegger standing in the middle of the parking area. She got into her blue Cutlass Oldsmobile, drove up to me, opened the door, and shouted, "Get in!"

"Whew! Thank you," I said. Dirty and sweaty in my gray baseball uniform, from an earlier head first slide into second base, a result of trying to steal a base on the pitcher, now I found myself cast literally into her lap.

"Let's go. I'll take you up the road a little ways from here. You can hide out in the bushes 'til your team comes by. I'm going back," she said. "The game's about over anyway. Big Robert is a jealous son of a bitch, that's all. He's been drinking too much of that alcohol he's been selling. I gotta go back and calm him down. Then, he'll be alright."

"But what will he do to you for helping me?"

"Don't worry about him. He listens to me. I'm the one who keeps his Black ass out of jail."

I surmised that Big Robert didn't know me from Adam and would hardly be chasing after me six months later. Waukeegan was a long ways from that little community outside of Venetian Creek. Big Robert wouldn't know where to start looking for me, anyway.

It seemed that all of my troubles happened off campus. Nothing to do with the classroom, or the well-manicured lawns; no food fights in the cafeteria, no panty raids in the girl's dormitories. I got into the kind of mishaps and near misses that happened to you when you thought you were making every effort to mind your own business. I'd be glad to get back in the classroom, finish out the semester and graduate just like my mother reminded me several hours ago.

But when you can't sleep, and you're lying in a hospital bed, with a flesh wound on your back under the left shoulder, and another deeper gunshot wound to the left cheek of your buttocks, you have plenty to think about. Maybe if I thought long and hard enough, I could figure out who shot me at the Mansion yesterday.

Then I looked back to the incident that happened in October. Wiley Jakes and I cruised over to the Legion Club just outside of town. The business operated a regular nightclub downstairs. Upstairs was where the gambling went on, mainly crap games played on two pool tables. Twenty to thirty men stood around the tables, making side bets as the players shot dice.

As soon as we saw the action, I whispered: "Man, I don't like this. Let's go downstairs." I had expected to find recreational pool games going on, not illegal gambling. My greatest fear in college was to get kicked out of school or put into jail; and then later try to explain it to my parents, the neighbors and the folks at church.

"Be cool," Wiley said. He's a teammate on the baseball team, a dark-skinned brother with a receding hairline like the famous Olympian track star Jesse Owens. And like another Olympian—Jim Thorpe—the six-feet two, two hundred pound pitcher was good at several sports. In fact, he played football at Waukegan. He really should've been resting at the dorm, since this was a weeknight during football season. But it was his idea that we go out in the first place. He would've gone without me had I refused to go. I had nothing else to do, but I wasn't looking for trouble either.

I went downstairs to the bar, ordered a beer and listened to the music. A few men and women danced on the dance floor. I didn't see anybody I recognized. These were working people, mature adults from local surroundings. It was the middle of the week. Still uncomfortable with the gambling going on upstairs, I went up and told Wiley: "Okay, man, let's go. Come on, man. Let's go."

Soon after we descended the steps and walked through the crowd of dancers, a half dozen policemen raided the club. Four of them ran up the stairs to the game room. One stood at the entrance, blocking the door, and another one was in a shouting match with the manager behind the bar. Who knows how many cops were waiting outside.

Two stories were out concerning the club's activities. One story had it that an unsuspecting police department heard about illegal gambling and came out to bust it and shut it down. Another story, which was probably the truth, was that the club owners had been slack in paying off the police their due cut of the 'protection' money. Nevertheless, a young man among the dozen or so men taken downtown to jail, pointed out that "Wiley Jakes and that dude that was with him, were the ones who ratted on us."

Two different men came on campus and quizzed Wiley. He told them he was just like everybody else there—just having a good time. He later told me: "I told them that you were my cousin from out of town who was with me that night."

Who knows? Maybe Wiley lied to me and told the goons who I really was, and they were looking for me now.

Chapter 6
Africa's Right Around the Corner

It was midday on Tuesday when I checked out of the hospital. Over the weekend, my roommate had brought me a change of clothes and some personal items from the dorm. Even though they had armed me with a set of crutches, a nurse informed me that I really only needed one. I had to pay for two anyway, so why not take both of them. Along with that, they gave me a ready-made, canvas cloth arm sling that I strapped across my neck and shoulder, to wear or take off as need be. Two medical technicians brought me to the dormitory in a white ambulance that had a Red Cross sign on each front door.

On the ride back to campus, I was consumed by the thought that somehow the dispute between Bakarie and Dr. Mansaray was related to me getting shot. I sat in the back of the van listening to the driver and assistant technician talk low. Both black men has low trimmed haircuts and wore white uniforms.

I knew I'd have to start with Bakarie and Hollie if I was ever going to get anywhere with this case. Somehow I'd have to find a way to interview Dr. Mansaray later on. Hollie wasn't harmed at the Mansion. So my first line of thought was to recall everything I knew about Bakarie. Was there some quirk about him, some chink in his armor that revealed what he was about?

Thanks to the crutches, I returned to the dormitory, half-way walking like a stilt-man in a circus, and half-way walking normal. I crossed the circular driveway to the glass double doors at the top of the concrete stoop.

42

The three-story brick building faced the circular driveway on the front. It was on this very stoop, on a cool evening back in November, where I met Bakarie outside sitting on the concrete platform rail that extended out like a bench from the side of either doors.

I knew he was a foreigner when I asked him, "How do you like it out here?" and Bakarie had answered: "I like it a lot. I like it a very lot." No natural born American citizen would say "I like it a very lot."

Presently, I heard that he was okay, but that he had sustained a slight case of pneumonia from being pushed into that fungus-infested, mildew consumed, loosely tarpaulined swimming pool, the day I got shot. I was going to check on him soon. I needed to ask him about the run-in he had with Dr. Mansaray over Adelaide. Whether or not the old man was capable of hiring someone to shoot him.

But on that previous November night, Bakarie, the foreigner, and his coterie, had played the host, by providing me with food one night at the dorm. It was a mild Saturday evening in November, a little cool; but for the time of year, it was normal. My roommate had gone to a concert in Montgomery. All was quiet in the dormitory that night, until a vending machine, like a slot machine, took the last of my money. In the hour leading up to the robbery, I woke up from a restless nap, only to watch the last fifteen minutes of a television show before the American flag, accompanied by the National Anthem, appeared on the screen to end the day.

So, at 12 o'clock midnight, the few viewers remaining, stood up to leave the wide, nondescript lobby of the dorm. Returning upstairs to our room, I

43

gathered the last of my pocket change—one quarter, two dimes, one nickel, and four pennies. These were lean times for college students, the early 1970's, when spending money to a poor student was hard to get, and even more difficult to hold on to.

On the basement floor two flights below our room was a multipurpose room containing a table tennis table, two square card-playing tables, and a dozen or so Army green folding chairs. A red soft drink machine and a snack machine, stood in an indented space along the wall at the base of the stairs.

"So I've got a choice. Something to eat or something to drink." I opted to get a "Honey Bun," a flattened, oblong rolled cake, brown and sugar glazed on the outside and textured like bread on the inside. Coins placed in the slot, I pulled the red, knobbed handle. The cake laying visibly on a rack halfway up the glass display window, fell to the bottom, got caught in the trap door and would not pass through the opening at the bottom where I could get it out with my hand. I shook the machine and rattled on the handle.

"Damn it, this thing took my money! Damn!" I gave it one last shove and left the room.

Hungry and defeated by that bandit red machine, I walked back through the dimly lit first floor lobby, where not long before, I had watched the TV channels sign off for the night. The Resident Manager's office lights were off and that made the lobby darker than usual. I passed through the glassed front doors and sat outside on the flat, concrete ledge on one side of the front steps.

I looked at the round turf lawn on an island out in the middle of the circular driveway. "What a night," I spoke to myself. "Nowhere to go, nothing to do."

The campus street ran east and west, and to get to the proper parking lot, you went west, circled around the adjacent dormitory and came to the back of our building. On the north side of the street was the main building of the School of Veterinary Medicine, a long single story brick building much older than the dorm. It loomed dark in the shadows, with its only light coming from the windows and doors of our residence hall.

"So, that's it over there," I mused. "The World's famous School of Veterinary Medicine, Waukeegan College, Waukeegan, Alabama, where just inside its lab doors, you are whooshed with the suffocating smell of formaldehyde that is used to pickle those dead animal specimens, mainly dead dogs."

The campus, like those poor little dogs, was dead. No party, no dance to go to. Football season had just ended, and the basketball team went out of town on its first road trip. Everybody worth his or her salt had ridden over to Montgomery, to see in concert, the hottest singing group out of Motown. Leonardo had been fortunate at the last minute and had gotten a ticket and a ride to the concert.

A young man who looked older than me, came through the glass doors to the outside and sat on the platform rail, the concrete ledge across from the one I sat on. He was dark and wore a blue collarless African print shirt and khaki trousers. I knew he was a foreign student, but was not sure if the man hailed from the Caribbean Islands or from Africa directly. The stranger

45

had been a roommate of one of my friends a couple of years back, and he spoke in an accent that revealed he was not from the USA.

"Hi, how are you?" the man in the collarless, blue print African shirt said.

"Okay. How about you? You like it out here, alright?"

"I've been worse places, but I like it a lot. I like it a very lot. This is a good place to be."

I was only asking about the evening, the weather, in general, but the foreigner answered giving a whole account of how he liked the country, the state, the town and campus at Waukeegan, altogether.

"Well, it's good you feel that way."

"Oh, yes, everything's fine. I've just come out of the laundry room. So that was you banging on the snack machine downstairs?"

"Yeah, it took my money," I answered.

"I'm glad you didn't tear it apart. You know how they like to make their inquiries," he nodded towards the Residence Manager's office just inside the glass doors. "Coming to everybody's room, asking a lot of questions."

"I sure as hell thought about tearing it apart." I was determined to find out where this brother with the accent came from. "You're from Jamaica, aren't you?"

"No."

"South America?"

"No."

"Nigeria?"

"That's close. Yes, I am from West Africa, but not Nigeria. I'm from The Gambia." He held out his hand. "My name is Bakarie Seesay." We shook hands.

"I'm Calvin Porch, from Venetian Creek, Alabama."

For a moment neither one of us said anything. Bakarie was looking down at his brown-laced leather shoes. I looked at the circular, lawn island out in the middle of the driveway.

"So you're a long ways from home? What brought you here?"

"Well, it was quite by accident, really. Actually, I had intended to go to Canada. But I heard that Waukeegan had a good forestry program. And I heard that the climate here was more suitable.

"The only problem I have is that I find it difficult to get all the different kinds of food we are used to. Do you like African food?"

"I've never tried it," I said.

"You should try it. Listen, one of our brothers has just returned from home with a lot of food we haven't had for quite some time. They're downstairs cooking some of it now. Why don't you come down and try some of it?"

"Okay."

We walked down the stairs to the basement, and turned the corner to go toward the laundry room, the opposite direction from the multipurpose room, in full sight of the bandit vending machine that took my money.

"Took my damn money," I said low.

"Forget about it," Bakarie advised.

In the laundry room, Bakarie got his clothes out of the dryer. His room was three doors down from the laundry room, on the opposite side of the hall, where the view through the windows gave you the sight of the green, rolling lawn outside, through which passed a long walkway that separated our dormitory's yard from the next one behind us. From the outside, the basement level on the rear appeared as a first floor level. On the front of the building, the basement windows opened out slightly above ground level.

I learned that these late night cookings were common within the circle that Bakarie moved. Cooking in the dormitory was not allowed; it was a violation of the fire safety rules. The foreign students were good at relocating their camps from one room to another, to stay ahead of the resident staff. The permanent management staff was off on weekend nights, leaving in charge student-workers who didn't go out of their way to find a problem.

The African's room, like all the rooms in the dorm, was furnished with the same things on the right and left sides. Just inside the door on either side, was a closet with a body-length mirror on its door, a bunk bed with pull out drawers below, and a desk in the corner facing the wall. All the wooden fixtures were of a varnished pinewood. In the back of the room, a white 'hot plate' with twin eyes, rested on a table. It was a portable electric stove.

While Bakarie made the introductions, I couldn't help but notice a putrid smell coming from the ingredients boiling in a pan. Of the four men in the room, two hailed from West Africa, one from Guyana, and the other from Jamaica. The smell that stunned my nostrils, came from the dried smoked fish, of which the fellow from West Africa, named Kojo, was peeling off the fish skin.

He tossed the brown smoked skin into the plastic trash can, removed the grayish brown strips of flesh from the bones, threw the bones in the trash can, rinsed the good part in a flat pan of clean water, then placed the cleaned fish in a boiling pot on the left eye of the 'hot plate' stove.

On the right grill of the small white stove, was a boiling pan of water with green leaves in it. A light-skinned guy named Neville from Jamaica, grabbed the pan by the handle. "Have some tea, Calvin."

"Thanks. What's that smell?"

"It's the fish," Kojo said. "You see, in our country, when the fishermen go out to sea to catch the fish, they have no way to refrigerate it. I'm talking about small, local fishermen. So to preserve it, and allow them to carry it back to the market, they have to smoke it. The whole fish is smoked intact, the head, the entrails, everything. But never mind the smell. As you will see, it is very sweet."

Pablo was the short, squat student from Guyana. He had on a white T-shirt and blue jeans. His round face and straight hair conveyed a composite of Africa and South American Indian. He spoke: "So, I see Bakarie has succeeded in getting you involved in the Pan African movement?"

"Not yet," Bakarie answered, waving his hand from left to right with the index finger pointing up. "We're just friends."

"Well, a friend of Bakarie, is a friend of mind," Neville said, bearing all his visible teeth.

I sat on the bed on the right side, near the teapot, sipping tea, wondering what green plant was used to make this tasty beverage. By itself, it was bitter, but with sugar added, it was delicious. I learned in conversation that the plant was a type of edible 'greens' commonly found in tropical climates. It was revealed among great laughter that the 'greens' were a 'cure-all' for various and sundry tropical illnesses—from malaria, to fevers, to constipation, to headaches, to anemia, to colds, to skin rashes, to stimulating a sluggish man to an erection when he wants to satisfy a woman.

"As for me," Kojo said, "anytime I'm ready to get with my woman, I have not one, but two cups of tea. Sometimes, three. To God!"

"Don't swear to God," Bakarie warned. "You know it's nothing but anticipation and expectation. The tea is only a mild stimulant at best. Like coffee."

"It works for him if he believes in it," Neville said. "It's all in your mind. Hah- hah-hah!" He held up his cup in a toast. "Long last herbal tea. Long last your hard-on, brother!"

"We're all alike," Pablo from Guyana said. "Strong believers in roots and herbs. Right, Calvin?"

"I know a few people who believe in stuff like that," I answered.

"Well, you see, we're all in agreement."

"It's ready," Kojo announced. "Let's eat!"

I learned that along with the common background of kinship with Mother Africa, food was the immediate concrete link that brought us all together.

I was curious about the ingredients in the stew. Such a delicious meal had to have a name. Bakarie noted that it was a simple meal, one that any of his African brothers could have prepared. He named the ingredients: water, palm oil, onions, green peppers, red peppers, slices of yams, dried fish, tomato paste, and a dash of salt. This reddish-brown stew, with small green and red vegetable cuts sprinkled throughout, with chunks of fish and yams, when poured over white rice, was a complete meal. No bread, no dessert, no sweet soft drink was needed. You only needed the food and a drink of water.

After we finished eating, we drank more tea and talked about African unity and the more encompassing Pan African student organization on campus.

"Calvin, how much do you know about Africa?" Kojo asked.

"Not too much. I know a little bit about the Trans-Atlantic slave trade. And I can name you fourteen or fifteen countries. But that's about it."

"He's got a lot to learn," Neville said.

"Let's not overload the man with too much information," Bakarie offered, sparing me of any further grilling and interrogation. "Let him relax and reflect on the things he has learned so far."

They agreed. I was glad. Within an hour of the meal, one by one, each student started drifting off, going back to his own room. When I got ready to leave, Bakarie spoke to me in the hall: "Look, you seem to be open to learning. Why don't you go by the International Students Center sometime? Look around, talk to different people. Then next semester, if you can work it in, you might consider taking an African studies course as an elective."

"I'll check it out," I promised. I walked back down the hall towards the east end of the building, near the multipurpose room, and went up the stairway near the scene where earlier the red vending machine had robbed me of my coins. I was not angry about the lost change now.

By 2:15 a.m., I was lying in bed. The light had been off ten minutes, when Leonardo came into the room singing a song by the Temptations. Ball of Confusion.

He turned on the lamp that was on his desk near the foot of his bed next to the window. His usual daytime clothes consisted of assorted sweatshirts with khaki pants or blue jeans. Always, he sported a white cloth tennis hat, the kind with the complete brim going around it, with the nylon quill stitched, air-cooled vents on the sides.

For the concert, he wore his absolute best—a navy blue double-breasted blazer and a metallic gray shirt with a large droopy collar that hung like hound dog's ears over the lapel of his coat. Just as exaggerated as his collar, was the width of his black, bell-bottom slacks.

"How was the concert?"

"I hope I didn't wake you up."

"No. I wasn't asleep, anyway."

He had his coat off and was sitting on his bed: "Man, I'm telling you, the Temps got down!" His brown face lit up. He talked while using hand gestures. "They did their thing. I'm telling you—they were slick. The brothers had their shit together! Every song—a dance—a move—bam—right on time. They sang their asses off. They were dealing."

Leonardo Tolbert hailed from South Carolina, and was a tall, brown-skinned student, who during the times when big Afros were in style, still wore his hair cut low, as he maintained it with a brush rather than a comb. Notably, the black dress shoes he had just kicked off, like his choice of haircut, upheld the traditional, conventional look.

"Well, we kept things quiet on the home front, you know. The usual stuff happened—the Rec Center closing at ten, visitation at the girls dorms *legally* ending at eleven, and boring TV 'til midnight."

"Hey, man, I wished you could've gone."

"Really, it turned out alright. I hung out with some Africans and some guys from the Islands, who stay on the basement floor. One of them cooked some good food.

"He took some smoked fish that smelled awful—put it with peppers and onions, boiled it in palm oil with sliced yams and tomato paste, and came out with a cross between a stew, Chinese food, and gravy. We ate it with rice. Then, we sat around drinking tea and talking about 'Back to Africa' and politics."

"You did alright," Leonardo said. He was now in his underwear. He turned off the lamp and got into his bed, under the covers. "My cousin, B.D.—we call him Beedy –gave me a dashiki from Africa, that's supposed to have powerful medicine in it. It's in the drawer under my bed. I haven't worn it yet."

We talked on for several minutes in the dark.

"Anyway, it's supposed to protect you from physical harm. A knife, a bullet—neither one is supposed to penetrate through it. And, you're never supposed to wash it."

"Sounds like bullshit to me," I said.

"Maybe you could have these guys look at the dashiki."

"I'll talk to Bakarie first. He might know a little bit about it."

Chapter 7
Conspirators Under the Bronze Statue

After the two medical technicians helped me out of the ambulance in front of our dorm, I stretched out my arms and legs as best I could.

"Good. I'm glad it's the middle of the day," I thought. Now I've got a chance to do two things. One, practice with these crutches to see how I'm gonna get about on campus. And, two, talk to someone about loaning me a gun.

The first task was easy; walk a little bit, rest, adjust the crutches and sling, shift my weight from one leg to the other, maybe sit and rest a few times. But the task of getting someone to loan me a pistol was a bit more difficult. It was unlikely that anyone on campus had a gun. I would have to ask someone who lived in town, off campus, possibly a student who still lived with his parents, or a non-student, someone who could keep a secret, a friend who could keep the whole thing in confidence.

I knew three guys that fit the bill—Deacon West, Charles Jordan, and Dwayne Norwood. If I got the search underway starting today, I figured, within a few days I'd have the gun I needed, in order to defend myself against that criminal out there who was still on the loose.

Having been in the hospital over the weekend, I had missed only two days of classes. I thought I'd go over to the 'Rec' and out by the fountain. Better to get the jokes and wisecracks out of the way, today. People can really make fun of you if you get shot in the butt.

The fountain, a square, brick and mortar structure, lay on the northward side of the main campus courtyard, if you could call it a courtyard, for there was no courthouse or municipal building nearby. The pool area containing the water stood three and a half feet from the ground, and we often sat on the top ledge of the fountain on all four sides.

Two concrete benches were attached to each wall of the fountain so that when we sat on one, the brick wall of the structure served as a backrest. A fixture on the campus landscape, like one on a town square, the fountain was surrounded by brick buildings and walkways on all sides; the Cafeteria-Student Union building on the southeast, women dormitories on three sides, and one lone, little-used academic building on the south side.

Test the traffic, I thought. Feel the pulse of campus here. I concluded that this was a safe post from which to warm up to the masses. A more sarcastic, jeering crowd, one less tame, existed among that camp sitting on the long bench known as the 'Breeze Station,' located up the lawn on the southeast of the courtyard. A considerable amount of lawn, trees and shrubbery separated me from the guys at the 'Breeze Station.'

More girls and romantic couples passed by the fountain than at the male-dominated "Breeze Station,"—a place for bullshit; hence, a place for bullshitters. Somebody along the way concluded that the "Breeze Station" was a cleaner name for college students to use.

Another place which I wished not to show myself first, was the billiard and pool room, located in the

'Rec' (Recreation Center) in the Student Union building below the Cafeteria.

It was like fishing. Splash! I got a bite. I sat on a bench facing a paved walkway that led to one of the women's dormitories. With books in their hands, they walked to and fro their afternoon classes.

"Oh, Calvin, I'm so sorry about what happened to you," Dee Dee said. "Are you alright? Can I help you with anything?"

"No, I'm alright. I'll be okay."

"Yeah, man. You look like you're in pain. Take it easy," a guy named Willie said as he overheard me and Dee Dee talking. Willie stood by the next bench talking to his girlfriend who was sitting on the top ledge of the fountain.

I felt better as more encouragement came from two other students. Now I was ready to test a swifter current of water. I hopped over to the recreation center, which encompassed most of the ground floor area of the student union building.

I passed through the glass double doors to the snack bar. By now the snack bar was closed to the lunch crowd, but the tables and booths were occupied by card players—bid whist enthusiasts; players who could talk trash, cajole, and taunt with the best of them, while slamming their cards on the tables, talking smack.

A few students paused to acknowledge my presence with a "Hey, what's going on?" or "What's happening, man?" But, for the most part, they carried on, too engulfed in their card games to pay any attention to a guy on crutches who hadn't done anything but spend the weekend in the hospital.

Alfred Brady Moore

I saw R. P., team trainer for the baseball team, standing behind a card player, looking on.

"Hey, R. P., I need to talk to you, man."

"What's up, Porch? I see they got you patched up pretty good. You look a hell of a lot better now than you did Saturday. What's the deal?"

"I'm looking for Deacon West. Have you seen him?"

"Yeah. I did see him about half an hour ago. Try the pool room."

More bullshit, more mocking, I figured. I entered through the glass-enclosed walls of the game room, greeting the attendant behind the counter. Then I responded to one table tennis player named Hank who yelled out "Hey, Cripple!"

"I can still beat you on one leg, and one hand behind my back."

"Aw, Porch, you couldn't beat me when you had two good hands and legs. How you gone do that now?"

I spotted Deacon West in the pool room.

"Well, look-a-here!" Country George Marshall said. He was the resident wisecracking, joking, jone-ing master. Country George was a good-natured, never-meaning-no-harm sort of fellow, who could make you laugh even if you were mad with him. He was a pretty good pool shooter who was hard to beat. As a 250-pound football player, he could handle himself well in a fight if he had to. His wardrobe was limited. He always wore blue jeans, a blue denim jacket in the winter, and sweatshirts, either with cut-off sleeves in the summer or long sleeves in the wintertime.

"Hey, y'all, here's the lover and the fighter! Yeah, Porch, I heard you and that other dude got to fighting over Hollie, and a rabbit hunter shot you in the ass, trying to break y'all up."

"Fuck you, George. You're full of shit, you know that?"

"I ain't lying. That's what I heard. If I'm lying, I'm flying. Hey, fellows, didn't y'all hear that, too?"

A few nodded and said yes they heard the same thing. I knew they were lying.

"Whatever you say, George. I don't have anything to come back at you with," I conceded. Everybody shared in the laughter, and then they left me alone.

"Hey, Deek. I need to talk to you."

"Let me finish this game, Porch, and I'll get right with you."

Deacon West was patient for a while, as I led him out of the student union building, down some steep, little-used steps between the Rec snack bar and a women's dormitory, that led to a narrow asphalt road that trailed behind all the buildings nearby. Smoke billowed out of the tall chimneys of the old brick laundry building. Up the steep incline to the south, stood the back walls of Bennington Hall, the main Liberal Arts building, with windows aligned on each floor level of the three-story structure. Up the hill just beyond a thicket of trees on the east, stood the old dormitory where Hollie lived during our freshman year.

Deacon West halted on the asphalt at the bottom of the steps, indicating, he wasn't going any farther. "Man, what is it that you want to talk to me about?

And why is it so important that we got to come way out here?"

"I just want to make sure nobody hears what we're talking about, that's all. Here's the deal, Deek. You know the town cops and the campus security ain't gone do nothing about me getting shot. Whoever the dude is, I think he might try it again. I need some protection, man. I need a gun, a good pistol."

"What you gone do, get him yourself? That's stupid, Porch. You ain't got no idea of what you're saying. First of all, the guy that shot you, is probably long gone. Y'all was trespassing on private property, you know. He probably mistook you for somebody else. Why would he hang around after that?"

"I got the same question for you that the police couldn't answer," I said. "Nobody could figure out why the man fired shots at me only. He didn't shoot at Bakarie or Hollie. So, why me?"

"The man was probably following after somebody that dressed like you. And when he saw Bakarie, he just shoved him in the pool. By the time he saw Hollie, he was sure he'd made a mistake. That's why he took off like a bat out of hell. He could've reloaded and killed you and Hollie both, if he wanted to."

"That's easy for you to speculate, but it's my life that's at stake."

"Take it from me, man. I'm older than you," Deacon West advised. "I've seen things in the Army. I've been to Vietnam and everything. I've bunked with guys and hung out with guys from all walks of life. Some of those dudes had done violent crimes and gotten away with it. When they got into the Army, they said it was safer in the Army than in the streets where they came from.

"What I'm telling you, friend, is this—you are a student, a small town country boy, a few months from graduating. You ain't nowhere in the ballpark with the kind of guys that would go out and kill somebody.

"You and me, we're just like those guys in the movies, in the Westerns. The farmers that come to town unarmed. The best way to keep out of trouble and stay alive among killers, is to be unarmed and avoid places where you can get into trouble. Stay around good folks like yourself, and mind your own business.

"I didn't get to be three years older than you, and survive Vietnam, by being stupid. It took a lot of praying and avoiding trouble, that got me through. And even when you do that, trouble will find you anyway."

"You talk a lot like my mother, Deek."

"Hey, if it's the truth, it must be alright. Yeah, Porch, I think that dude that shot you was an amateur. But even an amateur is dangerous once he crosses that criminal line of no return. And his next time out, he's no longer a rookie at it. He is a pro then."

"So I'm expected to hang around like a sitting duck, waiting for something to happen?"

"Nobody can say they know how you feel. You're the one that got shot. All I know is that if it were me, I'd try to go back to normal and put it all behind me."

"All I know is I'd feel better with a gun."

"I'm not gone give you a gun, Porch. But suppose you found someone that did? How would you carry it? Ninety-five percent of the time, you're here on campus. Ain't nothing gone happen here, but how would you get a hold of it when you needed it?"

"I'll carry it in a grip bag with my books. I'm lugging a grip bag around most of the time anyway. It's baseball season. Between books and gym clothes, I could easily keep it with me."

"You couldn't carry it everywhere, all the time." Plus, you know that any student found with a weapon on campus, is expelled, no questions asked.

"Deek, I appreciate everything you're saying, but I'm still going to get a gun."

"Suit yourself. I'm through with it."

After this request failed, I considered my other prospects, namely, Dwayne and Charles. I would see both of them before the sun went down. Just about every student passed through the student union building after classes and before the end of the day. Of the two, Dwayne was least likely to own a gun. He hailed from Selma, Alabama, and had lived in the dorms three years. It was only this year that he boarded in a house off campus with two other guys.

Charles, on the other hand, actually lived in Waukeegan. His family owned a home in town. Charles was an Air Force brat. His dad, long since retired, moved the family to the area to accept a job at the nearby V.A. Hospital. So the white family moved into predominantly Black Waukeegan.

I had seen the white boy on campus since our freshman year, and we had become friends our sophomore year from the time we took a psychology course together. I got along with Charles because I never called him derogatory names like cracker, honky, red neck or peckerwood. Of course, with the shoe on the other foot, and him being in the minority at Waukeegan, he dared not call Black folks names. To save money, for two semesters, we loaned each other one another's books, depending on our curriculum schedules.

So the day after Deacon West told me he wanted "no parts of that mess," I got Charles to come through for me. We met in the forecourt of the statue that stood on the west of the campus' main intersection. A circular driveway stood out from the statue on the front side of the fixture. Waist high, manicured shrubbery outlined the court, and evergreen trees buttressed and overhang in the rear of the elevated, bronze man, a relic of the founding president of the College. The trees aligned the statue in such an order, that a photographer couldn't do any better in arranging a backdrop.

"Man, you picked a hell of a place to meet," Charles said. He wore a green Army fatigue jacket and blue jeans, and he looked around in all directions.

"Do you have it?"

"Yeah, I got it. Take your time, Porch. Just hold on." He led me off to a bench beyond the bronze statue. There was nothing unusual about the two of us, each carrying an athletic grip bag on campus. No one would suspect us of being spies or conspirators. He reached inside his grip bag and pulled out a brown paper sack that contained a weighty object.

He held the brown paper bag with both hands, and opened it at the top for me to peep inside. "This is it, a .38 pistol. I only got the four bullets that came with it. If you want more, you have to buy 'em yourself."

"Let me hold it."

"Okay, but don't take it out of the bag. You can look at it later in your room, when ain't nobody around."

We transferred the gun to my athletic grip bag.

"You don't have to do this, you know," Charles said. "I mean, this is serious stuff. You get to a certain point, and ain't no turning back. Then again, where you gonna start at? I mean, we came to college to get an education. We're not gangsters."

"I know what I'm doing," I said. "I'm going to use the same procedure as the counselors and the police. I'm going to start at the beginning, and consider everybody a suspect, if they know me and had something against me, going back six months.

"Then I'm going to look into stuff relating to Bakarie Seesay and Hollie Drummond."

"Why them?"

"Because they were the ones that figured in prominently in my mind, on the day everything went crazy."

"That's a lot of people. Even me? You think I'm a suspect, too? You see how stupid this is getting? Just remember what I said," he reminded me. "I'm doing this because I'm your friend, and you asked me. I ain't got nothing to do with it. I'm not charging you anything. I'm loaning it to you for two months. And if you don't come up with anything by then, I'm gonna have to return the gun back to my Daddy's old tool room."

"I'm hoping to solve this thing without even using the gun," I said.

"You better!"

'Don't worry. I'm not going to do anything stupid."

We finished talking about the pistol. Like two espionage agents, we successfully completed the exchange. Then, in the forecourt of the bronze statue, we parted company.

Chapter 8
A Bulletproof Dashiki

I walked across campus feeling more secure in myself now that I had that gun in my grip bag. Now I'd have to negotiate when I would or would not have it with me. It would be so much simpler if I would've had a bulletproof Dashiki that really was bulletproof. My roommate has an African Dashiki that Bakarie once said had "medicine" in it to protect a man from his enemies. But that was all JuJu. As Bakarie had pointed out, people all over Africa thought well of President John Kennedy because he started the Peace Corps. It was said throughout the land—"If we had known that they were going to kill him, we would have sent him a gown with medicine in it." Of course the President was shot in the head, and the Dashiki wouldn't have done him any good.

It was back in November when Bakarie told us that story. He had come by our room one night. I'd had a long day before he came in.

At 6:40 a.m. on the last Sunday in November, I got up to get dressed for breakfast. For this one-third of a mile hike across campus, I dressed in a beige, zip-up windbreaker jacket over a blue gym shirt, a pair of blue jeans with white socks and white, converse All-Stars basketball shoes.

Pulled down over my head was my favorite hat—an Army camouflage hat, green with black and brown streaks that blended in with the terrain. It had a floppy brim like a cowboy hat and a tie string that I could use to secure it between my chin and neck. The hatband had stitched loops around it, that could store bullets vertically one next to the other, around the crown. The hat was four years old now.

While in high school, I had seen the movie "The Green Berets." About that time, I decided that I had to have an Airborne Ranger hat. These type hats were considered 'cool' because they were not easy to get. You had to live near an Army Surplus Store (of which some stores did not like to sell their goods to civilians) or be right out of the military, directly.

Philbert "Rec King" Cupp was another student who had regular fellowship with the International student body because he participated in campus-wide, table tennis matches. Virtually every country with a student on campus had a top-notch ping-pong player. At 7:00 a.m., he came down the hall and knocked on the door. "Hey, Nardo, Porch! Y'all going to breakfast?"

I opened the door. "Yeah, I'm going. Leonardo said he's gone sleep awhile."

Cupp was known as "Rec King." Sometimes shortened to Rec. Today he had on a worn out orange sweat suit with his white socks and tennis shoes. In three years, he had gone from a hapless, laughable beginner to becoming an expert table tennis player. Though awkward and ungainly, he had put in his time in Rec-ology. Our student recreation center was known as The Rec. With sheer desire and determination, the mahogany brown competitor emerged among the card players, pool shooters, pinball wizards, and ping-pong enthusiasts, as the undisputed Rec King.

"I've got a tournament this afternoon," Cupp said. "You ought to be there, Porch."

"I can't. I'll be at the library studying."

We walked across campus to breakfast. Cupp was animated the whole time, he feigned strokes and shots, and described how he would defeat his opponents in the table tennis tournament.

According to him, this one was to be international in scope—a fellow from Africa named Kojo Tarawallie, a student from China named Chou Lee Su, and a turbaned scholar named Rajib Patel from India, and a Jamaican called Neville. I had met Kojo and Neville with Bakarie that Saturday night at the late night dinner in the basement of the dorm. Cupp and a hand full of Black Americans made out the competitors list.

"These foreign guys are advanced students, and some of them are college professors. They're playing for their countries. They're playing for blood!" Cupp said. "We gotta kick their asses!"

The whole time, he demonstrated his strokes and shots, feigning and turning, displaying his forehand, backhand and serve.

"We're gonna kick their asses. Man, you gotta be there." Other students were walking across campus, either going to breakfast or heading to Sunday service at the campus chapel. While they might have glanced at the competitor, Cupp was oblivious to their curious observations.

We stayed in one of the cluster of dormitories on the northwest corner of campus, where five three-story brick buildings were turned at peculiar angles to each other, due to the slopes in the landscape and the curves in the roads. It took a brisk eight to nine minutes to get from our second floor rooms to the Cafeteria. Cupp talked about his strategy continually.

We walked along with the crowd from the northwest side of campus, and then cut across a field, using a dirt path that was a shortcut across two streets that circled around in an oblong semicircle. At the street that was considered the interior through road, we passed beside an old dormitory on our left, and journeyed through "The Valley," a sparsely grassed, vast gulch, almost the size and width of a football field. The higher points of "The Valley" were flanked on all sides by the posterior walls of old brick buildings, several of which were girls' dormitories. So from every corner, "The Valley" was somebody's backyard. In the old idiom—"If walls could talk"— "The Valley" held its own legends, hundreds of stories, asides, footnotes, and sidebars.

It was something to see the Cupp emerge victorious in a tournament. Awkward and clumsy, he used the whole floor on his side of the table. He had mastered the coordination of arm, wrist, hand, and paddle, with quick hawk-eye reflexes, but the rest of his body followed slower. So he won the hard way— made it look difficult. As was said of a deliberate, drudging, misfiring, and error-proned boxing match— "He won ugly!"

When it was all over, if he won, I'd see Cupp in gym shorts and a T-shirt, pull a gray sweatshirt over his head and hang a towel around his neck to absorb his success. It was akin to a Baptist preacher standing in his pulpit after a "bang up" sermon, with a white towel around his neck, knowing he had "got 'em going, had kept the faith, had fought the good fight, had run the good race, had fired them up, and had 'em shouting all over the place." In this quiet repose, standing there with a white towel around his neck, the Rite Reverend Rec King Cupp showed that he had done his job. Then he would let others shout their joys, encouragements, and amens.

As for the champions, their rewards were generally no more than to have their names posted on a list in the Rec room, or to win table tennis paddles that were of slightly better quality than the ones provided by the Center. When you won a tournament at Waukeegan, you were one of the three best players on campus—coming, going, staying, or just passing through.

The significant fact concerning Cupp, nickname aside, was that he single-handedly elevated the tournament to the level of a true athletic event on campus. Students came to see him play his game.

I was not surprised to find a routine Sunday morning breakfast menu. It consisted of a packet of cold cereal with milk, a glass of orange juice, and a large fried hush puppy ball of bread, containing sprinklings of corn, that you poured syrup over and ate with a fork. The College saw to it that half of its cafeteria staff got the weekend off, and it showed in the food preparation. I wondered if it was worth the walk from the dorm for this. Then I spotted a Shirley, whom I had taken a class with in the past, and I had talked to her from time to time. I got up to move my food tray over to her table.

"Hey, Cupp, I'll see you back at the dorm," I said.

Around 9:45 p.m. that Sunday, I returned back to the dorm. I had gone to dinner at 4:30 p.m. and had been at the library from 5:00 until 9:30 p.m. studying, among other things, Lorraine Hansberry's play—*A Raisin In The Sun*. In just a few days, Maureen Ezell and I would act out a touching scene as Walter and Mama. Our ensemble of seven had held one rehearsal and would have two more before our performance in the Speech and Drama class on Thursday.

When I entered our room, I met Leonardo, Cupp and Ivan, a student from down the hall. Leonardo was narrating Saturday's trip back from the concert in Montgomery. I greeted them. Leonardo changed the subject for a moment.

"Hey, Porch, did you ask him? You know, the African guy?"

"Yeah, Bakarie said he'll be up here around ten o'clock."

Leonardo was sitting in the chair near his desk, which was built against the wall near the window on his side of the room. Ivan sat on Leonardo's bed, and Cupp sat in my chair.

"Anyway, let me tell you what happened," Leonardo said. His brown face was alive, the eyes moving, the hands gesturing in punctuation to his words. In the room full of Afro hairdos, the South Carolinian with the low-cut, brushed hair style, held the audience.

"Charles Jordan's folks were out of town for the weekend, see. He knew he was gone get some. He was gone drop me off after the concert, take Geneva home and screw her, then bring her back to campus in the morning.

"Y'all know ain't but a few white girls on campus, anyway. So white boy had to get on the stick to line up this date. Man, they got to arguing on the drive back from Montgomery. She kept talking about how cute the lead singer was, and how she wished she could've been closer down front to see the singer, where he had come down off the stage and held one girl in his arms and sang into the microphone, looking at the girl.

"It really pissed Charles off when Geneva said, "'I wished that had been me. If only we'd had better tickets,'" Leonardo mimicked.

"And Charles said, "'Look here. I might not be a good singer, and I may not be too good-looking, but you're the one's been chasing after me out on the yard all over campus. And for your information, those were pretty damn good tickets.'"

"Anyway," Leonardo continued, "I sat my black ass back there in the back seat of that blue Volkswagen and kept my mouth shut. It was none of my business. I let them two white folks argue. I didn't say shit! It got kinda sticky after a while. He reminded her of the money he had spent on the dinner and the concert, and all Geneva kept saying was 'Take me back to the dorm.'

"So he took her little fine ass back to the dorm. The reason I was along with them in the first place was that another girl, a friend of Geneva's, was supposed to have gone with them. At the last minute, she couldn't go, so they let me tag along,

"When Charles dropped me off, he said he had prepared everything at his crib—wine, music, some smokes, everything! He was pissed off. When I talked to him today, he was cool about it. He said, "'Hey, you win some, you lose some. When you play the game, you gotta take your shots. The more shots you take, the more games you win.'"

"You have to give it to old Charles Jordan. Yeah, he's got a car and a little money to spend. And, with his philosophy of taking your shots, he probably get more pussy than all of us in this room put together."

"Speak for yourself," Ivan said. Ivan was a stout guy from down the hall, a member of the Kappa Alpha Psi fraternity, and he always wore something red—a hat, shirt, jacket, pants, drawers or T-shirt. Red and white were the frat's colors. We sometimes called him Kappa Red Ivan.

"Ah, Ivan, you ain't had none in so long, it's a shame." To this, we all broke out laughing.

Before Ivan got a chance to say something, someone knocked on the door. It had been left ajar, and Bakarie stuck his head in the room, amid all the laughter.

"Come in, Bakarie. This is the right room," I said.

Bakarie entered the room dressed like a college professor. He sported a brown tweed sports coat that had dark brown patches on the elbows of the sleeves. No necktie accompanied his white shirt. Black dress pants and brown loafers made out the attire. I made the introductions as the dark man—clean shaved, no beard, and no mustache—nodded to each person.

"Oh, I know you," Cupp spoke out. "You're a friend of Kojo's, the table tennis player. We whupped up on y'all today, huh-huh-huh!" In scoring this point, he and Ivan slapped each other's palms, in that 'give me five' congratulatory hand salute.

"Well, what can I say?" Bakarie answered with a smile as he hunched his shoulders. Then he demanded seriously: "So where's the garment?"

"It's under my bed," Leonardo said. He pulled out the drawer that was made into the bed's lower frame.

Bakarie help up the shirt, a brown hip length poncho with a V-neck cut out on the front. It was shaped like a folded blanket and was sewn together at the bottom corners on both sides. The West African felt its fine gritty texture, as a person would rub a composite of rich farm dirt.

"Aahh! Very nice, interesting." Bakarie held the shirt up with both hands on the shoulders of the attire. Then he ran his index finger along the interior stitches of the neck cutout. "You Americans call it a Dashiki, but I can assure you, it's more than that. It's authentic!"

"So, what do we have here?" Leonardo questioned.

"What you have here is a gown made of otherwise, common country cloth found in many parts of West Africa. Only now, it is endowed with powers or "medicine," if you will. Because the dye used to color it with, is a secret formula of which only few know of its contents."

The expert's eyes rolled, and his brows expanded. "Whatever you do," he punctuated the air with his index finger as he admonished, "don't wash it. And avoid wearing it during the rain."

The poncho-type shirt was dyed a light, tannish, khaki brown, containing as designs, small chocolate colored brown, geometric circular "O's." An angular, heart-shaped pocket, the same chocolate color as the "O's," was sewn off center, and was affixed at the front of the shirt just below the V-neck cutout. The bottom hem, the same color as the pocket and the letter "O's," reached four inches in height from the tip of the fringed ends, up the body of the garment. The hem and fringes constituted a band that ran around the entire bottom of the outfit.

Bakarie took off his European jacket, and pulled the cultural heritage garment over his own head, and showed us how to wear it.

"Our people believe that, worn by the right person, the shirt will protect one from the thrust of enemy daggers, spears, and even bullets. Ahhh! Powerful medicine, you say? Even today we believe in it.

"Traditionally, during tribal wars of years past, this garment was a favorite of men when they traveled to unknown territories." He folded the shirt back in a pleat on the top of both of his shoulders. "This," he said, "means a challenge! It says you are more a man than the next man. Unlike your slang 'to have a chip on your shoulder, and to dare anyone to knock it off,' this type of shirt is normally worn by a man of character, self-discipline, a leader, a warrior, a wise man, a chief.

"You must be strong, but not boastful; confident, but still humble. The truth of the matter is, if you don't have those qualities, the medicine in the shirt won't work for you."

"For a moment there, you had me thinking all a man had to do was put on this Dashiki, and he's covered for just about everything, like wearing a bullet-proof vest," I said.

"Oh, no. This shirt carries a lot of responsibility. You have to be up to the task."

"Maybe that's why they gave it to my cousin B.D. when he visited Africa," Leonardo said. "Old B.D. is a pretty good guy, and he gave it to me. Tell you what— to keep in good standings with the rest of y'all, I'm

75

going to make sure I wear it when I'm on my best behavior."

"You do that, and all the spirits will be happy. I've got to go now," Bakarie announced.

"Thanks for coming by," I said.

"Yeah, I really appreciate you telling me about the history of the shirt," Leonardo added.

After he left, we started talking about other folks who believed in witchcraft, juju, voodoo, hoodoo, roots, magic, and other forms of the supernatural. Each of us cited at least one person from our hometown who held those beliefs.

A few days later, Bakarie invited us to an international students' food bazaar at the International Student Association building. There would be no conflict in our schedules, he reminded us, as the event was scheduled during the same hours as lunch in the cafeteria. The end of November had been the beginning of my friendship with Bakarie.

Chapter 9
A Friend of a Friend

Now it was the first day of March. It was dusk. Lights on the cars were dimmed yellow. It would get dark any minute now. Then all the lights would go on bright. Less than a half-hour had passed since I had placed the pistol in my closet and was informed by Neville of the impending news.

Adelaide Mansaray drove the car. A real cutie, always looking as if she stepped out of *Vogue* magazine, Adelaide wore a short Afro hairdo and had on triangle-shaped, ivory earrings. The petite, chocolate complexioned African was Bakarie's girlfriend. Neville, the Jamaican with a medium length Afro, sat up front with her. I was in the back seat with the crutches crossing my lap. The base of the crutches rested on the floorboard behind the driver, with the cushioned end armrests protruding upwards, just short of reaching the ceiling of the car.

In the mid-sized gray Chevrolet, we passed an old, little used airfield on our right, and then a two-story motel on the left, flanked by small service stations on the right and left of the motel. Then, we approached the Interstate Highway to Opelika.

"I don't think he's going to make it," Adelaide said. "I think he's going to die."

"You shouldn't talk like that," Neville said. "Let's just hope for the best."

"Does Bakarie have any folks in the states?" I asked. No one answered.

"People think that just because we speak with a different accent and come from developing countries, that we're all the same," Adelaide complained.

"I didn't say that."

"I know. But still, I don't know how you handle anything like this. Maybe you call the country's embassy. Maybe you call the International Red Cross. I don't know."

Kojo is knowledgeable in international business," Neville offered. "Let's rely on his experience."

"I feel so responsible. I wish I could do something about it."

"Nobody's blaming you, Calvin. What happened to Bakarie could've happened to anybody, anytime," he said. "Being at the wrong place at the wrong time is a fact of life. It happens everyday."

Then it was quiet. Nobody said anything more, lest his or her remarks come out stupid. What could you say? A friend was expected to die. Then it was night, and the car lights were turned on bright. We rode on the Interstate Highway heading to County General Hospital in Opelika.

Less than an hour ago, all I hoped for was just to take a nap. There was a plain concrete stairwell between the dorm's first and second floors. Replete with white painted walls and a lone light bulb hanging from the ceiling, this room with its stacked rows of concrete steps remained the last obstacle to surmount leading to our floor. When I put my key in the door, Ivan appeared in the hall just from the bathroom.

"Hey, Porch, a guy named Neville came by a few minutes ago looking for you."

"Did he say anything or leave a message?"

"No. He just walked away, mumbling something to himself like "'Oh, man, it's not looking good. Not looking good at all.'"

I stepped into my room. Ivan, ever present in a white football jersey with the number ten in red and a red baseball cap, came in behind me: "What's going on? I've never seen him on our floor before."

"Neville lives on the basement level. He's a friend of Bakarie and Kojo. I know him. He's a pretty good guy."

I coolly set the grip bag in the corner in my closet behind the door. The gun lay in the bottom of the grip bag, under two tennis shoes turned upside down, beneath a folded white towel. I had just gotten the weapon from Charles Jordan. Ivan is one nosey-assed dude, I thought to myself. You can't tell him anything unless you've got all the facts. He's subject to jump to conclusions without knowing what the hell is going on.

"So what gives?" Ivan quizzed.

"I don't know, but I'm going to find out. I've got to go," I told him, motioning to the door. "I'll see you later."

I hurried down the stairs as fast as I could, considering that the crutches were still a part of my mobilization. When I passed through the lobby, I saw Neville enclosed in the phone booth, talking on the telephone. Neville spotted me and waved. He finished speaking and came out of the phone booth.

"Man, it's not looking good," he said. "They had to rush Bakarie over to County General Hospital. He was released from the hospital a day before you were. Now he's in again. I just got off the phone with Kojo. He's over at the hospital now. They've done all they can, and now they're waiting on an outside chance that the medication might take effect.

"According to Kojo, Bakarie is semi-conscious. It's some kind of bacterial infection from being thrown into that pool at the Mansion. I'm waiting on a ride to come by. Would you like to come along?"

"Yeah, of course."

"Good. Adelaide is coming over to give us a ride."

When we arrived at the information desk, a nurse told us where to find Bakarie. Upon entering the assigned room, we found it empty.

"They must have moved him," I said. "We'll just go back to the information desk."

As we exited the door and looked down the long corridor, we saw Kojo and a doctor walking towards us, the doctor talking and Kojo solemnly nodding his head. The doctor, a middle-aged white man in white surgery garb, talked conciliatorily to the West African student. Kojo wore a bluish-purple, tie-dyed long sleeve pullover shirt with a matching 'pillbox' type hat with dark pants and shoes.

"I just can't understand it," Kojo said throwing up his hands. Then he focused on us who waited in the corridor outside of the room. "He didn't make it," he called out, shaking his head from side to side, indicating 'no' in body language. "Brother Bakarie is gone."

When Kojo got closer to us, he was incredulous. "A simple thing as an infection caused by bronchial pneumonia, and now he is dead. I just can't understand it."

"Man, I'm so sorry," I said.

"Lord, help us," Adelaide cried out. She searched without reward for an answer: "How do you explain this to his family who has worked so hard to support him? It's just not fair. Oh-oh-oh-oh-oh!!!" she kept crying. "All these years, only to have your life taken away. It's not fair."

Neville had a more stoic opinion: "Life is not always fair. Some people have good fortune, others don't. We can't do anything for Bakarie, now. All we can do is pray for his soul, pray for strength to his family.

"And, if we can just remember the good qualities he had and carry them on, that's all we can do."

"I know that doesn't make it any easier, but he's right," Kojo said.

They kept Phillip Bakarr-Seesay Momodu's body in the hospital morgue for the evening, in preparation to ship it over to Montgomery for an autopsy the next morning. Kojo followed up with the student affairs office and found out that Bakarie had life insurance, and he left the matter in the hands of the proper authority. No funeral took place in the United States. The remains were sent to West Africa.

The African students got together and planned a Fortieth Day Memorial Service in honor of Bakarie. I learned that this, by definition, was a sending off party held in honor of a deceased loved one, a common festive event in much of West Africa. It is basically a Muslim custom of service, planned forty days after someone passed. As per Kojo, this was a party that started in the afternoon and went long into the night, and there were plenty of food and drinks, and a

Libation ceremony thrown in at some point during the occasion.

Sometimes, a goat or a cow was killed and prepared, cooked and served. Always at these events, the menu included roasted, peppered chicken, rice, fufu, and some type of greens *plasas* and stews, beer, palm wine, soft drinks and other alcoholic beverages. The custom was that you came and sat and visited with the family and shared pleasant memories of the deceased loved one. Sometimes, there was dancing and singing.

West Africans had male and female Secret Societies, like the Free Masons. For these occasions, they dressed alike for songs and dance performances. The criteria used to gauge how elaborate to make a Fortieth Day Memorial Service was determined by whether or not you were a "Big Man" or a "Big Woman." Bakarie was not a "Big Man," so his associates agreed to just put on a nice party.

For a few days after he passed, I felt miserable, couldn't eat, couldn't sleep, couldn't concentrate. I was in a state of being that mimicked a flu-like funk, a weak feeling without the hot and cold changes. A listless, gloom covered me like a blanket that I couldn't fight off. I took only one day off from classes since I had already lost two days due to my own wounds. Guilt was eating at my gut because I felt responsible for choosing to go to the Mansion that day. I wanted to cry but the tears wouldn't flow. I paid little attention to the time of day or my surroundings. My friend was gone.

After a few days, the demands of college life beckoned again. Sometimes you have to compartmentalize bereavement, put it in a cubbyhole and revisit it later. Then one night, about two weeks later, I was down in the lobby and unconsciously I walked out of the front door, sat on the stoop where I first met Bakarie. There in the cool of the night, I put my face in my hands and cried, whimpering involuntarily. Then for only a few minutes, a breeze rushed through the air and the trees in front of the dorm. I spoke to the rustling wind in the leaves of the nearest tree; "Oh, man is that you? I hope you're alright where you are. A surge of relief touched me like a burden lifted off my shoulders. It was as if Bakarie spoke through the wind—'Yes, I'm alright. Don't worry.' From then on, I was not sad anymore.

Even before Bakarie's death, I had already decided that I would let the Waukeegan Police Department and the campus security office debate the merits of the more viable, probable theory, and that I would pursue the "weak, remote" one. It was my life they were theorizing over, anyway. The great theory was 'isolated crook chases isolated man on the run; crook shoots Cavin Porch, then discovers has shot the wrong man; and hunter and hunted vanishes.' The weak, remote theory: Gunman follows Calvin Porch for some reason; shoots him at the Mansion; possible mistaken identity involving a friend or a friend of a friend; and possibly Calvin Porch not telling all that he knows.

"If it were me, I'd go back six months ... and see how they fit into the picture."

"It could be related to a friend of yours, or a friend of a friend. Lord knows who that could be."

They hadn't considered Professor Mansaray in the equation at all until I told Roland Trotter about the feud. And now with Bakarie dead, and the after knowledge that the two finally did reconcile their differences, that was now a moot point, or was it? I still needed to check it out.

A new theory I had to consider was that I may have been a mistaken target of Hollie's jealous boyfriend. Oftentimes, college girls dated guys who were not students, who lived around town, and lived by their wits. Some unsavory guy out there may have a campus guy on his hit list. After I thought about it longer, I concluded that that theory was no stronger than the other two.

Lately, I hadn't had a girlfriend since Maureen, though I was in the process of rekindling the flames with Hollie. I hadn't seen Hollie since the day at the Mansion. All I had of her existence was the note she left in my hospital room. I wondered why she hadn't checked back with me at the hospital like she promised, or called on me.

Why did that song always pop up in my mind whenever I thought of her? I'll be there. I'll be around.

Chapter 10
Like A Bazaar In Casablanca

A few days after Bakarie died, I begged Aaron Aldrich to cover a cultural topic on West African societies in the general interest column that he wrote in the student newspaper. He was active and wore many hats—he played on the Baseball team, was the assistant student ombudsman, and wrote a weekly column in the campus paper. He had already written an article about African and Caribbean music that was well received on campus, but he wasn't too interested in this topic at the moment.

"Good," I said. "What I had in mind in the first place was for you not to do the article at all. I'll do the legwork, put it all together and let you get the credit for it."

"How're you going to do that? You're not on the newspaper staff."

"Aaron, all you have to do is call Dr. Mansaray's office, tell him you want to do the article, arrange an appointment with him, and send me out in your place." Aaron is a skinny, mahogany-toned guy who wears black-framed, tinted lens glasses and sports a thin scraggly beard. He shaves it off during the Baseball season.

"I couldn't risk that."

"No, I don't mean pretend I'm you. I'll go as myself. I'll tell him you couldn't make it, that you sent me to do the interview. He won't know that I'm not on the staff here. Send me out with a set of prepared questions. I do the work, you get all the credit."

"I know you told me you needed to check this out for your peace of mind, but what's in it for you for real, Porch?"

"All I want to do is slip in a few questions about cross-tribal conflicts. I won't be specific about Bakarie and Adelaide. I'll keep it general. I promise."

"Alright, you got it." Aaron made the appointment for two days later. I'd have to go to Dr. Mansaray's house off campus.

As I thought about it, it occurred to me that our campus life was like that of a small town community. It was such a small world. Here I was going to visit Adelaide's dad "fronting" with the very feature article that Aaron wrote during the time when I ran into him at a function where Bakarie and Adelaide were present. It was back in November. In some uncanny way, now it seemed that my friendship with Aaron and Bakarie was connected. But how? And to what?

I clearly remember that day back in the fall when I went to that Food Bazaar sponsored by the Pan African Student Association. It was a day when I'd planned to skip the bland, institutionalized meal in the cafeteria.

The night before, when I returned to our room after visiting Maureen, I saw a note sticking through the door. It was from Bakarie:

> *Hello Calvin and Leonardo,*
>
> *It's me, Bakarie Seesay. We're having a cultural cuisine bazaar tomorrow at the social services building. It's between 11 a.m. and 1 p.m.*
>
> *I thought it would be a good idea if you would forego lunch tomorrow at the*

*cafeteria and join us instead. You can
expect good food from the tropics –from
the Caribbean Islands to Africa.*

> *You are invited,*
> *Bakarie*

I halfway expected to see Leonardo and Cupp at the function, but I was really intrigued by the presence of Dee Dee Pelham and Aaron.

The Social Services Building was actually a white, wood-framed house with a wide, low to the ground porch floor across its front. It stood just northeast of Bennington Hall, separated from the grounds of the former by a quiet winding road that trailed behind the dormitory where Maureen lived. The white, wood-framed house faced a drive-around lawn court to the east. Directly across the court stood the ROTC complex, twin two-story asbestos veneered barracks that looked more at home on a military base. And on the north flank of this lawn stood an old brick relic that served as a women's dormitory.

I entered the house and greeted everyone who looked in my direction. Specifically, I searched for the few people I knew—Bakarie, Kojo, Pablo, and Neville—the guys I met at the dorm, cooking a late night dinner on a portable, electric 'hot plate' stove.

Any group or organization on campus could use the Social Services facility upon request. The cultural bazaar had a decidedly Afro-Caribbean theme. They had brought their own posters and decorations. The slick, colorful posters on the walls, not unlike the ones seen in a travel agency office, depicted everything from fishing boats along a beach, to bandana head-covered women carrying items in bowl-pan containers on their heads, to the scene of street revelers and party goers at a carnival festival. The colors of the deep blue sea, the rainbow prism, the peacock, and the butterfly were all represented.

Various students had their food laid out on white cloth-covered tables. Some had stainless steel pans borrowed from the campus lunchroom. Smiling, talkative attendants, each representing his or her respective country, stood by the food samples. It appeared that the foreign students had gone to great lengths to make their food palatable to the uninitiated Western World student visitors. There was a great display of meat pies, shish kebobs, Spanish rice, and jallof rice dishes—familiar looking food, easy to handle for the awkward novice.

Among the first group of familiar faces I saw were Cupp and Dee Dee. In the past three years, Philbert "Rec King" Cupp hadn't really spent any more time in the Recreation Center than anyone else. "King Crab" and "Rec King" were nicknames usually given to freshmen students who were failing or flunking out, but Cupp's passion and development as a table-tennis tournament player, had extended the ownership of the moniker in the minds of his friends and associates.

An ordinary homely fellow, he was captured in a romantic, "cutie" pose as he and Dee Dee exchanged spiced shish kebobs—beef cubes-on-a-stick—that each one held up to the others mouth.

"How nice, Cupp. I didn't know you had it in you," I joked.

"Hey Porch."

"Hi Calvin," Dee Dee said. "You should try these."

"I will."

Cupp sauntered over to another table. Dee Dee was short and fine, a butterscotch brown dancer who sported a short Afro and wore a blue denim outfit, a basic choice of many girls on campus.

"I didn't expect to see you here," I said.

"Cupp's African friend, Kojo, invited us," Dee Dee answered. "Half the time, they're tournament rivals. The other times they play as a duo."

"The last time I saw you out at "The Breeze Station," you hinted about giving Dwayne Norwood a little play."

Although Cupp and Dwayne were both my friends, Cupp was actually Leonardo's best friend. Whereas Dwayne hung out with me more and we took classes together by virtue of having the same major, I saw this as a moment to lobby for Dwayne.

"Dwayne's alright," Dee Dee said, "but he's a little silly and full of bullshit to go with it."

"Cupp's kind of dufous, though, don't you think?"

"That's part of his charm. That's why I like him. Actually I like him more now than before. He's teaching me to play table tennis, and I'm introducing him to modern dance.

"In fact, he's going to be a spotter and assistant on our dance routine during the half-time show at the basketball game this week."

"I'll be there," I promised. "I hope y'all do good. Cupp is an alright guy."

Just then Cupp returned: "You ought to try some of this stuff, Porch."

"Hey Porch!" someone called out. "Where you been, man?"

89

I looked around and faced Aaron. "What's happening, Aaron?"

"All kind of stuff is happening, man." He took a bite from some finger food he held in a small paper plate.

My association with the vegetarian Aaron went back to our sophomore year. Chief among his accomplishments was the acquisition of a nickname a teammate bestowed upon him. "Streak-O-Lean" or "Strick" was the name that rang in bad humor to Aaron's ears. I knew that Aaron detested the nickname, so I never called him that. Basically, the nickname was used by a few of the guys on the team when they wanted to get a "rise" out of him. At first, it was like an inside joke, exclusive to us on the Baseball team, until a few Football and Basketball players in the locker room got hold of it. Then the tag ran the risk of becoming a full-fledged nickname.

"My column is going well," he said referring to his weekly column in the campus newspaper. "And my new job as Assistant Ombudsman is exciting. So, tell me, what brought you here, mingling with the foreigners?"

"Bakarie Seesay, a friend from West Africa. What brought you here?"

"Oh man, I've got an article coming out tomorrow on Afro-Caribbean music. You have to read it."

"I'll check it out."

Aaron, an eclectic writer, always sought feedback on his articles, and I usually chipped in my opinion when asked. One time, I commented that one of his articles appeared to be rather mundane, as if "right out of a book," whereby the author's feelings were hurt.

After that, I was more guarded when he asked for my point of view.

"But let me tell you. I've got some stuff hotter than my articles, and I can't even report it," he whispered.

Aaron Nathan Aldrich was a Political Science and History major with the ambition of some day becoming a lawyer. Failing that, a major league baseball career would come in a close second. The baseball part had slim possibilities, as he, like I, was not a starting player. He had speed and quickness and was the best fielding outfielder, but his throwing arm strength was only average, and his batting average below average.

"My new job as Assistant Ombudsman puts me in touch with all kinds of campus problems," Aaron said, "real, legal problems. Stuff that involves the whole college."

"How do you manage to get so much done?"

"It's not too hard. One thing is usually related to the other. And if you work it right, it's as simple as keeping an appointment. While I'm thinking about it— I need your help with a situation that's getting a little messy right now."

"What's it about?"

"It's about a mutual friend of ours that's gotten himself in a jam. I can't talk to you about it now, but I think you'll want to hear about it. Come by the Ombudsman's Office between three and five this afternoon."

Aaron believed in extra curricular activities, and he moved around on campus documenting his observations in his weekly column titled *Meandering*.

To an ordinary student, someone who did not participate in activities on campus other than studying, it seemed that these campus newspaper scribes were, in a laboratory sort of way, practicing their profession with an earlier start on their craft than the rest of us. Radical Liberal Arts 'types,' History-Geo-Socio-Political-Economic-Technocrat-inclined students flourished on the weekly campus news staff. To an uninitiated freshman or unsuspecting sophomore, they came across as relevant and militant. After you had been around them to know them personally, you learned that behind the militant rhetoric the authors put on paper, hid regular, mild-mannered students, more often than not, the sons and daughters of well-to-do parents. Aaron blended in well with this group.

I had been at the gathering about seven minutes as I waded my way through the maze of people and food stations, before I reached Bakarie's table. He was dressed in a brown, short-sleeved safari suit, holding court and looking professional, as he talked to several on listeners.

"You see, here's a person with an unbiased view of what I'm talking about," Bakarie said, shaking my hand with one hand, and patting me on the back with the other.

"Tell us, Calvin, is jallof rice better with chunks of only one kind of meat or with several kinds of meat in it?"

"I've only had it once, and it was good then. I'd rather think that the more, the merrier."

"You see … that's exactly what I believe," Kojo said. He had his table set up next to Bakarie, and they were talking about something I knew nothing about.

"My friend, you are not helping me," Bakarie light heartedly warned me.

The discussion concerned matters of seasoning and taste that varied among African Nationals. A particular dish might vary due to the application, or lack thereof, of onions, tomatoes, peppers, palm oil, cooking oil, ground nuts, beef, chicken, fish, goat meat, etc. To the Sociology or Anthropology student not acquainted with the subtleties among Africans, this was a lesson. Age old likes, dislikes, suspicions, associations, disassociations, war and peace, all had their existence rooted in subtle differences one group had from another.

With a simple dish like jallof rice, one tribe (a word Bakarie had taught me not to use, substituting Nation or National), might use only one kind of meat, or only one meat at a time, never including two at a time in the same dish. Another Nation might use fish, beef, and chicken, in the same dish, much like how the Louisianans employ variety in their gumbo soup.

"This is all in good fun and camaraderie," Bakarie stated, ending the bantering that had gone on for several minutes. He held up a cup, indicating a toast. "Let's have some tea."

This was the same herbal tea I remembered from the first meal I had with them when we first met at the late night dinner at the dormitory. Kojo's specialty, I remembered, an all-purpose tea, guaranteed to make a man more virile if he drank enough of it continuously.

"As you can see, we have a lot of fun when we have these gatherings," Bakarie said.

"It's alright with me," I said. "I'm all for it."

"Good, because this is only the beginning! We're having a party on Saturday night. Food, drinks, fine women, everything."

'What's this I hear about fine women?" a young woman asked. She nudged up against Bakarie affectionately and held his hand. She was petite, wore a short Afro with small circular earrings, and modeled a purple and blue tie-dyed dress.

"Adelaide, this is my friend Calvin. Calvin, this is Adelaide. What about the party on Saturday?"

"I'll check back with you on that," I said. "My girlfriend mentioned something about another party for Saturday. I'll see what she's thinking."

"Bring her. She'll like it," Adelaide said.

"I'll see."

When the conversation ended the word *girlfriend* reverberated in my mind. Though events had been leading up to this point with Maureen and me, our relationship hadn't been defined. That was my first utterance of the word girlfriend.

After I left the gathering, I went to two classes. I was anxious to hear what Aaron was going to tell me, since he made it seem like it was important and too confidential to speak of in a place that was "crowded like a bazaar in Casablanca."

Chapter 11
A One Dollar Bet

At the end of the day after Aaron gave me the okay to interview Dr. Mansaray, I called Hollie. I had gotten her phone number the day at the Mansion before the bullets flew. I'd hoped she would call me, but she never did. She lived off campus in a rented house that she shared with two other girls.

After I brought her up to date on my condition since the shooting, I questioned her.

"Hollie, I need to ask you something, just gathering all the facts, you know, trying to put two and two together."

"What do you want to know?"

"I heard you had some trying times with Ed. Do you think he would've had someone follow you?"

"You mean like at the Mansion? Hell, no. He's too much of a coward for that. If he did anything to anyone, it would be in private, out of the way of people." Hollie had come a long ways since our freshman year. She was tough and no-nonsense then, but she'd gravitated to and embraced the spice of vulgar and profane language, using it like salt and pepper—a sprinkling here and a dash there.

"No, he wouldn't operate that way. He wouldn't have someone else do his dirty work; he'd do it himself. But he's too chicken-shit scared to even think of doing that." Hollie was giving me more than enough information, and I let her continue uninterrupted. "I had to get away from Ed. He's a jealous son-of-a-bitch. Whenever we went out somewhere and some guy smiled at me or greeted me, Ed thought I'd led him on.

95

More than once, he's tried to provoke another guy into a fight, especially if the guy was smaller than him.

"If it was somebody his own size or bigger, he wouldn't say anything, but would later pick an argument with me. He wants somebody who's weak that will put up with his shit. My mother told me, 'If he hit you, he don't love you.' And I told him that when we first started going together.

"Well, he hit me one time, gave me a black eye, and that was enough. I hit him up side the head with the biggest skillet in the house. I left him dazed on the floor. 'Motherfucker, you will never hit me again,' I said. Then I walked out the door with that skillet in my hand. He probably had a cartoon knot on his head after I left, but I didn't stay around to see it."

"That bastard!"

"Don't worry about it. That's history now. But you know what Calvin? I think you ought to leave this thing alone. You're on a wild goose chase that's going nowhere. Nobody's after you. Just leave it alone. You're wasting your time."

"That's what everybody's been telling me, but I can't let it go until I know for sure what it's all about."

"Well, since we're talking, I need to let you know something. I'm dating a friend of yours now."

"Who?"

"Luckie."

"That's the story of my life. The girl I like chooses my friend. You tell me we're not compatible, yet I've seen you with a couple of guys who I know are not compatible with you."

"I was at the point of starting an intimate relationship with you that Saturday, but you're a special friend and I just don't want to spoil that."

"Oh really? So if I hadn't got shot that day, we would've been tight by now, huh? Tell me, when did y'all start hanging out together?"

"The day at the Mansion. Luckie walked back to campus with me when they took you to the hospital in my car. He was considerate and well-mannered."

"Well, if you need me, I'll be around." We said goodbye. When I hung up the phone I could've kicked myself. That was weak. Basically, I told her I'm available on the rebound whenever she's between boyfriends. Weak, weak, weak!

By now it was a week after the shooting and I put away the crutches. There was still a little tightness and nuisance pain in my buttocks, and I favored my left leg. Thanks to Coach Benson's arrangement with the V.A. Hospital, I 'rehabbed' at their Physical Therapy Center. The first two sessions were out of the way. For the next four weeks, I'd have to go over there three days a week. I also returned to the Baseball team, even though all I did was exercise, run laps and play catch on the sidelines.

On the walk to Dr. Mansaray's house, I crossed the Southwest section of campus, observing the old buildings that were built during the turn of the century. All the old square-cut relics, the sidewalks and pavement were constructed with bricks manufactured by the institution itself when it was no more than a Trade School—a 'Normal School.' It was documented that our founding president had a philosophical difference with the well-known Dr. W.E.B. Dubois.

While the doctor sat in his Ivory Tower theorizing about the concept of the 'Talented Tenth,' taking a tenth of the population of ex-slaves, grooming them, and making them the leaders of the future, our founder focused on the 'Normal Nineties' who needed clothes on their backs and food on their tables right now.

The old brick structures stood as monuments that represented the 'hands-on' approach. Now since the beginning of the Twentieth Century, Waukeegan College has made the leap into the present, where the talented tenth can thrive without leaving anybody behind if they were willing to try. Someone like me, for instance. I'd come to college on a student loan, armed with mediocre scores on the ACT and SAT tests. So in the end, our founding president and the 'educated' doctor both had their philosophies satisfied.

Neither of my parents had finished high school, but they understood the value of an education; which is why my mother reminded me that night at the hospital that I should leave this foolishness alone about trying to find out who shot me. Once I talk to Dr. Mansaray, I *am* going to leave it alone. That's the promise I've been telling myself anyway.

I'd crammed up on the Anthropology and Sociology necessary to do the interview—rather, the amateur interrogation. As credentials, I carried two copies of Aaron's article on African and Caribbean music. I'd give one to Dr. Mansaray if he didn't already have one. I'd written, in my own handwriting, the ten questions Aaron insisted that I stick to. As far as the Professor was concerned, this was going to be a follow up to the cultural music article. I'd have to find a subtle way to ask him—"Did you hire someone to harm Bakarie Seesay?"

The Mansarays lived in a modest neighborhood off the western border of campus in a white, wood-framed house that stood on a hill up a steep driveway. Since I'd gotten that pistol from Charles Jordan, I wore sweat suits and carried a grip bag whenever possible. The gun lay in the bottom of the bag under a pair of tennis shoes and a white towel. Of course I never took the gun to the V.A. Hospital, and I didn't have it with me today. For the interview, I dressed casual—ordinary shirt, pants and shoes.

Mrs. Mansaray answered the doorbell, attired in a green and white matching head-tie and dress set. I saw where Adelaide got her looks. The mother's face was rounder and fuller, but the resemblance was there. She led me to the sunroom, an extension of the den on the back of the house.

Wusu Mansaray was a middle-aged man with salt and pepper gray hair on his medium-length Afro and thin beard. Except for a one-inch gap on each side of his face below the earlobes, the beard would've connected from ear to ear.

"Have a seat," he said after he shook my hand and greeted me. "Can I get you anything?"

Before I could answer, he called out to his wife, "Howah, bring him something—a Coke or Seven-Up and some plantain. Would you prefer Coke or Seven-Up?"

"Seven-Up," I said.

Along with his dark trousers and shoes, Dr. Mansaray wore a beige, short-sleeved shirt, a garment cut like a jacket at the waist, that he wore outside of his pants. Bakarie had once told me that it was the kind of shirt you could wear to any event, whether formal or casual; every serious-minded West African had at least one of them. "So, how can I help you?"

I told him about the article Aaron wrote, and that we, the Campus Newspaper, were looking to do a follow-up topic. He was familiar with the paper, but had only heard of the article from his daughter. I showed him a copy and let him peruse it. By then, Mrs. Mansaray returned with the soft drinks and two plates of snack food that looked like friend bananas, sliced lengthwise. She set a fork on a napkin on the coffee table beside each plate.

"It's good, try it," Dr. Mansaray said.

"It really is. How do you get the bananas to keep their shape after frying them?"

"It's plantains, not bananas." He proceeded to tell me the difference. The plant was larger than a banana, not naturally sweet, and could be processed in a variety of forms; you could bake it, fry it, pound it, flatten it and eat it like a potato, bread it, cake it, or shred it into smaller pieces. What they gave me was battered in flour, fried and covered with a sugarcoated icing. "Not bad, eh?" he said as he sliced a second piece with his fork.

I learned that the Professor was living in exile in the United States. A decade had passed since he'd fled his country. A military coup, headed by non-commissioned officers who made themselves generals, caused him to lose everything he had worked to achieve. The college professors fell out of favor with the semi-literate generals. He escaped with nothing but the clothes on his back. Six months later, relatives helped the wife and daughter get out.

"It's just me, Howah and Adelaide here in the States. As for the relatives back home, I can't do much to help them on a teacher's salary. Oh, I can send a little money home from time to time, but that's about all I can do. My daughter is a student on campus. Do you know her?"

"Yes, I've met Adelaide. She a beautiful girl."

"Well, thank you. You see, if we had never left Africa, we probably would have had a lot of children by now. But because things have been so uncertain since we came here, my wife and I avoided the hardship of having a large family here. That's why we put all our care and concern on Adelaide. But that's not what you came here to talk about."

Yes it was, but I couldn't tell him that. "I'm not in a rush Dr. Mansaray. I've got some prepared questions, but they can wait."

"Very well. Just to give you an example of our lives here, I've had to protect our daughter from suitors who I feel world derail her career and ruin her life. I cannot afford to let that happen. She is not ready to be out on her own.

"I finally did give in to her with her recent boyfriend. My wife and I agreed to put on a big engagement party. Well, we've spent money on an event that's not going to happen now. The boy is dead.

"I know. Bakarie was a friend of mine, too."

"I know. You're here to find out about him and me, how we got along."

"That's crossed my mind, but the feature article is a priority."

"Priority for who—you or Aaron Aldrich? When you called for directions and said he couldn't make it, I knew it was not important to him. I did some research, too, you know. You're Bakarie's friend and you're looking for clues as to how that incident happened. Is that not so?"

"Dr. Mansaray, I'm only a student trying to complete an assignment. May I proceed with the questions?"

"Your failure to answer my question means that I am right. Howah!" he called out to the other room.

Howah Mansaray came in the room. "Yes darling?"

"Pay me the one dollar bill that you owe me," he said lightheartedly. "He came here to quiz me, alright. I won the bet!"

"I feel so embarrassed by this," she said. "Mr. Mansaray playing a game, when he should be serious. Forgive him. He's not normally this way."

"I told her before you got here that the purpose of your visit had nothing to do with writing an article. That article will never be printed, will it?"

"Oh, yes sir. We have every intention of printing it," I said. "We usually have two weeks lead time. It's definitely going to be printed."

"Huh-Huh-Huh!" he laughed. "I have to tell you that we had been prompted by Mr. Roland Trotter of Campus Security. He spoke to me in his capacity as a part-time employee of the police department. He told us we could expect to be questioned in the future, if not by the police then certainly by someone from the newspapers.

"I half-way expected someone from a real newspaper—huh-huh-huh! This is not a knock on you, but the campus paper is a small fry when you consider all the stuff we've been through."

I thought to myself—my first venture into investigative reporting and he was making me look like an ass. Well, at least Roland Trotter did his job. He checked out the Mansarays based on what I told him from my hospital bed.

"So, I'll tell you what I told him," Dr. Mansaray said. "At first Bakarie and I didn't get along for two reasons. First, we are from different tribes. Secondly, I love our daughter too much to let someone take advantage of her. When I saw that he was sincere and only wanted the best for her, just as we do, well, I changed my mind.

"And as far as the tribal war at home is concerned, that is beyond our control. Our tribes have not always been adversaries. Greed and power has corrupted our leaders. If we're ever going to rebuild our country, it has to start with somebody. Why not us?"

Wusu Mansaray pointed out to me that he had ordered food, drinks, and party supplies for the engagement party. But more importantly, he had to eat the cost of two plane tickets for out of town guests, as he could not return the tickets for a refund.

"We can still have a party with the supplies. But the out of town guests will now have to wait and visit us for a memorial service." He then told me about the event called the Fortieth Day ceremony. I'd already learned about that from Kojo.

Still not conceding that I only came out to "interrogate" him, I reminded him that I had the

103

assigned questions from the campus paper, and that I was responsible for completing the list. He was a good sport and complied, knowing full well that I already had the information I came for.

This was the last tangible trail to pursue in the case of 'Who Shot Calvin Porch.' Now I had to leave it alone and accept the theory of the town police department—an unknown assailant pursuing an unknown victim, nothing to do with three students who just happened to be on the scene.

Goodbye to Yesterday

Part 2

Round Up the Usual Suspects

Chapter 12
A Behind the Scenes Kind of Guy

I felt that I could trust Aaron to keep his word about printing the African cultural piece, because I sure did go out on a limb with Dr. Mansaray. I promised him that the article would be printed.

Aaron "Streak-o-Lean" Aldrich was a behind the scenes kind of guy and sometimes it's hard to keep your word after you've negotiated concurrent deals in confidence with various individuals. Sooner or later, a deadline or a scheduling conflict will interfere with a promise.

He and I were pretty good friends, dating back to our sophomore year on the Baseball team. Since both of us were "walk-on" athletes trying to make the team, we talked about different things before and after practices. Then we'd hang out on campus sometimes. I tried out for the team and got cut my freshman year. The second year was round two. That year was Coach Benson's first year with us; and, in essence, he still regarded me as a brand new freshman. Aaron transferred to Waukeegan at the beginning of his sophomore year. The fact that I'd made it through spring training and dressed out for two games the season before didn't count for anything with the new coach. Aaron's complete season at his first college didn't help him any, either.

That head-to-head collision on the ball field with him last week freed us up from practice that day, and that free time ended up placing me at the Mansion in the line of fire. What's that old expression? "An idle mind is the devil's workshop."

The only time I can honestly say Aaron did something that bordered on the unethical was back in the fall when he used his position as Assistant Student Ombudsman to help Nehemiah Luckie get out of a students exams scandal. I was minding my own business at the Pan African Association Food Bazaar when he asked me to come by his office at the newspaper suite to help him carry out a plot. It was toward the end of last semester, when Maureen, Luckie, Charles and I acted in some scenes from a play for our Speech and Drama class.

At 3:10 p.m. that day, I descended the red brick-colored, ceramic tile steps that led to the cavernous entrance to the Student Union Building.

Aaron ensconced himself in one of the three small offices that I saw when I entered through the larger glass-walled general office where a half dozen or so students occupied desks with typewriters on top of them. While the interoffice belonged to no one in particular, they had some unwritten understanding that whoever used the interoffice, had more personal or private business to handle than the dwellers in the outer offices. For this very reason, nothing permanent was ever on the walls or desks to show that the office belonged to any one person.

"I'm really impressed with your office," I kidded him, as I looked from one side to the other.

"Hey, whatever it takes to get the job done," Aaron said. "Have a seat."

After some brief small talk, he informs me in his official capacity as the Assistant Student Ombudsman, of the reason for our meeting.

"I'm trying to get one of our buddies off a list of athletes alleged to have received passing grades through immoral acts. Most of them are football players with a few other athletes sprinkled in. I know that Deacon West, Wiley Jakes, and Austin McCoy are on the football team, too; but Luckie is the only one on the baseball team that is being investigated—so far, knock on wood.

"This is some heavy shit, man. Jeff, the Ombudsman, and me are working with the Office of Student Affairs to resolve some charges filed by some Nursing students.

"Nehemiah Luckie—Brother Luckie, has been included on a list of culprits, who have earned "A's" by letting that faggot Professor Carlos Morgan suck their dicks."

"I've heard stuff like that from a lot of guys," I said.

"Everybody has. But, when we get them one-on-one for an official record, nobody speaks. It's some kind of arrangement they've got with the good Doctor."

Luckie played on the baseball team with us, and he was a well-liked, happy-go-lucky student who had prospects of playing Major League Baseball.

The particular class in question was a Chemistry class required specifically for General Science and Social Science majors, Nursing students, Physical Education, and Health and Nutrition majors, among others. As difficult as some students found the course, there were some athletes on various teams, taking the course, who were not even required to take it. Why would anyone take a difficult course he didn't have to?

What especially made the Nursing students angry was the idea that certain athletes flaunted their deal in front of everyone. The sports stars showed up for classes a few times during the semester—generally arriving late, and often leaving early—and they never attended the independent lab sessions. But on exam day, they showed up with more confidence than the ones who had "burned the midnight oil."

"I really don't care if all of their asses get punished," Aaron said. "They ought to be earning their grades like you and me. I'd like to see Luckie make it to the pros. The thing is, I'm trying to get him out of this, without helping the rest of them."

"I don't know," I wondered. "Sometimes you try to be your brother's keeper, and he don't even give a damn."

"They say Dr. Morgan has some kind of arrangement where the guys show up for exams, take the exams with everyone else, and later, re-complete the tests in his office, where he give them "A's". The failed tests are thrown away and the good ones are kept as the permanent record."

"Have you talked to Luckie, yet? He's in my Speech and Drama class. We're practicing some scenes from a play. I could tell him you guys are on to them."

"So, what kind of grades did you get from the Professor?"

"I edged out of there with a "D" the first semester, and a "C" the second one, thank God. That was two years ago and I'm not looking back either.

"Man, he wrote notes on my quiz and test papers about three times: "'Calvin, you seem to be having difficulty understanding the course. Please come see me.'"

Aaron got a big laugh out of that.

"Believe me," I admitted, "I didn't tell anybody those notes were on my papers until I heard other guys say they had the same thing written on theirs. Then we laughed about it, and wished and prayed for a "C," but would accept a "D" on the finals if it came to that."

"Lord, just 'C' me through!" we both said it at the same time, laughing at this idiom, because it was a campus-wide saying.

"Seriously," Aaron said, "we're going to wrap this thing up within the next two weeks, before the final semester tests are over."

"What's the big deal?"

"The problem is—and I know it seems unethical— I'm trying to get Luckie out of this mess without Jeff, the Ombudsman, or the College Officials knowing about it."

He revealed his plan. The only witness the Office of Student Affairs had was a former student who had graduated and moved on. The student's sister, a present Nursing student, had learned of the names from her brother. Luckie's name came up on the list. Because on paper, each young man's grades and exam papers were considered legitimate, the only avenue available to the Inquiry Panel was to apply pressure to the individuals and hope that at least a few of the athletes cracked and named specifics—times, dates, descriptions, etc.—of the incidents.

"Luckie will have to keep a low profile for the next two weeks and avoid the loud and boisterous crowd he is accustomed to running with. Every student named will receive a notice to appear at an inquiry.

"All Luckie has to do is say he never received a notice when his buddies ask if he did," Aaron said. "Then, he's gone have to leave campus for some kind of emergency in the middle of finals."

"He's not going to want to do that," I warned. "That would be the same thing as flunking out of school."

"Ordinarily, yes, but he's got to make it look real."

It occurred to me that old Streak-o-Lean Aaron might some day become a good lawyer. He was calculating and thinking ahead and putting himself on the line as well, when he could have chosen not to get involved.

"I'm curious," I said. "First, why don't you just have Coach Benson get him out of it? And, second, why are you telling me all this?"

"Because Coach Benson or any other coach wouldn't be able to save them all, without getting himself into trouble. And, if he tries to pick and choose who he wants to help, that wouldn't go over well with team unity among other athletes.

"The reason I'm telling you, Porch, is that it's going to take a couple of Luckie's friends outside of his running buddies, to convince him my plan will work. He would listen to you."

"So here I am, trying to help a guy out who made an 'A' in Chemistry."

"Look at it another way. Nehemiah Luckie could be Waukeegan's first athlete to play Major League Baseball. And years later, you and I could ask ourselves was it worth it, and we could say yes."

So in Luckie's absence, Aaron plotted out the athlete's career. Luckie would stay around long enough to initiate final exams. After taking two or three exams, he would need to go to the remaining professors, notify them of his emergency need to leave campus, willfully solicit "I's"—Incomplete grades— with the promise of taking the exams when the second semester resumes. When registration began, for a few days to a week, he would be a student without a scholarship.

Once he fulfilled his obligations to remove the Incomplete grades during the first week of the second semester, he could then register late and be back in school, having lost only a few days of actual classes. The semester finals would begin the second week of December with the Christmas break ensuing immediately afterwards. Add Luckie's one-week delay in registration, and in Aaron's estimation, that gave them roughly a month to resolve the inquiry and smooth over the situation.

"By then," Aaron said, waving his index finger in the air like a magician saying "presto," "we'll have the mess cleaned up. Hopefully only a few students will get expelled. And, just maybe, that pervert Dr. Morgan will get fired."

"I'm not playing the Devil's advocate, but if this thing blows up in your face, it's going to be a bunch of guys out there mad enough to kill you."

"Oh, no!" Aaron said confidently. "Ain't no chance of anything going wrong. Let me worry about that. Most of these guys have been jocks all their lives, any way. They got a sense of rules and regulations. To them, this would only be a bad call by the referee, in a game the players had been cheating in all along."

I left Aaron, agreeing that I would talk to Luckie.

Though the rehearsal for the Speech and Drama class took place on the third floor of Bennington Hall, we the participants first gathered in the hallway near the front doors.

"So how do you feel?" I asked.

"Good," Maureen said smiling. "How about you?"

"The same. This evening ought to be a good one. Everybody's going to have to be ready. You're not going to forget your lines, are you?"

"If I do, you can whisper sweet nothings in my ears."

"I heard that," Millie, the white intern student assigned to Sister DuMaine, said. "Y'all better be thinking about nothing but that play."

"Okay, Sister DuMaine, we hear you," I teased.

Charles, Gail, and Luckie came in together. When Millie suggested that we go upstairs to get started, I used that time to speak to Luckie. Luckie was a slim, muscular athlete, about six feet two inches tall, about my height. In fact, I once borrowed his blue double-breasted blazer. He was wearing an older maroon team cap with the "W" logo on the front above the bib.

"Hey Luckie. I need to talk to you, man."

"Yeah, alright. What about?"

When the other students went ahead, I spoke low, "That stuff about those "A's" that guys have been getting in Dr. Morgan's class, is getting ready to hit the fan."

"Man, that's just talk. They can't prove anything."

"I don't know what they can prove. All I know is that Aaron Aldrich is on the Inquiry Panel, and he said your name is on the list."

"I ain't worried."

"Listen, we need to talk about this after practice. You're going to have to keep quiet about it though, because Aaron says he's going out on a limb trying to help you without helping the rest of 'em. He's trying to help you get drafted for the Pros."

"He told you that? Damn!" Luckie seemed worried for the first time.

"Let's go practice. Ain't no need to worry about it now," I said.

The rehearsal began as usual with Charles cracking jokes to get everyone loosened up. Millie, the appointed facilitator, took her job seriously, as she had been more schooled and practiced in acting than the rest of us. Her job was to make sure the rehearsal started and ended on time, account for the few props required, and to generally allow each participant to bring his or her own skills to the play.

Everyone seemed sharp, except Luckie. His lines were few in comparison to the rest of us amateurs, but he seemed as though his mind was somewhere else.

"Okay, okay, let's do it again," he begged. "I got it now."

"Come on, Luckie," Gail said. "What's the matter with you? Can't you get it right? It's only a small part."

"There are no small parts," Charles jested in a pretentious British accent. "Only small 'ock-tors'!"

Everyone laughed at Charles' statement, augmented by his Shakespearean sleight of hand gestures. He succeeded in getting us to relax, and the rehearsal went smoothly from then on.

At the conclusion of the rehearsal, I told Maureen I would catch up with her before she got back to her dormitory. "I've got to talk to Luckie about something important." Luckie had hung back near the exit door.

"What do they know? What do they have?"

"They have names, dates, and incidents, Luckie. They're waiting on guys to start telling on each other. I can tell you everything Aaron told me, but it's complicated. You need to get with him and work out the details."

"I appreciate you telling me. I wish I had …"

"Just talk to *him*," I cut him off. "I've got to go."

I cut the conversation short because I didn't want to hear the details of Luckie's involvement. Between the guys—all of them athletes—always kidding and joking on "The Breeze Station" bench outside the Cafeteria or in the locker room at the gym, I had heard several of them say that they had earned an 'A' by letting the Science Professor perform oral sex on them. But these same young men, in a serious setting where no humor was involved, would deny that they had done it. So you couldn't be sure who was or was not lying.

The conversation went something like this: "Man, you better go get you an 'A.' All you gotta do is let him suck yo' dick. Y'all crazy, sittin' in class everyday and still failing. Better do like I did. I got me an "A!'"

After this declaration, everyone broke out laughing. You had to consider whether the jokester had actually done it, or was he trying to solicit participants who would either say—"I did it, too," or "I'm going to do it." Once the prankster got a volunteer, he would convince the other laughers that he himself hadn't really done it, and the egg would be on the face of the volunteer like a punch line in a joke. I remember this same scene was put to me by another athlete two years ago.

"Porch, man, you taking a chance. You barely got out of the first semester with a "D." With baseball season coming up, you know you gone miss some labs. You might mess around and make an "F.""

"I'll take my chances," I answered. I studied hard that semester and made a "C."

It was dark and chilly outside, and the campus light posts, distanced and far apart, seemed inadequate to cover the landscape for which they were designed. When I caught up with Maureen, she was standing on the walkway near the long concrete benches at the entrance to her dorm, talking with Mille and two other girls who were on their way out of the dorm. When I got near them, Millie said she had to go across campus to the Theater building where the real Performing Arts students hold their rehearsals.

"I don't know what's happened to Charles. He was supposed to walk me to the Theater building."

"Oh, really?" Maureen questioned.

"Yes. Here he comes now."

Charles walked up in a double-time pace, almost running. "Hey, I'm sorry I got side-tracked, Millie. I see you're in good company, though. I'm ready. We can go now. See you later Maureen, Porch."

The Caucasian couple took off. "Now remember what I told you two," Millie teased. "Save the sparks for the play!"

"Girl, go on," Maureen answered, grinning. Then she spoke to me: "I like her. She's alright."

"So, what do you think—birds of a feather, huh?"

"It's a logical situation, since it ain't but a few white students on campus anyway."

"Yeah," I commented, "Charles told me that first day she was assigned to us, that he was going to ask her out. Enough about them. It's getting chilly out here. Let's go into the snack bar. We can get some coffee. Come on. We won't be there long."

She mentioned something in protest, reminding me that she had something to do shortly. We backtracked our steps on the walkway without Maureen taking time to drop her books in her room. I offered to take her books and she conceded.

One of the largest buildings on campus was Jenkins Hall, a three-story brick structure with steep segmented roofs and a large bell tower housed on its highest peak. In an earlier era, the bell served as an alarm, but now it served to remind the observers that the college was indeed an old school, built and designed during the Nineteenth Century.

The top floor housed the Cafeteria. On the front side facing west to the square, we had to enter a mountain of exterior red ceramic stairs with a landing about a third of the way up before we reached the door to go inside. The Student Union sector occupied the ground floor, a series of glass-enclosed rooms, with the Recreation Center in the middle, and the Snack Bar on the left.

I ordered two cups of coffee and returned to our table. Along the wall, out from the food counter, stood a jukebox. Someone had played a popular song two times in a row. The Temptations song, Just My Imagination Running Away With Me. A cozy little house out in the country with Maureen and two or three kids seemed like a pretty good idea. But it was—.

"This is nice," Maureen observed. "Sitting here with you, taking a break from everything."

"It sure is. Listen, Maureen, a friend of mine from West Africa invited us to a party Saturday night. It's going to be a good one—an international party. Everything from calypso to the limbo. I'd like for us to go. Will you go with me?"

She held my hand on top of the table next to the white styrofoam coffee cups. It was like a gesture to let me down easy. "Oh, Calvin, I've been planning to tell you. I'm pledging AKA next semester. We've got a rush party Saturday night."

"Couldn't we go to both of them?"

"I don't think so. We've got a meeting for new sorority pledges before the party begins. We're not even going to be at the basketball game."

"Well, we'll just deal with what comes up. First things first, anyway," I said. "We got the play Thursday. I think we'll be ready."

"I think you'll do better than you ever imagined you would. You've got the best part."

"You think so?"

"I know so. You're not as good as Sidney Poitier," Maureen revealed and grinned. "But, you really should consider joining the Drama Club. Talk to Sister DuMaine. Millie thinks you're good, too."

"Maybe I should. I'll think about it."

We finished our coffee and left. When we got to the entrance to her dorm, I posed an invitation to her.

"You know, you should walk me home sometimes. Don't you agree?"

"Sure, I'll do it," Maureen said. "But then you would have to walk me back again."

"I wouldn't mind. It would be worth it."

"Okay."

"How about Thursday evening?" I said. "After the play, we could have some wine and cheese in my room. Just the two of us."

"Okay."

"Unless you got other ideas. You could invite me up now."

"Not tonight, I couldn't. Nor tomorrow night. There's no privacy in the room. I'm scheduled to study with a couple of girls from down the hall."

"Then I'll hold you to Thursday," I said. I kissed her, and we said goodnight. Then, I walked across the lawn, going west, passing by the fountain where she and I had on another night, shared a long intimate conversation that culminated with us making love in her room. 'What a night,' I sighed. Recalling that night, I mused to myself—sometimes a moment presents itself and it is the right time, and actions and events flow better then than if you had planned it that way. In my usual plodding, roundabout way, I hadn't figured to lure her into bed as soon as it had taken place. It must have been the right time.

So far, the end of last semester has been better than the first two months of this semester. After the Mansaray interview, I returned to campus.

I walked through the door of the glass-enclosed, sparsely furnished newspaper office. "How did it go?" Aaron asked.

"I found out what I needed to know. There's no *smoking gun* there. The information will be good for your story, but nothing for me to go on."

"A story that you talked me into covering. We can still do some good with it. That's why we're here—to educate the masses. Tell you what I'm going to do. I'll share the by-line with you. I'll do the introduction and the last paragraph of the piece, but the body of it will be yours. It'll read—by Aaron Aldrich and Calvin Porch. How does that sound?"

"Pretty good."

"Well, if you ever become a writer or a reporter, you can always say you got your start here."

"You know, that's got me thinking, Aaron. I might want to put this on my resume. Do you think you could let me work on a few more stories just to make it legit?"

"Yeah, we can work something out."

Chapter 13
Shooting the Breeze

It was about time I used some common sense. The police, my parents and my friends had told me that it made no sense for me to be thinking that I could find the person who shot me. I was chasing a mirage. But when I think about what the police officer said about going back six months to recall disputes, arguments or disagreements I might've had with others, it occurred to me that nothing clear and concrete came to mind.

Still, in some kind of vague pattern that I couldn't put my finger on, I felt that the recent past contributed to my present calamity. All I could think of were the good days we had during the end of last semester. Things were going good with me and Maureen, Cupp and Dee Dee were just getting together, Charles was threatening to quit school to go into show business, and Aaron was his usual self, working on some behind the scenes student government function. Why couldn't those days come back again?

The first hint I received that Maureen really liked me came not through my own eyes and ears, nor through any words she had said. It came from her friend Shirley one Sunday morning after breakfast. It was in that span of time right after Thanksgiving but before the first of December. Maureen was not a suspect, but our acquaintance fell within that six-month timeframe the police detective had spoken about—*It could be related to a friend of yours, or a friend of a friend.*

It was that Sunday morning after the concert, where Leonardo had slept in, and Cupp and I had paced across campus to meet a cold cereal breakfast. I told Cupp, "See you back at the dorm," then I went over to sit with Shirley. After breakfast, Shirley, a cute, dark-skinned girl usually given to wearing bell-bottomed jeans and casual tops, grabbed her clear plastic cleaner's bag off the hat and coat rack near the cafeteria's entrance. Inside it was a black choir robe. That Sunday, she wore light make-up, a blue and white dress with a blue waist jacket, and, neatly in place, a well-trimmed mid-length Afro hairdo.

"Look at me. I wished I was dressed better," I said in casual clothes and my green Army floppy-brimmed, camouflaged hat. "You don't mind if I walk with you to the chapel like this, do you?"

"No, come on."

"Y'all gone sing good, today?"

"We sing good every Sunday."

We walked down the wide, reddish tile steps of the Cafeteria and crossed the lawn of the main campus square to the street that ran along the southern terrace of the wall of the gulch known as "The Valley." Trees hung over both sides of the street, and it was shady all the time.

"I saw you from a distance yesterday, when you and some other girls were walking over by the Fountain," I said. "It would've been just too countrified for me to yell out at y'all."

"That was me and Maureen and some girls from my hometown. So, what have you been doing lately, Calvin, to attract a secret admirer that a little birdie told me about?"

"Who?"

"You know, I'm talking about Maureen. Since you all have been working in that play together, that's all she's been talking about. You and her in that play, *A Raisin In The Sun*."

"She hasn't said much to me."

"Take my word for it. She likes you."

"I'll have to pay more attention."

Her next remark after that was: "Well?"

I had shown some interest in Shirley myself, but had not wholeheartedly pursued her because previously she had not shown me much consideration or attention over and above what she had shown to a few other suitors. In other words, she was a serious honor student who made the Dean's list every semester and although she went out on an occasional date and would let you visit at her dormitory once in a while, you weren't going to get far with her. Having a boyfriend was not on her priority list. And as far as sex was concerned, she wasn't giving up any booty. A guy with a lot of patience could marry a girl like Shirley, but who was looking to get married?

"So what do you think about it?" I asked, referring to Maureen.

"It's got nothing to do with me, one way or the other."

I left the topic about Maureen alone. At least Shirley wasn't jealous of this newfound prospective relationship.

We crossed the intersecting street, where just beyond on a well-manicured lawn to the northwest, stood on a small court, the bronze statue of a by-gone College president. Running to the right and left of the landmark was a permanent masonry wall that was actually a bench with a backrest. We kept to the paved walkway across the lawn and stopped on the gravel-paved entrance to the chapel.

"Well, this is as far as I go," I said.

"Somehow, I get the feeling that you used to go to church."

"Yeah, there was a time."

"What happened?"

"Nothing. I just need to get back in the habit."

"Well, don't take too long. Oh, I've got to go now. Bye."

"See you later, Shirley." I went back to the dorm feeling good about a tidbit that 'a little birdie' had told me about. Tomorrow I would see Maureen and go from there.

Our campus was laid out in a series of squares and rolling lawns and was populated with assorted oak trees. Its' character existed in the old brick buildings built in the late 1800's. Constructed with hand-made bricks of a by-gone era, each original structure—whether an academic building, a dormitory, or a business office—was defined, stamped, and identified by white painted window frames, doors, and porch columns, and brick red tile floors at their entrances. On the shady sides of these same buildings, moss grew in the grooves of the bricks and mortar where dampness had accumulated. Of these main structures, at least a half dozen had quaint little courts in front of them, replete with asphalt walkways and trimmed, square-cut shrubbery. The newer three-story buildings, built with modern, indistinguishable assembly-line bricks, had rows of windows in line on each floor, their only color scheme was the reflection of a shadowy, light and gray 'sleight of hand' fixation, created by Venetian blinds in the windows.

Nevertheless, no fixture on campus was more popular than "The Breeze Station." Situated on the southern border of a main east-west street, it was a forty feet long concrete bench, with as a backrest, a retaining wall that ran east and west in a convexed angle, and it served as an embankment to the terrace behind it. Behind and above the bench-retaining wall loomed a series of low-spreading Juniper trees, connected together in a far-reaching umbrella over the heads of the occupants.

At 12:25 Monday afternoon, Dwayne Norwood and I found seats at "The Breeze Station," among the oglers, philosophers, and general bullshitters. We had finished lunch and had about a half-hour left before classes resumed.

Maureen and two other girls came through the double-glass doors of the cafeteria that faced us. The landing outside the doors was above ground and had red tile flooring laid on top of the concrete steps. Underneath the porch landing, was a cavernous entrance to the Recreation Center below the cafeteria. A wide concrete parapet aligned the landing and trailed down the steps, serving the same purpose as a guardrail.

Maureen walked over to where we sat. Smiling and looking radiant, the cute honey brown-skinned young lady wore a soft red-blue-brownish-combination plaid wool skirt that stopped about knee length. Complimenting the skirt, she sported a long sleeved, tan knit blouse under a blue button-down sleeveless vest-type sweater.

"Hi, Calvin. I didn't see you in the cafeteria. Have you had lunch?"

"Yeah, a good while ago."

"I really like the way the play is shaping up," she said. Her smile was still inviting. Maureen's hair was thick, with soft curls, yet it passed as an Afro, and it covered her ears and extended to the nape of her neck.

"I'm glad we made the changes," I said. "I like my new part."

"I'm looking forward to seeing you this evening. See you."

"I'll be there," I promised.

She walked away to catch up with the other girls she had come out of the cafeteria with.

"Old Calvin trying to be cool," Dwayne teased. "I'll be there," he mimicked me in a comic high-pitched voice, that was nothing like mine. Then in his regular voice, he pointed out, "Man, that girl really likes you. You ought to go for it."

"I'm working on it right now. I can't lose, see? I got the part in the play that Sidney Poitier played in the movie."

"What's that got to do with it?"

"Cause the hero always gets the girl in the end. Don't you know that?"

"You're full of shit, Porch," Dwayne said laughing.

"Hey, I'm telling you the truth. Watch me."

We ended the discussion on Maureen and paused for a few minutes to listen to other theories from the philosophers sitting out on the long bench, known as "The Breeze Station."

"Oh, man—look! Time is getting away. Come on, Dwayne! Man, you got to help me with this." I held an

127

abridged novel in my hand, of that variety, where the book jacket is colored "caution-light" yellow with black lines crossing it. I was scheduled to meet with Sister Margaret DuMaine in conference at 1:00 p.m., and I needed to cram some information fast. *From Here to Eternity* was the name of the novel I selected for the oral book review.

Dwayne Norwood hailed from Brantley, Alabama, a little town near Selma. A medium brown complexioned fellow with a thick Afro, Dwayne, like in the present, was fond of wearing floppy-brimmed cloth hats atop his Afro, more toward the back, with frontal crown hair showing under the hat, suggesting he was not a serious hat wearer, sporting it only for style.

He had witnessed the Selma-to-Montgomery Civil Rights March, made famous by Martin Luther King, Jr. In his own words, Dwayne's claim to fame was: "We went as far as the Edmond Pettis Bridge, then we took our asses home."

"Okay. I'm going to help you out the best I can. Remember this," he advised, "Sister DuMaine's going to ask you a lot of questions. Take these down first, and then I'll give you the answers." He had his one-on-one conference with the nun earlier during the morning.

"Why did Prewitt leave home? Comment upon the background of Prewitt's mother and father. Why did Prewitt refuse to continue boxing? What did Warden suggest Prewitt do to resolve Prewitt's AWOL problem?

"During the attack on Pearl Harbor by the Japanese, what were Prewitt's choices when he was stopped by patrolmen, while trying to return to his company? Compare Robert E. Lee Pruitt's character before he entered the Army, with his character, as it were, towards the end of his military life."

In a matter of minutes, we had gone over the questions and answers. If Dwayne hadn't come into the picture on this one, I would've had to beg off for another conference date with the old white woman, reducing my overall grade for the semester. Sister DuMaine taught English Literature, Speech and Drama.

"I'll bet you're thinking the same way I was," Dwayne guessed. "How are you going to be able to clean it up good enough to talk to a nun about it? Don't worry, Sister DuMaine can handle it."

James Jones' book, *From Here to Eternity*, had in its content fornication, adultery, prostitution, vulgarity, profanity, and murder. It had been on a selected list of a dozen or so books recommended by the English Literature Department to provide diversity in the modern concept of Realism. But no one figured that the white, mid-western, past sixty year-old nun would willingly cover it in her classroom.

I didn't set out to use this particular novel for my oral book review, but the deadline to report on a book had come sooner than I anticipated. Having seen a lot of war movies, and armed with the abridged copy of the novel, I figured this one was easier to cram on short notice.

"This is exactly how she starts out," Dwayne said, the blue, floppy-brimmed cloth hat, comically atop his head. "'We can talk intelligently about anything, as long as we use the proper vocabulary. So now, we'll begin.'"

"That's when she start to grill your ass, right?"

"There you go. You see, Porch, now you're catching on. She throw a ton of questions at you, and you can't say shit, piss, or fuck. You got to work hard to dress it up. Now you gotta say defecate, bowel movement, urinate, fornicate, adultery, prostitute, carnal knowledge, he knew her, and stuff like that."

By then, Della Dianne Pelham came walking down the steps from the street along the terrace above "The Breeze Station." Dee Dee was a short, average looking girl with a fine ass and not much breasts, who wore her hair in a short Afro, that framed her face well and made the butterscotch, brown fireball look cute, more attractive than she really was.

A Social Science major like me and Dwayne, the sprite senior hailed from the rough parts of Chicago, Illinois where, as a youngster, she played sports in the streets with her older brothers. Her street vocabulary belied the lithe softness and delicacy, which she displayed on the stage as a dancer in the Modern Dance Club.

"Hey, Dee Dee, come here!" Dwayne called out.

She had on a blue denim jacket over a white T-shirt that had Waukeegan College written across the chest. The Navy-styled, blue bell-bottom pants fit her excellently. Within seconds, she was in our faces: "Hey Dwayne. Hey Calvin. What you want, Dwayne?"

"You took Speech and Drama last semester. Tell Porch he can get through the nun's conference if he'll just be cool and act like he knows what he's talking about."

She looked at the notes I had on my notepad, then back at the "caution-light" yellow and black striped handbook in my other hand.

"You're up shit's creek without a paddle if that's all you got."

"Damn, Dee Dee, I thought I had a chance."

"Well, Calvin, you're a pretty good looking guy. Maybe you can charm the hell out of her. Okay. Let's add a few more questions to this. Maybe you'll have a chance to make a 'C.' I've read the book before even though I didn't review it in her class."

We took several minutes and rehearsed more questions and answers on the novel. One o'clock in the afternoon was approaching.

"Boy, I'll tell you," Dee Dee said. "That Sister DuMaine thinks she's slick. Old, wrinkled, white woman, sitting in her office between classes, sipping her liquor, getting just tipsy enough without anybody knowing it.

"If she could reincarnate herself, she'd probably be a whore, you hear me? A hoe'!"

"I don't believe that," I said.

"I ain't lying. You Southern Baptist Negroes are all naïve. Y'all don't know anything about Catholics. Let me tell you," she continued. "My home girl had a work study job in Bennington Hall last year, and still does now. Part of her job was to empty wastebaskets, clean off desks, run errands, and stuff.

"It was nothing to see liquor bottles and mouthwash in Sister DuMaine's desk drawers. She sips it out of a coffee cup. She always keeps a pot of coffee going on a little corner table as a decoy. Hell, her favorite drink is 'Southern Comfort,' something she can drink straight or with the coffee."

By then, some other students sitting on the long convex bench within earshot of Dee Dee, joined in the laughter.

"You would think that the average self-respecting woman would avoid a book like *From Here To Eternity*. Not her! She'd rather discuss it with you guys. Ever notice that more guys review this book than girls do?"

She held up the yellow and black book. "I'm telling you, it gives her a chance to live vicariously as a whore."

"Vicariously?" Dwayne asked. "What you mean by vie-care-ree-us-ly?"

"I know what that means," I volunteered. "That's like if a man was a ball player, see? And he didn't go, or couldn't go, as far as he wanted to with it. Then he has a son, and he puts his son in sports early, gives him a ball as soon as he can walk. And on up the ladder, he pushes the child to success.

"When the child is successful, the man is successful. He relives his sports life through the child. That's called vicarious."

"That's right," Dee Dee concurred.

"Dee Dee, I don't want to get with you vicariously," Dwayne flirted. "I want to get with you for real!"

"Well, Dwayne," she paused. She calmly lifted the blue, floppy brimmed cloth hat off his head, where he had been wearing it playfully on the back of his Afro with frontal hair sticking out from under it, and she placed it level and right: "You play your cards right, and we'll see what happens. But one thing though." She put her left hand on her hip and punctuated the air with her right index finger as she spoke: "You see, 'cause I hang with y'all and talk a lot of shit, don't mean I don't like to be sweet talked to and given a lot of attention. That don't mean I'm easy."

The drama of street savvy and the demand for respect was played out in the span of a few seconds. Dee Dee, a lone woman, standing before a long bench occupied by men, clearly put Dwayne in his place, without a scene, and at the same time, allowed him the opportunity to end the conversation decently, setting up the possibility that their next encounter might be a positive one.

"'Cause I ain't a quick, easy piece of ass," Dee Dee said. Then she put the ball in his court. "But, you know what? A little serious dedicated time put in and a little consideration can go a long ways."

Dwayne, challenged, gave a good answer—one that not one of the signifying jokers, hecklers or instigators at "The Breeze Station" could find fault with. "I'll see you later," he promised.

"Okay," she replied and was gone. Dee Dee went down the brick-red tile steps to the cavern entrance of the student union Recreation Center. Above the cavernous entrance was the porch landing with steps descending to either side of the building's exterior wall, the very entrance/exit where Maureen and two friends had left the cafeteria less than a half-hour ago.

"Well, brother man, you ain't the only one that's got something going on," Dwayne said. "I'm a step closer to tightening her up. Take my word for it. Me and Dee Dee gone get together."

Chapter 14
From Here to Eternity

It was now time to meet with Sister DuMaine. Bennington Hall was approximately seventy yards due east of the Breeze Station bench. That bit that Dee Dee alleged about Sister DuMaine was just too much! The idea that the nun drank liquor and, through Literature, was living vicariously as a whore. As good-natured as Dee Dee was, you couldn't believe everything she said.

Then I remembered how Hollie had once said that she had a bad experience with a nun. According to Hollie, who had attended a Catholic elementary school, her desire to play the piano was snuffed out by an unsupportive nun. Constantly admonishing the child that she was not learning fast enough, the woman smacked Hollie's knuckles with a twelve-inch wooden ruler, to which young Hollie ran home to tell her mother. The ensuing Parent-Teacher confrontation resulted in Hollie being taken out of the class, never to seriously study music again.

I remembered my freshman year when Sister DuMaine taught English Literature. She was in her first year at Waukeegan and had offered that her students call her "Sister Margaret," and we duly obeyed. But in the student handbook and registration schedule, she was always listed as 'DuMaine' only, where last names were used exclusively. So, now after three years, no one called her Sister Margaret anymore. We addressed her as Sister DuMaine.

Our College, like many predominantly Black colleges, maintained its accreditation by employing professors of diverse cultures and backgrounds. Each department had its share of Caucasians, Europeans, Asians, Africans, Indians, Pakistani, and other groups. Though the majority of professors were African-Americans, these other nationalities provided international perspectives, so to speak.

My first year at college, it was Sister DuMaine who instructed me to 'articulate, speak clearly, and enunciate!' "Don't talk in your throat. Articulate! Speak through your teeth."

At 12:57 p.m., I entered Bennington Hall, the main academic building on campus. I left the yellow and black "Cliff Notes" handbook with Dwayne. Now all I had was a three-ring binder notebook in my hand. Inside the building, the wide hallway ran parallel—east and west—to the street outside on the south wing. Classrooms aligned the wall on the north side of the hall. Professors and administrative heads occupied the offices on the south wall.

I entered through the door to an outer office where two administrative desks, a small, flat, black cushioned type office couch, and a few chairs adorned the waiting room. Inside, Brenda, a student worker, faced me as I entered. Brenda was Dee Dee's homegirl and a Journalism Major. She wore glasses and had a short bang over her forehead, with the rest of her hair pulled back and held down on the sides and back with hairpins.

"Hi, Brenda."

"Oh, hello there," she greeted. Immediately, the phone rang: "Excuse me. Hello, English Department. May I help you? Yes, she is. One moment please."

Brenda walked softly, almost tip-toeing into the nun's office to the right of the room. I sat on the black, cushion-sectioned, synthetic leather-covered waiting-room couch. It was like waiting in a dentist's office.

Brenda returned to her desk. "I'll tell her you're here when she gets off the phone."

"No problem, I'm not in a big hurry anyway."

Brenda whispered: "She's excited because an Italian priest from her last school is passing through to pay her a visit on his way to New Orleans."

We heard Sister DuMaine's voice precede her: "Brenda, mark it on your calendar that we're expecting a visiting priest on Thursday. His name is Mario Giacomelli. Wherever I am at the time, you are to direct him to the classroom where I'm teaching."

"I'll do it," Brenda answered.

"It's so exciting. He's going to Africa to work as a missionary. Oh, hello Calvin," she said entering the general office.

"How you doing, Sister DuMaine?"

"I'm find. Come on in."

I followed after the elderly Professor, whose Navy blue two-piece jacket and skirt outfit was more befitting a hostess at a restaurant or a hotel than the traditional garbs worn by a nun.

"Sit down. We'll get started."

I sat down in the chair across from her desk feeling nervous, hoping the nauseating, queasiness inside me didn't reveal my true discomfort. I hoped she would ask the right questions, rather that she would ask the questions to which I knew the right answers. A quick glance around the room showed that the office was just as Dee Dee had described it when she had claimed that the nun was a drunkard and a vicarious whore.

Beyond the two-tiered bookcase in the rear corner, stood a small, brown, wooden cabinet that served as an end table. On top of it stood an electric coffee pot, a few cups, spoons, a jar of dairy creamer, and a sugar dish. I wondered if the old girl kept the alcoholic beverages in the cabinet below.

"So, why did you select this long novel," Sister DuMaine asked while peering behind her wire-rimmed glasses, "when you could have reported on a shorter one instead?"

"I figured it would be easier, considering my ROTC background and having watched a lot of war movies."

"Fine. As you know, we can talk about any subject in Literature, as long as we use the proper vocabulary. With that said, now we'll begin. How do you feel about the period of time the novel deals with, as compared with today's military life?"

"From what I gathered," I said, "the Army during that time had to struggle to use sports as a means to occupy the men, to keep them busy. There were no Black characters in the novel. And I suppose that's because the Peace-time military had little use for us then.

"Nowadays, there's a real war going on in Vietnam, and they can't get enough of us to fight."

"Why do you suppose that's the case?"

I looked at the elderly, stately white woman, the alert, light blue eyes, and the face un-made up behind the wire-rimmed eyeglasses. No longer was Margaret DuMaine's face veiled as in the days of old. The old vestige to that period was the blue scarf-like headwear, outlined on the front with a white border, which rest atop her head.

"I don't mean to be disrespectful, Sister DuMaine, but I think you know the answer to that one." I was never one to outwardly protest or demonstrate injustices unprovoked, but if the topic presented itself in the due course of conversation, I would, as the educator's say, make use of this "Teachable Moment."

"Black folks have always been the last hired and the first fired. Always the ones sent out to do the dirty work for the white folks. Then, when everything's fine again, we're put back in the corner to be forgotten about."

"I see."

"Do you, really?"

"Yes, I do," Sister DuMaine answered. "In my own way, I try to push for freedom and equality for all people. You see that photo there?" she pointed to the wall on the right at a color photo of herself, dressed like a college graduate in black cap and gown, receiving a handshake and a certificate from a Black man who was also dressed in a black cap and gown.

"That picture was sent to me just last week. And, today is the first day it's been up there on the wall."

She pointed out that it was an Honorary Degree she received from a prominent African-American organization of higher learning for her contribution to the community in which she worked.

"You see, Calvin, sometimes we do our part by fighting for a cause. Other times, it's by encouraging others to bring out their own thoughts and ideas.

"I believe in the freedom of the press, that the English Language be used to express oneself, using one's own grasp of the language. This very novel we're discussing—when faculty members felt it should not be used as Literature, I fought to have it studied, to the chagrin of the Department head, who reminded me, for Christ's sake, that I am a nun, as if I had forgotten the fact that I am.

"As uncomfortable as I am with the banal and vulgar vernacular that James Jones used, I should never let my personal discomfort get in the way of literary expression.

"That's not to say that I approve of vulgar and profane speech," Sister DuMaine pointed out. "The Writer Jones didn't invent this language in his book. He showed real language as people in that situation spoke it.

"Oh, I've heard various and sundry accounts of how I came to champion such a book."

It sounded as if the nun, accustomed to hearing confessions, was now getting relief, removing a burden off her own shoulders in the form of a confession. As she went on with this discourse, I half heard it and half imagined something else entirely at the same time.

Well, well, which one was she? I thought to myself. I almost laughed out loud at the allegation that Dee Dee had made about the nun's vicarious life. Was she the dilemma ensnared Karen Holmes? The subtle, virginal Lorene? Or the house madam herself—Mrs. Kipfer?

If it were possible that Margaret DuMaine were a vicarious whore, in my imagination, she would have been Alma, incognito as Lorene, turned good to return home undetected, a demure, actress-goddess, a prodigal daughter returned home unscathed, her past life only a fog in the minds of distant soldiers, who wouldn't remember if Lorene was real or imagined. That was the fictional Alma. This is the real Margaret—a nun, safe and tucked away in Waukeegan, Alabama.

"In the moments when I am truly able to be objective," Sister DuMaine said, "able to distance myself from the job at hand, I find the speculations silly, comical, completely laughable. Huh, huh!" she chuckled. "No doubt, you probably have heard some version of this amusement."

"No, ma'am, I haven't," I lied.

"Well, I digress. Let's get back to the matter at hand. I want you to think about the question before you give me your answer."

"Okay."

"What was Prewitt's mother's deathbed request?"

"She made him promise her that he would never willfully or deliberately hurt anybody unless it was necessary."

"Good answer, Calvin. Now, what character trait or traits distinguished Warden from the officers of whom he had an opportunity to become?"

"Oh, I know that. He thought officers were hypocrites, that they played politics with people's lives. As a non-commissioned soldier, Warden saw them as liars, saw them as self-promoting opportunists, who flattered their superiors, as a means to gain favor. He was a practical man, and he didn't like playing their games."

"Hum-mmmmm! And, do you think men in our current military system feel the same way?"

"Yes, I do. In fact, there is a common slogan in the civilian world that came from the military. It says: 'It's not what you know; it's who you know.'" Now I felt I was doing well, on a roll, that her questions could not stump me.

"How did the song 'The Re-enlistment Blues' get started ... and who completed it?"

That question had a vague reference in my mind. I was thinking fast, which character had not been mentioned yet? I hazarded a guess: "Maggio and Prewitt came up with the idea, but Prewitt finished it." Was this a trick question, I wondered?

"Are you sure?"

"Yes."

"Really, now you only have half of the answer right. Which half?"

"No, Prewitt began it, and Maggio finished it, I think." I reversed my answer. "No, Prewitt finished it. They found it on his body."

"Prewitt did complete it," Sister DuMaine corrected "But the idea of it was conceived of during a night watch in the field, where three other men were present. Maggio was not present. Now, Calvin, I get the feeling that you are guessing. Did you really read the entire book?"

"Yes, I read the whole book," I lied.

Then she asked me a question I thought was obscure.

"Of the three characters—Prewitt, Warden and Malloy—which one was articulate in Social,

Philosophical, and Spiritual issues? Give an example to support your position."

"I'd have to say Warden, because his view of life was more clear cut. He had a practical approach to everything."

"Now, this is getting ridiculous," she said, her hands cupped together in a resting position on the desk. Her blue eyes stared at me. "You obviously didn't read the novel in its entirety."

"I'm sorry I missed that one. Please let's go on," I begged, not saying I did or did not read the complete novel. Two lies were enough at this point.

"Alright," she relented. "For your information, Jack Malloy was Prewitt's stockade or jail mate. Somewhat of a Renaissance man, Malloy influenced Prewitt with his ideas. He talked about meditation, eastern philosophy, non-violent protest, passive resistance, and other things. Prewitt was quoting Jack Malloy when he decided not to fire his guns at the guards. But we'll go on."

Sister DuMaine finished the oral book review with two easy questions that I knew. "What was Lorene's real name?"

"Her real name was Alma."

"What was Karen Holmes dilemma?"

"She wanted to divorce her husband, an officer, and marry Sergeant Warden if he were to complete Officer's Training School and become an officer. It would be a mess for all three—Karen Holmes, Captain Holmes, and Sergeant Warden. All three careers or futures would be ruined if Karen Holmes divorced her husband and married a non-commissioned soldier."

"Alright, Calvin. You've given a fine account of yourself today. I'm looking forward to seeing how you'll perform in the play, *A Raisin In the Sun*. How are the rehearsals going?"

"Oh, it's coming along fine, Sister DuMaine."

When I left her office, I said a silent prayer, "Lord, I'm sorry I lied to Sister DuMaine. But please don't let her take points off my final grade." Three weeks remained for the semester's ending. I wouldn't know if my prayer was answered until then.

Chapter 15
A Raisin in the Sun

At 6:00 p.m., it was time to return to Bennington Hall. A hand full of us had to rehearse a few scenes from a play. On the front of Bennington Hall, the white porch columns and the double glass doors faced south to a boulevard crossing its front. Farther out beyond the sidewalks lay a flat lawn, arranged with tall orderly, oak trees squaring it out; and still father beyond the lawn southward, another road; a main public road that ran through campus, and ran parallel with the boulevard that passed in front of the building.

The big room on the third floor of Bennington Hall was set up for multiple uses. It doubled as a lecture hall for various professors during the daytime. In the evening time, it doubled as a small theatre for plays or movies.

Maureen and the intern student Millicent Yates talked while they looked out a window to the rear of the building to the area below. A steep incline along the academic building's rear led to a quiet, narrow road behind two flanking dormitories that snaked around the north of campus. If you stayed on the narrow road, it brought you back full circle to the front of Bennington Hall.

"It's a quiet, quaint little area. I'll have to check it out sometime. You know, I'm still learning the campus," Millie said.

"The best time is during the middle of the day, when everybody uses it as a shortcut. It's just quiet now because it's getting dark outside," Maureen commented.

144

I approached them as they talked. 'Nice shape,' I said to myself as I assessed Maureen from behind. She wore a blue denim outfit—a half-cut jacket that stopped below the waistline, and jeans that had no pockets. Millie wasn't bad either. She was a senior, an intern student from Auburn University, who was assigned to the English Literature Department under Sister DuMaine's tutelage. One of the few white students on campus, Millie Yates was a Performing Arts Major. A big part of her internship at our school, was to coordinate and facilitate rehearsal schedules for students who participated in acting scenes from plays, as part of their Speech and Drama classes. Her role was similar to that of a graduate assistant, like a tutor or a lab assistant. The dark-haired young woman wore a long, beige sweater that covered her butt like a waistcoat, along with vertically-striped, blue and khaki bell-bottom trousers.

"It's getting darker by the minute," Maureen said.

I stood behind her and leaned over her shoulder. "I like the night," I said softly into her ear.

"You do?"

"Yes."

Just then a voice sounded out, coming through the double doors to the rear of the auditorium. "Alright, everybody," Charles Jordan shouted, "let's get this show on the road!" This was vintage Charles, a confident young man, not shy to speak up or attract attention.

"We've been waiting for you, Great White Hope," Luckie shouted back to him from his position on the stage near the green chalkboard. Everyone was present

145

except Gail Davis. Just as Charles had done, she entered the room talking: "I'm sorry I'm late."

Down front stood an eighteen-inch high platform, the width of the center aisle. A large green chalkboard rested on the wall facing the students. It was this precise location where Luckie had greeted Charles as he entered. The props were already on the stage, thanks to a few volunteers who came in early. Borrowed chairs from downstairs, a pair of storage cardboard boxes, a woman's straw hat, a briefcase, a small table, and a drinking glass made up the set.

All the chairs in the audience were bolted down to the floor, and they had desktops that could be folded down on the sides to hang vertically between the armrests of adjoining seats.

"I've been working on my redneck cracker accent," Charles announced. He had grown up as a military brat and had lived in many states apart from the South—even abroad in Europe for a short time. He had no trace of the Southern drawl in his speech. But he was patterning his accent for the role after George Wallace, then Governor of Alabama. The character of Lindner would have a Southern dialect.

"He's supposed to be a Northerner," Millie said.

"Yeah, but it's more fun to play it with a Southern accent. Ain't that right, Porch?"

"Yeah, I think so."

"We'll see," Millicent said.

When it was time for me and Maureen to do our scene, Millie directed us: "Alright, Calvin, Maureen—loosen up! Have fun with the roles. Maureen, don't try to act so proper. Be receptive to his hug."

146

I observed a tenderness in Maureen's demeanor each time after Walter, the character I played, commanded the white visitor Lindner to get out of our house. That moment had called for a decisive statement, and any woman would appreciate her man taking a strong action against an adversary at the appropriate time.

Charles' line: Well—I don't suppose that you feel...

My lines: Never mind how I feel—you got any more to say 'bout how people ought to sit down and talk to each other? ...Get out of my house, man.

Maureen played the part of my mother in the play and there was a place in the play for a mother-son hug, and I liked the scene because it put me in close proximity to her because I liked her anyway. "Kind of official and legal-like," I mused to myself. "Kind of put me in the right." I put a little extra in the hug the first time we did the scene because I thought I could get away with it.

"What are you doing, Calvin? She's supposed to be your mother, not your wife," Millie corrected us. Then we did the scene over.

"Alright, cut!" Millie shouted out. "That's a good scene. Looks like y'all got it down pat. Let's give some other folks a chance to practice."

Not one to let grass grow under his feet, Charles quickly got interested in Millie Yates. As everyone in the play was a junior or senior, the intern's age was approximately the same as ours. That made her a contemporary, a peer. What Charles and Millie had in common were obvious. Both were white on a predominantly Black campus. Both of them had

147

performing arts experience in some capacity. Millie would do her intern stint for the remaining semester and return to Auburn to graduate.

Charles had more real life performing experience than everyone rehearsing on the stage. The tall, collegian wore his dark hair parted on the left side and it tapered over his ears and was longer on the back than on the top and sides, and he wore a thin mustache that curled downward on the corners of his top lip. Chief among his wardrobe was a green Army fatigue jacket and faded blue jeans. In addition to his college life, on weekends he performed as a stand-up comedian and emcee at small local clubs. He also had experience as an announcer at football and basketball games and had worked part-time as a radio disc jockey.

More than once, Charles had confided to me that he had a notion to give up school and get into the entertainment business, full-time. He had numerous album collections of comedians such as Pigmeat Markham, Moms Mabley, and Redd Foxx, albums with blue language deemed unsavory for the respectable crowd; not a bad collection for a white boy military brat.

At 8:30 p.m., we called it quits. I left Bennington Hall with Maureen. The others drifted out on their own. Charles stayed back on the platform stage talking with Millie.

Once we got to Maureen's dormitory, I asked her to tarry outside: "Don't go in yet. Let's go over to the fountain."

"Okay."

Maureen's dormitory faced west to a large rectangularly squared lawn, the central, social pathway across campus. From the double glass framed front door of her dorm, you could look directly out to the middle of the lawn and see the campus fountain. A landmark on campus, the fountain was a square, raised brick structure that stood three and a half feet high. Its top ledge was a one-and-a-half foot wide rim that ran around its entire length. Inside it, we saw a murky pool of water. Concrete benches affixed on all four walls allowed us to sit down lower than the pool above, or we could step up on a bench and sit down on the top rim above the water. This night, the fountain lights were off. The only light touching the fountain was that from the distant light posts on the corners of the lawn square and the low, dimmed glares coming from the buildings facing the square. We sat atop the fountain ledge, with our legs dangling above the bench we used to step up on.

"This is nice," Maureen said. "For a moment, you can forget about all the things you have to do."

"Like what?"

"I have to study, Calvin."

"I do, too."

"No, I didn't mean to make it sound like that."

The murky water in the fountain behind us mirrored the minimal light of the distant light posts. Sometimes the assorted red, yellow, blue, and green lights inside the pool were on and the water percolated in the waves. More often than not, though, like this night, the lights were off and the water was dead and gloomy with various pieces of debris—a fallen tree branch here, an aluminum can there, an apple core somewhere else, laying in the midst of the pool.

"I'm the oldest child in a large family," Maureen said. "When you're the first, a lot is expected of you."

"My family is big, too; but I'm a middle child. I can see what you mean, though."

"You see, I was thinking of my grandmother. She lived with us when I was a child. In the part of the play where I play Mama—well, I patterned it after her. I couldn't do it in that loud, boisterous, overbearing way that y'all wanted me to do at the rehearsal."

"Play it the way you want to. I think you do it good," I encouraged her.

"My grandmother had dignity, quiet dignity."

"I'm sure," I said. I leaned over and kissed her on the cheek. "Tell me about your family—where you grew up."

It was revealed through conversation that we both had some things in common—both of us had grown up in small, white-painted, wood-framed houses that were crowded with siblings and two to three beds in each bedroom; shared dresser drawers where each child was allotted only one drawer; with shoes kept under the beds; where indoor plumbing only became available to our homes after we were past the age of twelve.

"Our house was so hard to keep clean," she said. "Saturday was the big day to do the cleaning. We started early to get it out of the way.

"If we had to go to town, it was after the cleaning. Going into town for us was to go into Meridian, Mississippi. We live so far out in West Alabama that Meridian is the biggest town around."

"We live on the East Alabama border, close to Georgia," I said. "For us in Venetian Creek, downtown is Neshobee, Georgia. When I was very young, I

150

thought all the states in the United States were separated by rivers, because a river separated Alabama and Georgia near us."

"What happened when you found out differently?"

"I thought the other states were missing something. Like they weren't complete. Kinda like growing up with trees and hills and valleys, and later on, having to live in a place without them."

Then I stood on the ground in front of Maureen and pressed up to her as she sat on the foutain ledge, her legs dangling against the exterior wall of the fountain. I positioned myself between her dangling legs and wrapped my arms around her, under her arms. Her breasts arched just below my chin. I leaned into her.

"I can hear your heart beating, Maureen."

"You can?"

"Yeah. It's telling me—I want you, I want you."

"No, it's not."

"Yes, it is. I want you for real. I want us to get together in bed. I want to get naked with you, make you feel good."

She held her arms around my neck with them resting on my shoulders. "You're serious, aren't you?"

"Yeah."

"When?"

"Now. We could go to my room. You could wait in the lobby and I could run my roommate out if he's in," I suggested.

"No. Let's go to my room. My roommate's boarding out of town on a practice teaching assignment. For the rest of the semester, she is here only on weekends. Come on."

"How come you never told me this before?"

"Because I didn't need to tell you."

None of our dormitories were co-ed, but some nights during a month, there were open house evening visitation with curfews. So resident students were used to seeing members of the opposite sex in the hallways without being surprised, even if it was on a night when there was no open house visitation going on. A young man could make a mad dash from the lobby when the Resident Manager wasn't looking, and within seconds be in a young woman's room.

Maureen's room was typical of the twin furnished rooms that Waukeegan provided—on either side facing the center of the room stood an identical closet, bed, and desk built against the wall. As was customary, record album jackets, colorful psychedelic zodiac posters and slogans hung on the walls. A small infrared or blue strobe light in place of the regular desk light, provided just the right mood when needed.

She turned on the low blue light that she had placed in her desk lamp. We sat on her bed.

"Let's undress each other," I said.

With the tossing of garments, came soft moans, caresses, playful snickering and long kisses. When we were barebacked and her bra was still in place, I beheld the sight and hugged her again. I reached my arms around her back and gingerly disconnected her bra. The bra rolled down her supple breasts, revealing a firmness brought on by our lovemaking.

"Oh-h-h-h-h, this is nice," I said.

"You like it?"

"Oh, yes."

"Now, it's my turn," Maureen whispered. She unzipped my pants, reached through my shorts and felt my hard-on, now pulsating. "Wow! It's got a life of its own," she said.

I unbuttoned her denim pants. I gently ran my fingers down the exterior front of her panties and cupped my hand at her base, and felt that she was receptive. Then, I felt behind the elastic waistband of her panties and explored below the soft pubic hair. Within the smooth, soft folds of her femininity, I felt a delicious sexuality that was all hers to give.

No longer able to finish the game of undressing each other, we both shedded our own remaining clothes. On the small bed built against the wall in her half of the dormitory room, below the blue tinted light, we lay and rolled and shifted one on top of the other, beside one another, astride one another, hands and lips, fingers and toes, caressing one another. Between catching our breath, our lips and tongues met for long sweeping kisses.

Then I was beside her, our legs crossing, touching, still exploring. When I entered her, she moaned: "Oh-h-h, this is good." As we connected, touching, feeling, and experimenting, we embraced all of the senses our bodies possessed. After the panting and climatic releases subsided, we lay spent, calmly at rest. She lay on the side of the bed against the wall. I lay to the side nearest the center of the room and faced her.

"What are you thinking about?"

"I was thinking about the scenes in the play," Maureen said. "I was thinking, in the beginning—how we hit it off, how we connected, the attraction and tension we brought to the play. I liked you a lot and I know you liked me."

"Yeah. Two love birds with the hots for each other"

"That's just it. Since we've just did it and gone all the way, I wonder if we'll still show the natural sparks that everybody say we were showing. Will we be serious or will we be too carefree?"

"Don't worry. We'll be even better. You'll see."

"I'm feeling happy and giddy now," she said. "Actually tingling. If I took what I'm feeling now to the stage, the play would be a light-hearted comedy, like we've got a secret that nobody knows about, that we're waltzing through it, grinning."

I kissed her on the forehead and got up to put on my clothes. "We will waltz through it. It's gonna be easier. Now that we're relaxed and the tension's gone, we can now focus on the actual lines, and not feel awkward and be stumbling all over each other."

Maureen got dressed, went to the bathroom and came back to the room. "I'll usher you out of the dorm, safely now," she said.

It was not curfew time yet, so the side entrance was still available as an exit. The Resident Manager had her hands full at the front desk in the lobby.

I hiked across campus, heading west by way of "The Valley," a passage that separated the northwest sector of campus from the center of campus. The evenings' cool breeze was typical for the first of December. "The Valley" was a dimly visible throughway at night, lighted only by the lights out of the rear windows of the surrounding buildings; it was a foot path down a field behind a set of buildings, that descended downward to a flat bottom and ascended up a hill again between and behind another set of old brick buildings on the west of the gulch, a terrain heavily trafficked during the daytime, but scarcely trekked across at night.

I felt pretty good, walking in the calm and quiet ambience that the evening provided. It was quiet—a passer-by here and there, a nod or a greeting to a known colleague, a sum total of four or five people, were about the total of people I saw. I was thinking about Maureen. Then it hit me from out of nowhere— an old Jerry Butler song from out of the clear blue yonder. He Don't Love You Like I Love You.

Then it dawned on me. Did she fall for me because I'm Calvin Porch, or was it because of the words I spoke in character as Walter Younger in the play, *A Raisin In the Sun*? I thought, either way, it's alright with me. If the part helped me to "get over," hey, what can I say? I was happy with the way things had worked out. I had this new feeling that we would become "an item."

When I returned to our room and got ready for bed, I put on my checkered blue and white pajamas and turned off my desk light. Then I went over to Leonardo's desk to turn off his light. The calendar on the wall below his desk light showed where he had marked off every evening during the week, where he would study late at the School of Engineering Library. So that's where he is now, I thought. I admired his ability to stick to a plan, for he wasn't so much a brilliant student as he was a disciplined and determined collegian.

As I lay in bed thinking about Maureen, that same old song crept into my mind. The similarities between that song and the play we practiced, converged in my mind. The reference to those words—"great quotations," "rehearsals," "Lover's play," "final act," "take a bow," "exit"—followed from beginning to end, suggested a budding relationship that somehow didn't have all the ingredients present. It sounded like a one-sided love affair. Of the two in the relationship, only one wanted to keep it going.

Now I understood how with movie stars, both the leading man and lady often carried their in-character love affair on the stage to the real world. Was this happening with us? Playwrights and songwriters can write words better than ordinary people can speak them.

I knew I liked Maureen to the point of developing a permanent relationship with her. I lay in the dark, recalling the smiling honey brown face of this girl from West Alabama, who wore her hair parted off center and wore it longer and curlier than the average Afro hairstyle, her own version of an Afro. She had told me that her grandmother was an Indian, and they still had existing relatives on the Indian Reservation in Philadelphia, Mississippi, near the town of Meridian.

Maureen's face livened up when she told how her grandmother in her youth had escaped the reservation and fled into Alabama and lived among sharecropping Negroes, where she married a Negro farmer and remained there for over twenty years without crossing back over the Mississippi state line. Though the grandmother eventually went back to visit in the Meridian area, she never again set foot on the Indian Reservation, less than twenty miles west of Meridian. And this was the woman Maureen said she visualized as she embellished and endowed her character as Lena Younger in the play.

Now I felt tenderness for her, who at the moment, was across campus in her room. I wonder if she's thinking about me right now? The month of December was definitely off to a good start.

Chapter 16
A Burning Desire

By ten p.m. Wednesday, Leonardo and I returned to our room. Cupp had come by not long after we had settled in for the night.

The door was ajar as he entered from the hall. I sat on my bed with my back resting on the wall, still fully dressed in blue jeans and a maroon sweatshirt. My black tennis shoes stood on the off-white tile floor. Only my stocking feet covered with gray athletic stocks showed that I was grounded and at home for the evening.

Across the room, Leonardo sat at his desk, attired in brown leather house shoes, khaki pants and a blue denim shirt, with the shirttails out. Vigorously, he brushed the waves in his low-cut hair using a soft, square hairbrush. He didn't seem to care that he was among a small number of young men on campus who still brushed waves into their hair, when the majority of men wore long, combed out Afros.

Cupp was preoccupied with the articles in the campus weekly newspaper that had just come out that day. He sat near my desk with the chair facing toward the center of the room, toward the door. Known to wear a sweat suit until it faded, he had on his reddish-orange sweat suit, under a green Army fatigue jacket and black low-cut tennis shoes. He had been in the Recreation Center earlier, practicing on his ping-pong game.

"Man, I'll tell you," Cupp said. "The basketball team is in bad shape. Guards can't shoot. Big goofy center play like he's 'flicted.'"

"You mean afflicted, don't you?" I asked.

"Flict-it, afflicted, who cares?"

"Cupp, man, you kill me with your words," Leonardo said. "I ain't heard that one in a long time. 'Flict-it. Huh-huh-huh!" he kept laughing.

"We've got to support them, though," I stated. "Can't let the other team come in our gym and feel like they're at home."

"Yeah, Cupp, tell us about the dance moves y'all going to be doing at the half-time show Saturday."

"I'm not really gone be dancing 'Nardo. I'm gone be a spotter, an assistant. See—me and two other dudes are there to lift up the women and help them glide and float through the air, hold them over our shoulders and help them turn fancy flips. Stuff like that. All we gotta do is sidestep, move up, move back, help them when they need us, stay out of their way when they don't. Good work if you can get it."

"So, how did they pick you?"

"I'm good, Porch!" Cupp jested. "No, really, it was Dee Dee that got me involved. We kinda made an arrangement. I agreed to teach her to play table tennis and she asked me to work out with the Modern Dance Club."

"Leonardo, you should've seen them yesterday at the International Students food bazaar. Cupp and Dee Dee were eating cake out of each others hands."

"She is fine, though," Leonardo admitted. "Looks like it's more going on than a song and a dance to me."

"We're hanging in there," Cupp allowed. There was a big "shit-eating" grin on his face. He was blushing. We all laughed at the understatement.

159

I had already read Aaron's article, but didn't say anything as Cupp read portions of it out loud.

Meandering
By
Aaron Aldrich

A fascinating question was posed to me recently. It concerns a question, no doubt, of which many of you feel you are experts. Bear with me as I present this scenario. About two weeks ago, I was casually listening to James Brown, Mr. Excitement, Mr. Showman, the hardest working man in show business, soul brother number one. Need I say more?

Anyway, the question took on an International flavor when one of my South American brothers pointed out to me, matter of factly, that there was a fellow with one name, called "Sparrow," who is just as good or better. So we sat and listened to his album of the great Sparrow. I have to admit, though I couldn't understand the words, the rhythm and the beat had an Afro-Caribbean-Latin tone guaranteed to get you shaking. No sooner than I opened my mouth to form an opinion, a West African brother pointed out in machine gun rapid fire: "NO-NO-NO-NO-NO! You are both mistaken. The man you seek is Fella Ransom-Kuti!"

"Fella who?" I questioned. It turns out that West Africa has a James Brown equivalent, too. So we listened to his rendition of Mr. Excitement. I must admit, Fella sounded more like James than Sparrow did. But it opened my eyes—and my ears.

What the three stars had in common was an "out front," individual presence, a charisma, born for the stage, backed by a band with a lot of punch, that matched and punctuated the singer's every move, strut, twist, turn, squeal, and grunt. Though James Brown is the only one of the three I've actually seen in concert, I imagined, from looking at the pictures on the album jackets, that the other two performers brought the same visual presence to their music.

And if the singer actually tried to sing (none of them in my opinion had a great voice), his band expertly created the perfect tone, ever reminding the know-it-all music critics that they too were professional musicians. Well, you say —Who is number one? Who is the man? The debate continues. Diplomatically, I must say—at a party—all three could hold their own.

"He played it slick in the end, by not saying who was the best," I said. "That's just like him—playing politics."

"It ain't over," Cupp promised. "Wait 'til those foreigners get a hold of him. They love to argue. Believe me, I play against them every week."

"I got an invitation from Bakarie to go to an Afro-Caribbean party Saturday night. Did either one of y'all get one?"

"Naw, I didn't," Leonardo said. "But I'm going over to my home boy's new pad after the game. He's like having a house warming, a sit down, wine and cheese get-together."

"They asked me," Cupp said. "I'm not going though. I'm gone be hanging out with Dee Dee. The Dance Club's supposed to be doing something after the game."

"Imagine that," Leonardo observed. "On this whole boring assed campus, we got a basketball game—and three separate places to be Saturday night. How often does that happen?"

"Not too much, more like never!" Cupp and I said in unison.

"I'm trying to get Maureen to go to the party with me," I said. "But she's got other plans. She's pledging AKA next semester. They got these pre-pledge meetings and a rush party to go to."

"Man, you better try to get tight with her before she gets too deep into that sorority stuff," Leonardo warned.

"I know."

"Yeah, they get all stuck up after they pledge," Cupp said. "Fraternities and sororities. They got their own tables in the cafeteria, their own benches to sit on, all over campus. And when they have a party, you can't get in unless you're a Greek—a Black Greek. It's the AKA's, Alpha's, Delta's, Kappa's, Omega's, Sigma's, and Zeta's."

I recalled to mind that Deacon West is an Alpha, R. P. a "Q," and George Marshall is a Sigma. "All of them aren't that way," I spoke.

"Damn near."

"One thing you can say about the Deltas though," Leonardo added. "When those sisters throw a party, they let non-Greek guys come in. You gotta give them credit for that."

Not one of us denied that. Of all the fraternities and sororities on campus, the Delta house, nestled down a shady-laned side street just west of the college tennis courts, was virtually a campus facility. Perhaps the close proximity of the sorority house to campus made this sorority more receptive to the general, non-pledging students.

"Too bad Maureen's not pledging Delta," Leonardo finished.

"I'm not worried about it," I said.

The door was still ajar and Ivan from down the hall stuck his head in after two quick knocks on the door. Fully dressed with a khaki trench coat covering his street clothes, he looked like he had just come in from the cold. On his head was a red baseball cap with white letters inscribed across the front—indicating his fraternity, Kappa Alpha Psi. Kappa Red Ivan always wore something with red in it.

"What's going on?" Ivan greeted.

"Speaking of the devil," Cupp said.

"What? What did I do?"

"You ain't done nothing. Come on in, Ivan," I said.

"We were just talking about you Frat boys," Cupp said.

"Oh, hell, I know what this is leading up to," Ivan answered, anticipating a familiar topic. He didn't seem offended by Cupp's remark. In fact, he smiled. "Let me get what I came for and get out. I'm in a hurry. Leonardo, I need to borrow a book from you."

"You don't have to go anywhere," Leonardo said. "Cupp is just talking. Don't mind him."

"You see, that's what I'm talking about. He needs something now!"

"Cupp, you know I'm not like that. I got friends all over. I hang out with a lot of folks. Yeah, I'm in the Frat, but I don't let the fraternity tell me what to do or who to associate with."

"We know you're alright," I said. "Cupp is just giving you the wrath of God 'cause you're the only one here."

"Yeah, when I see red, I charge like a bull," Cupp teased. "Ivan, maybe you need to get rid of that red hat."

Everyone laughed except Ivan. Cupp had through serendipity arrived at a true pun, a neat punch line to an unplanned joke.

"Touché, Cupp—good shot, you jive-ass June bug. I'll give you credit for that one," he responded good-naturedly. "But the hat stays right where it is. I wear this cap proudly. I'm proud of what it stands for.

"I don't know why I'm talking to you anyway. There's nothing to prove to you. I gotta go. Porch, Leonardo, see y'all later. Cupp, you can go to hell." He walked out of the room.

"Hey, wait up, Ivan!" Cupp yelled. He lowered his voice. "See y'all in the morning." He went out into the hall to catch up with Ivan. They had been good friends for our first two years on campus before Ivan joined a fraternity, and became known as Kappa Red Ivan.

Due west of the fountain square just beyond the expansive lawn-cut, concaved gulch known as "The Valley," lay a circular road that separated Waukeegan's central campus from the buildings on the west and northwest. On this road, Cardwell Hall stood facing east, just south of the caution-lighted crossroad that sent you east or west.

The old brick building, once a versatile academic hall, now housed the Agriculture and Industrial Arts Department, mainly. On occasions when classrooms were overfilled at Bennington Hall, the Liberal Arts Department deigned to use this facility. Among Cardwell Hall's attractions was a Lecture Theater just as good or better than the one on the top floor of Bennington Hall. In this room, Sister Margaret DuMaine conducted her Speech and Drama classes.

The industrial-sized, rounded-off angles of the restroom fixtures depicted an era like that of the early auto industry, where purpose and utility suggested that ovals were better than angles, that aesthetics, if they existed, had been incidental and clearly secondary to functions. That era gave us the crow's feet bathtub that the wealthy now place in their modern homes as a status symbol.

At Cardwell Hall, when someone flushed the white porcelain toilets in the restrooms, a gush and vacuum sounded out in the hallway. Ancient radiator heaters, spaced periodically along the walls in the rooms and hallways, had pipes attached that ran along the walls. In the attempt to heat Cardwell Hall, when turned on fully, the pipes rattled in an un-intrusive refrain. In the quiet of the evening, one might think the place was haunted.

I walked into the restroom carrying a vinyl blue and white gym grip bag. This was the day we performed scenes from the play. It was only minutes before Sister DuMaine's class started.

"What's going on, Brother Porch?"

"Hey Charles. Looks like you're getting ready."

"Man, we gone knock 'em dead. We gone turn it out! How you like it? Look at my outfit." This white boy over the past few years had become comfortable using Black folk's jargon and idioms. He had on a brown sports coat, black slacks, white shirt, and a black bowtie. He pointed to his pants legs.

"You see I got these plain, black Army shoes and my pants legs jacked up high so you can see my white socks," Charles noted. "And when I sit down to cross my legs, the bare skin of my legs show. That's just like white folks do, you know."

"You should know."

"I'm going for the laughs," Charles said. He had the one part in the play where the scene called for a white character.

I took off my sweatshirt and put on an old long-sleeved plaid shirt of assorted red, green, blue, and white colors. That one garment was my sole costume piece to depict the historical time period in which the play was to have taken place. I was glad Charles saw a way to play his part comically.

He warmed up and practiced in front of the bathroom mirror. But it was not his lines from the play. He mocked the Governor of the State. "My fellow citizens of Alabamuh, this is your Gov'nor speaking. As I promised y'all before, I stand for states ri-ights. No outsider or Johnny-come-lately's gone come in he-ah, in the state of Alabamuh, and tell us what tah-du. I promised y'all I was gone keep the nigras in they place, and that' what I intended tah-du."

In the middle of the governor's speech in the mirror, two other young men had entered and were just as amused as I was. "See, I got y'all laughing," Charles said. "I'm good! I know I can be an entertainer."

"I've got to give it to you," I said "If I'd heard you on the radio, I would've thought you were George Wallace for real."

Then he got serious. "Mark my words, Porch. This is my last semester in school. I'm going out on the road. Gonna tour with bands, work the concerts and night clubs.

"I feel like I'm ready," he continued. "I've already done some gigs as an emcee, announcer, and stand-up comedian."

Charles had been working the local spots—the Elks, roadhouse cafes, and high school dances. This past football season, he had filled in as the half-time announcer for the marching band at home games.

"I don't know," I said. "You'll have three and a half years of college out of the way. One more semester and you get your degree."

"Other folks have made it without a degree. I can't keep turning down opportunities, man. If I don't take my shot now—who knows—I may never do it. Hell, I

167

could've gone on the road with Lionel Richie and the Commodores, but I didn't. And look what's happened to them—on their way, headed for the big times. And look at Tom Joyner—playing records in that little old booth in the Cafeteria. Now, he's got a regular gig at a radio station."

"It's a tough decision."

"The problem with you, Porch, is that you're too cautious. You like to play it safe. You're one of those people like my parents, who think a bird in the hand is worth two in the bushes."

"I just know what I would do if it were me."

"I was watching the late show a few nights ago," Charles said. "They had an old famous actor on there who had a similar situation like mine. And you know what he said? He said 'Sometimes it's best to take your chances when you've got something to lose. You have to remove the safety net, burn the bridge, strip yourself down to nothing but your talent and a commitment.'

"You see, I said to myself, that's me! I need to be out there—going for it, putting myself on the line. Education is good, but that would be like having a safety net, having something to fall back on."

Luckie had quietly entered the restroom while Charles described his personal plight.

"I think you should go for it," Luckie said. "It's not everyday you come across somebody that's got it together and has confidence to go with it."

Luckie had a grin on his face, as he looked in the mirror to adjust the cap on his head. His part in the scene from the play was that of a preteen-aged boy. He wore a simple white shirt with black suspenders and short blue jeans, cut off above the knees, with white socks and white tennis shoes. A young man, at twenty-two years of age, he fitted the green baseball cap on the back of his head with his frontal hair sticking out, affecting a child's appearance. He was just as tall as us, but he had been assigned the part of a child.

"I appreciate that, Luckie. See, Porch, I do have some supporters. I gotta go. Gotta mess with Mille Yates before class begins."

"I never said I didn't support you," I spoke as he headed out the door.

"Don't worry about him," Luckie said. "He's a survivor. He'll be alright."

I finished buttoning up the front of my costume attire. It was a workingman's shirt.

"You know it's kinda strange," I said, "when you see somebody that's really got a burning desire to do something, and they know exactly what they want to do. It makes you think, 'how come he knows what he wants to do and I don't know what I want to do? How come I don't have that burning desire?'"

"It's like a gift," Luckie said, "like a calling. You can't give it to yourself, and you can't make yourself have it. Look at me." Apparently, he had forgotten about the pre-teen outfit he had on for the play, short pants and suspenders, and green baseball cap resting far back on his head.

"I'm a good baseball player," Luckie added. "I got confidence, and I'm sure of myself on the field. But I don't have that same confidence in the classroom.

"You're an all-around student, Porch, you're getting by. Maybe your gift is simple—just to have common sense, to be the voice of reasoning among us crazies out there."

"That makes me look kinda ordinary, don't it?"

"Not really. You're the one who helped me decide to go through with Streak-o-Lean Aaron's plan to deal with that mess I'm in. If I'd had confidence in my own smarts, I could've passed that course on my own."

I never asked Luckie directly whether he had taken part in that scandal involving the homosexual Science Professor, but Luckie's willingness to undergo the program outlined by Aaron showed that the word Y-E-S was written all over his face.

"So you are going through with it?"

"Yeah. Aaron's scheme is slick, but one slip up, one bad move, and I'm out on my ass, expelled, gone, no hope of being scouted by the Pros.

"I hang out with some wild folks—some of 'em stupid," he said honestly. "And I'll keep hanging out with 'em. But if I'm ever in a corner with my back against the wall, you better believe I'm gone listen to somebody that's got some sense."

"The only thing wrong with that, Luckie, is that one of these days, you're going to run into a jam, and ain't nobody gone be around to help you."

"That's why they call me Lucky," he said, heading for the door to the hallway. "I always find a way out of a jam."

"They call you Luckie 'cause your name is Luckie."

Then we walked in the hallway, toward the Lecture Theater. "Maybe that works for you," I said. "but to me, it seems like a hell of a way to operate."

"Don't worry about it," he replied.

To enter the Lecture Theater of Cardwell Hall, we entered from the rear on either side, much like the doors that waiters go through in a restaurant when they carry serving trays above their heads. Inside, approximately thirty of us sat near the front facing Sister DuMaine, who stood at the lectern on the stage, announcing that the beginning of class was underway. True to consistency, the bespectacled, elderly nun girded her loins with the armor of a two-piece outfit— a Navy blue jacket and skirt with a white blouse. Her scarf-like hair attire was small in comparison to those of by-gone days. Navy blue like the other garments, it had a white band across the front edge, and it fit far back on the middle of her head—bangs of hair sticking out, akin to a woman's "head rag" worn during the Saturday morning housecleaning.

"Alright, everyone. Today we're going to need your full attention and concise critique," Sister DuMaine announced. "We have scenes from three plays to cover. And I must admit, this is one of the areas I enjoy most as a teacher—to see acting talent emerge that before now, we never knew existed."

"Also, I would like to introduce a special guest, Father Mario Giacomelli. He's not a critic. He's only passing through, traveling to Louisiana to receive a brief assignment before embarking on a trip to Africa to work as a missionary. Would you please welcome our guest with a round of applause?"

A young white man with a full head of dark hair stood up in the back of the room and said hello and that we had a beautiful campus. Then he sat down. He didn't look like a priest. He had on ordinary street clothes, a beige windbreaker jacket over a brown casual shirt, paired with dark trousers.

We sat through scenes from the plays *Death of a Salesman* and *The Prince and the Showgirl*. Then came *A Raisin in the Sun*.

When I saw Maureen in her costume as Mama in the play, I was glad I knew her as the fine young woman she was when she wore her regular clothes. The garbs for the play didn't flatter her at all. She wore a gray, drab, oversized dress with a brown belt around her waist. A darker shaded gray felt hat, shaped like an upside down kitchen pot was pulled down over her head. To round out her character as Mama, she wore a pair of black eyeglass frames that had no glass inside.

I got to hug Maureen in one place in the scene. But in the next moment, she finds out that my character has squandered a portion of our insurance money and she flails at me, beating me over the head, and pleading, "Strength Strength!" just like Mama in the play did to Sidney Poitier.

After the class was over, we walked together back to Bennington Hall. We had just crossed the street at the four-way crossing where the blinking yellow caution light directed the traffic that separated the western campus from the main grounds on the east. Below the sidewalk terrace on our left, beyond the steep, downward lawn, stood the campus museum, an old brick cottage with ivy growing up the exterior front wall. Looking down the gulch behind the museum, we got a northward view of "The Valley," the shortcut across campus.

"We did good in the play," Maureen said. "Everybody said so. I didn't mean to hit you that hard, but I wanted to make it look real."

"Yes, you did. I can't complain. I got a hug and a few licks out of the deal. The hug was worth it."

We were now back into our regular casual clothes.

"You really did it up in your old lady costume, but I like you better as you are now."

"I should think so," she said and smiled. "I want to always look good to you."

When we reached the entrance to Bennington Hall, I walked with her through the double doors.

"So, is our private wine-and-cheese get together still on this evening?"

"I meant to tell you," she said. She touched her index and middle fingers to her lips, kissed them, and softly touched my lips with the two fingers, completing the kiss. "Something's come up, my sweet. We'll have to postpone it. But come by the dorm this evening anyway."

"But I had planned ...."

"Oh, Calvin, you look like a wounded puppy. Don't worry, I'll make it better."

Other students passed in and out of the building and our little private world was encroached upon. I tried to appear undaunted. "I'll see you later," I said, turning toward the doors.

That evening in the lobby of her dorm, while sitting on a lounge couch, she revealed her physical state of mind. Her menstrual cycle had begun that morning, and had not the class play been important, she would have stayed in during the day.

"You have no idea what it's like," Maureen said.

"I don't want to know," I answered, waving my right hand, palm out, gesturing, "Stop! I've heard enough."

173

"Don't laugh. I can hear it coming," she said. "If Eve hadn't eaten that apple in the Garden of Eden, we wouldn't have this problem today."

"Well?"

Together we laughed it off and talked of other things. This weekend coming up would be the first one in December, and within a week, the first semester final exams would begin. I had heard that this was a pivotal, landmark time of the year for graduating seniors like us. When I bidded her goodnight, I left humming the words to the song. Just My Imagination Running Away With Me.

Chapter 17
Victory for the Home Team

The Saturday evening basketball game was the main event on campus, followed by a half dozen or so house parties scattered about the sleepy residential areas of town. The Waukeegan Tigers prepared to face State U., our biggest rival in basketball. At the Toland Hall gymnasium, our team had their bench on the south side of the court, in front of the stage and to the right and below the clear-glass backboard and goal. All that existed for us was the hope that our boys would get lucky and win the game. At least they always played hard against hated State U. The Tigers wore the home court white uniforms with maroon trimmings and numbers.

But Toland Hall had a legend and reputation of its own. In the words of Hollie who was tight with me during our freshman year: "Toland Hall smelled like a pair of funky white gym socks that had never been washed, had been worn too long, turned rank and yellow from sweat, with their fibers and mesh hardened to the point that the socks could literally stand up on their own."

The building was a gym, athletic complex, and an all-purpose facility for campus-wide activities. It was built in the style of the city auditoriums commonly seen in medium-sized American cities. Got a concert, a dance, a job recruitment conference, a Greek show, a Red Cross blood drive? Have it at Toland Hall.

We entered Toland Hall from the front entrance on the north side, and we passed through a narrow hallway that ran left to right, furnished with two small

175

offices, the size of toll booths on a highway, on one corner, and restrooms on the other. Continuing to the left or right, we passed through swinging doors on either side that took us into the gymnasium. The entrance to the balcony was a passage up steep, concrete steps through a narrow doorway on the east corner across from the toll booth-like offices.

Permanently in place was the basketball court that faced north and south, with a stage complete with maroon-colored curtains, occupying the south wall. The second and third levels above the first floor comprised a wrap-around balcony spaced with anchored, adjoined theater-type chairs. The high windows on the ground level prevented lookers-on standing outside from seeing anything inside.

So when you made your grand entrance through those swinging doors to view an event in this building, you expected excitement. The more outgoing and fashionable students used their grand entrance as an opportunity 'to see and be seen.' Unless you arrived early, the seats on the first floor were filled. The metal, folding chairs on both sides of the building, faced the court. To facilitate a courtside view, the concrete floor, starting from the walkway next to the hardwood floor, rose six inches in elevation behind every row of chairs.

'To see and be seen.' This might consist of wearing the right hat cocked a certain way, a fashionable jacket, a pair of hip hugging bell-bottom pants, a great inviting smile, the double-take observation, the confident swagger in your walk; each one of these points had a place in making a 'cool' entrance. And you dared not walk in with books in your hands as if you were just from the Library.

I sat with Dwayne Norwood in the first row crowd at half court. Dwayne wore his characteristic white floppy tennis hat, which rested more on the back of his head than on the front of his Afro.

"I can't believe it!" Dwayne said. "I should've acted sooner. I don't understand what Dee Dee sees in Cupp." The previous Monday, sitting out on "The Breeze Station" bench, he had made a half-hearted attempt to show some interest in Dee Dee, and he told me he had been to Dee Dee's dorm once since then.

"They got something going on," I said. "Cupp's teaching her ping-pong and she's smoothing out his clumsy ways. Wait 'til you see them at half-time."

When the half-time buzzer erupted, both basketball teams—tall men with big feet—trotted to the locker rooms. Then the lights were dimmed. The Modern Dance Club entered the court, amid cheers and hoots and whistling from the crowd. They came out running in that sprite, lunging, floating-in-the-air, swimmingly smooth way of running to position, as dancers are known to do.

Suddenly, standing in place at center court, facing the spectators on the western side, stood a dozen shapely women, Dee Dee among them. They were dressed alike in black tight-fitting dance outfits of the bathing suit variety, where underneath black leotards covered their fine legs down to their ankles, just above their bare feet.

Della Diane "Dee Dee" Pelham, the short, well-proportioned dynamo from Chicago, Illinois, stood in the dance line, Afro hair-styled and attired, identical to the other dancers, doing a knee-bounce shimmy to an instrumental version of "Papa Was A Rolling Stone," a popular song at the time.

In front of the dancers, positioned on the gym floor, stooped with one knee on the floor, and one hand coolly, finger popping to the rhythms of the music, kneeled the spotters—Cupp and two other young men. Each male had on black pants, a white sleeveless athletic undershirt, and was barefooted. Each had to be a well-conditioned specimen with upper body strength enough to lift a dancer above his shoulders, or better still, carry a young woman on his shoulder.

"That lucky dog!" Dwayne repeated. "That lucky son of a bitch."

"Why begrudge him? Cupp was just the right man at the right time. Knowing you, you wouldn't have danced with the Dance Club even if they had asked you. You would've said that was sissy stuff."

"You're right," he conceded. "She's just too fine for him, though."

I watched the dancers and was reminded of the feelings I often had when observing talented girls perform their skills. And I tried to articulate this feeling in my mind, thinking that somehow, this feeling was universal. To an ordinary high school boy or an ordinary college young man, in his mind, there is a mystique about beautiful young women when they are displaying their talents in a public arena. This group of the opposite sex include cheerleaders, majorettes, actresses, singers, dancers and graceful athletes.

To a smitten boy, his dream girl seems out of reach to him, close in view, but yet distant in intimacy returned. He is like a shy sixth grade boy with a crush on a pretty lady teacher. Why would so fine a woman like her, like a plain ordinary guy like me? What would she see in me? If I was a popular star athlete or a popular playboy with a good rap, a good conversation—maybe, just maybe. But she won't even look my way.

Was this a universal feeling, or was it just the way I used to feel? I thought to myself. And do girls and women feel the same way, too?

Then the music stopped. The lights came on bright again, and the basketball game resumed. The highlights of the game weren't reached until less than seven minutes remained on the game clock. Our coach, a salt-and-pepper haired, middle-aged man in a gray suit and maroon turtleneck shirt, beckoned with a crooked index finger for a first-year player to move up from the end of the bench. Springing to his feet, a tall, little known player walked up to the scorekeepers' table, half pimp-walking, part strutting, part prancing, and part trotting. At the sight of his entrance into the game, everyone in the gym, especially the small town and country people, knew that John Gooden was different, definitely "Street," hardened by big city life, and had probably been around the block more than a few times. That walk and those mannerisms were so ingrained in the inner city young man that the coach— it was said by a nearby spectator—knew better than to take on the task of smoothing out the ghetto nuances of his find, his "diamond in the rough," a good player that through no recruitment on the College's part, literally fell into his lap.

John Gooden, a tall, brown complexioned athlete with a wiry, uneven Afro hairdo and a goatee beard, dashed out onto the court to cover his man 'like a cheap suit.' The team had created a cheer for him based on an old Rock and Roll song called "Johnny B. Good." The players on the bench started singing, and it caught on, and fans all over Toland Hall started singing along:

Go Go Go Johnny Go!
Go Go Go Johnny Go
Go Go Go Johnny Go
Johnny B. Good

According to R. P., the athletic trainer for the baseball team, who hung around the gym with the basketball trainers a lot, he had heard the whole scoop on Johnny B., and he shared the information among us. Like Deacon West on the baseball team, Johnny B. entered college later in life, after a stint in the Army, and a tour in Vietnam. He had knocked about aimlessly in the streets of Chicago and Gary, Indiana for a year and a half, playing recreational basketball. During that time, the rugged war veteran moved in and out of bad company. His main accomplishment back then was that he avoided getting put in jail and creating a criminal record, because he loved playing basketball too much to be stuck in a prison. Playing basketball saved his life. He was on the brink of getting into serious crimes; the temptation and the money were too appealing to turn down forever. He did a few things—sold a little pot, shoplifted every now and then, snatched a purse once in a while.

Then one night at a YMCA Rec tournament, a Waukeegan College alumni who was the Executive Director of the 'Y' took notice of the hard working, hustling defender, who seemed to thrive in the unpopular aspects of the game—rebounding, blocking shots, stealing balls, and passing the ball when he could've taken the shots himself. The Director chatted with Johnny B., called Waukeegan's Athletic Department, and the rest was history.

His reputation among his Tiger teammates was that it was bad news for the opponent's top scorer when they put Johnny B. in the game. Even though our team played zone defense, the coach turned him loose to stake out, shut down, and hound only the leading scorer of the other team, with his hands up, legs kicking, and 'trash talking' all the way. He could frustrate and reduce a thin-skinned opponent to inconsequential proportions.

Johnny B. Good chased his man with a vengeance, psyche-ing the player out and spewing out non-stop trash talk. Once, when he came near the half court foul line, I heard him bark to an opponent: "Whatcha' doin'? Gimme that ball. You can't handle me. Gimme that ball—you don't know what to do with it!"

Socially on campus, he hung out with a tight knit group of guys from Augusta, Georgia, actually a bunch of Aaron Aldrich's home boys that let him tag along because one of the guys in the clique was a fellow Army veteran and an associate of the basketball player.

I remember greeting John Gooden and two guys from Augusta a few evenings before at Aaron's Ombudsman's Office. They were leaving as I entered. I greeted him: "Hey, what's happening, man?"

"Not much. You got it."

"I heard you were doing a pretty good job on the team."

"Aw, I don't do nothing. I just kick a little ass every now and then. Hee Hee Hee Hee!" he chuckled on his way out.

I asked Aaron, "Is he one of your home boys?"

"Nah! He's just a good friend of Tyler's. Vietnam vets. You know how that goes. I don't trust him, though."

"Why not?"

"I just don't trust him. He's got those eagle eyes, always looking around like he's gone steal something."

"Well, you can't judge him by that. He's probably a good guy."

"He probably is, but I don't trust him."

That was then. As far as the Saturday night game was concerned, Johnny B. was a hero. When the game was over and we counted up the casualties, our Tigers had scored a hard fought victory over State U. by one point—88 to 87—due mainly to his "take no prisoners" style of defense. He amassed the statistics of three steals, two rebounds, two key passes, and four points in which he "dunked" the ball in over taller defenders, all with less than six minutes remaining in the game. Go Go Go Johnny Go!

Part 3

Resolution

Chapter 18
Man, You Must Be Trippin'

By the end of the third week of March, I had been going to the Veterans Administration Hospital for two weeks. The rehabilitation on my left shoulder and back, and my left hip and thigh progressed well. True to his word, Coach Benson arranged with the V.A. Hospital Physical Therapy Department to allow me to rehabilitate from my injuries under their auspices. The Athletic Department had a working relationship with the V.A. Hospital.

This arrangement on paper, listed me as a Volunteer Recreational Program Assistant, whereby I had to do one hour of volunteer work for ever half-hour of therapeutic treatment I received. If I had arranged this at the beginning of the semester and signed up for a related course, I could've received academic credit for this volunteer work. Of course at the time of registration, I didn't know that I would get shot a month later.

I looked forward to the progress report and review at the end of the day with Miss Belinda Ward, the supervisor to whom I was assigned. In fact, I was infatuated with her, but didn't know how to tell her about my feelings. One more complete week on the program and they would determine if I needed any further workouts.

I stood by the road to the V.A. Hospital. It was quietly traveled during the middle of the day. Two weeks of experience had taught me that I could hitchhike a ride to the V.A. Hospital within ten minutes. In just ten minutes, I could reminisce about a lot of things while standing beside the road, daydreaming.

The two lane, black asphalt road wound through the landscape. Fields on both sides revealed springtime development. Green, grassy brush and shrubs almost knee high, came up to the red muddy ditches on the roadsides.

Wild plum trees with green leaves and early stage foliage stood close by. Strung along in no particular order, honeysuckle vines with white and yellow petals sprawled along the branches of the plum trees, like unplanned garland on a Christmas tree. When ripened in a few weeks, you would have to skirt through thorny briar patches to get the red fruit.

Out in the fields beyond the plum trees, stood young, low and scarcely branched pine trees. Still out farther, the landscape was walled in with thickets of tall pine trees in all directions to the point that local folks in the area had described the area as the Black Forest.

I could reminisce about a lot of things in ten minutes, even a whole lot of things that happened last semester. I had exhausted all avenues and pursuits concerning who shot me that last week in February. And Bakarie had died a few days later, indirectly related to the incident. It was apparent that my own personal style of detective work had gotten me nowhere. I remembered the police detective's words: *"If it were me, I'd go back six months and write down the names of everybody I had an argument with, or had a serious disagreement with. And, I'd see how they fit into the picture."*

The detective's words hadn't netted any results. I was thinking of returning the pistol to Charles. Remembering insignificant events from last semester, I had scrutinized my friends and associates.

For instance, even the budding relationship between me and Maureen was recalled to memory in search of a clue. Our romantic season that carried over from last semester ended in a trickle, actually a whimper, and like the passing of a summer rose, it dwindled away. The words of a previous conversation with Leonardo and Cupp had proven to be prophetic: "Man, you better try to get tight with her before she gets too deep into that sorority stuff," Leonardo warned.

"Yeah, they get all stuck up after they pledge," Cupp said. "They got their own tables in the cafeteria, their own benches to sit on all over campus, and when they have a party, you can't get in unless you're a Greek—a Black Greek."

I thought it was mainly the Christmas holidays that interrupted our relationship. From my hometown in Venetian Creek in east Alabama, I had talked to Maureen out in west Alabama only three times by long distance telephone calls. Francine Porch didn't like the idea of her unemployed college student son running up her telephone bill. Two days after New Years Day, registration began for the second semester. We had a day and a half on campus without much privacy to try to rekindle the flame we had a few weeks ago, before six weeks of Sorority pledging started for her.

So when she got on the initiation line with the Alpha Kappa Alpha Sorority, things cooled off between us. It came on gradually. Then it was complete. I had sat in the same area in the Cafeteria, so that when her pledge line marched in, she'd see me. For about two weeks, she'd given me a wink or a smile. I knew things between us were going bad when she started looking straight ahead, cold and stoic, never looking my way. I started to wonder—could it be? It was too painful to contemplate. I shuddered to think about it. Could it be this is the end? The palpable sting in my heart and the anxiety in my gut came with a reeling, nauseating feeling that I was rejected, put aside like an unwanted toy. It was like being stood up for the big dance, all dressed up, and standing on the street curb, awaiting a ride for a double date, watching a lot of cars pass, until finally you see your girl ride by with three other people in the car, and one of them is in your place. Then it was time to slink back the way you came.

The AKA Big Sisters kept Maureen and the other pledges together at all times, except for the time they had individual classes or were asleep in bed. Six weeks of initiation and hazing climaxed with a "Greek Show" in the gym at Toland Hall, when the newly initiated Greeks "crossed the burning sands," their description of "going over," completing the rituals giving them full membership and fellowship into a more worthier fraternity or sorority than the next one.

This was the big show on campus, where the pledges performed step shows to the cadence of hand claps and foot stomps, and they sang and danced with the choreographed moves of the popular singers of the day. Three to four weeks of weekend parties, exclusive to the Greeks, followed the "going over" rituals.

Needless to say, by the end of February just before I got shot at the Mansion, I had lost Maureen to a fraternity guy named Eric, a "Q-Dog" member of the Omega Psi Phi Fraternity. The old idiom: "Out of sight, out of mind" was apt here. I hadn't had a decent conversation with her the whole time she was "on line" and had only glimpses of her around campus. I can honestly say that during the entire initiation period, I never, but once, talked to her alone for over ten minutes, and that was for only fifteen minutes. Out of sight, out of mind.

Now I had this rehabilitation to go through to get my muscles and limbs reconditioned to optimal motion and strength. The V.A. Hospital therapy program—in radio disc jockey jargon—was supposed to "put a little pep in your step, a little glide in your stride, and a little cut in your strut." In other words, "make you run like a brand new car" so that you could "purr like a kitten and run like a scalded dog." But due to the gun shot wounds, the injury had "put a little hitch in my gitty-up." Radio Disc Jockeys. My friend Charles Jordan, clothed in a white man's body but with a Black man's heart and soul, had done a little part-time disc jockey work at a local radio station.

Now it was the fourth week of March. Earlier in the month, I adopted the habit of wearing a sweat suit on campus and to and from baseball practice. All total, I owned three sweat suits. I kept up this dress attire even on days after I returned from the Physical Therapy sessions. This allowed me to inconspicuously carry the pistol in a grip bag under a pair of tennis shoes and a folded towel. There were young men all over campus wearing sweat suits and gym suits and carrying grip bags every day.

On the days I went over to the V.A. Hospital, I wore regular casual clothes, as there was no time to go back to the dorm to change into a sweat suit before hitchhiking a ride to the hospital. Plus, as part of Coach Benson's arrangement with their people, I'd have to do volunteer work in the social services department as a trade-off for time spent in Physical Therapy.

If anyone knew I was carrying the pistol, he might've thought I was paranoid, but I kept the gun just in case the gunman decided to strike again. But I never decided what I'd do if I did discover the culprit: shoot him, beat him up, make him confess, call the police? What exactly would I do?

Off campus, I only went to three places and I took the grip bag with me to two of them—to the campus bookstore where I could get provisions, on the edge of campus, and to the corner food store two blocks off campus. A third place to which I decided against taking the gun was to the Chicken Shack sandwich shop on the southwest edge of campus. I feared that by some strange twist of fate, I could be mistaken for an armed robber, since it was nighttime when I ventured there a couple of times per week. To a hungry student at night, the Chicken Shack was a refuge for a meal if you had a couple of dollars on hand. Dozens of students—males and females—from all the dormitories on campus made the long walk down dimly lit campus sidewalks in route to the Chicken Shack.

On the last Tuesday night of the month, I returned to our room. Leonardo was sitting at his desk studying.

189

The neon light affixed to the wall above the desk was on above his head, and his record player on the table end of the desk was turned down low, but not so low as to not hear the lyrics clearly. An old harmonizing male group out of the sixties sang some lovesick song that had a simple rhyme.

Leonardo spoke immediately: "Hey Porch. Man, did you hear what happened to Charles Jordan?"

"No. What happened?"

"Man, you wouldn't believe it. He ran off with a Rock and Roll band. Gone tour the country with 'em. Not gone stay around to finish school."

"When did it happen?"

"Yesterday, according to Nadine Fuller. You know her, Nathan Fuller's twin sister, the cute girl with the big eyes who wears glasses. We take classes together."

"Dog! He's gone and done it," I said. "I've heard him say it before, that he wanted to get out there and see what he's worth, put himself on the line, test out his talent. But I thought he was gone wait 'til he graduated first."

"Well, according to Nadine, things got speeded up some. You see, Nadine and them live next door to Charles' family. Sunday night, they heard Charles and Old Man Jordan arguing about something, like they were getting ready to fight. The old man threatened to call the police and Charles threatened to leave. Then, they quieted down.

"The next morning when everybody was gone, Nadine Fuller's mother saw a blue van with fancy writing on it, something about a Traveling Blues Band, pull up in the yard. Charles gets out of the van, goes in the house, and comes out with a suitcase, and they leave."

"So, he went and did it," I said. "Mr. Bo Jangles."

"What?"

"It's something Charles referred to once when he was talking about going into show business. Just something about Sammie Davis, Jr." I was nervous, felt like I had said too much.

"Let me tell you what caused everything," Leonardo said as his face lit up in excitement. "Nadine's mother went over to talk to Charles' mother later on. The whole thing was about a gun, a pistol, that was missing.

"Mr. Jordan, the old military man that he was, had a bunch of rifles in the house. But for some reason, he kept the pistol out in the utility room in the garage in a service toolbox, mixed in with screwdrivers and wrenches, and everything. Charles got the gun, but he refused to tell his dad why he got it, or what he did with it.

"All he could tell his dad was that he would return it later and that it's in good hands.

"According to Nadine, she herself don't cuss much, and her mother don't cuss at all. So if Nadine was blushing, you know her mother had to wash out her own mouth after she repeated what Old Man Jordan had said: 'Good hands? Good hands, my ass!'

"That had been the reason for the argument. Charles said he was loyal to his friend. Old Man Jordan said that loyalty to your family comes before loyalty to a friend."

"So with Charles already chomping at the bit to leave home," I surmised, "this just gave him the opportunity to get on out of there."

"Exactly."

"Well, I hope he make it," I said.

"Yeah, that's something, ain't it?"

I knew one thing for sure. If Charles could keep a secret and not tell where the gun was, I had the same obligation to keep it a secret. I couldn't tell anyone— not even my roommate.

I put on my blue bathrobe and got my toiletries and went into the bathroom down the hall. It had been a long day and now this, I thought while brushing my teeth in front of a mirror on the wall above the sink. A row of six sinks and mirrors made up the entrance area of the bathroom. To the left around the corner wall were the toilets and urinals. The shower stalls occupied the space on the right side of the room. Charles' flying the coop had not complicated anything with me. It was just another cloudy element thrown into the whole scheme of things. I got into the shower, turned the water on as hot as I could bear it, and relaxed as it rained down on me.

Earlier during the afternoon, I'd confided with R. P. about a theory that had been shrugged off by Roland Trotter, the head of Campus Security, and laughed at by Aaron Aldrich. In the gathering up and rounding up of suspects, it finally dawned on me to consider only what happened that day at the Mansion from the time I woke up until the time I got shot. In the past few weeks I had only considered what happened from the time I met Hollie and Bakarie at the Library to the time of the shooting. Look at all the patterns and coincidences, I told myself. That Saturday I went to breakfast, left there and went to baseball practice. Coincidentally, I had worn the same kind of practice outfit as Aaron.

Just that one time only, I had dressed like him. I normally wore the team issued garbs. Aaron liked to dress in his own self-styled practice gear. The team colors were maroon and gold. That Saturday, we both wore blue and white sweat suits. Colors other than the college colors were generally worn by freshmen, rookies, and walk-ons, not by upperclassmen like us. I collided with him in a head-butting accident on the field. Both of us were taken to the gym in Deacon West's car for ice packs and aspirins. Deacon West had said of us knocked out on the field that we looked like the Doublemint Chewing Gum twins on the TV commercial.

After receiving first aid attention, Aaron had put on his street clothes and went to sit in the gym on the bench with the basketball team trainer and some basketball players and watched the team practice. He told me that was his plan as we got ready to leave the gym. Other than the basketball team, we were the only persons in the gym. R.P., the baseball trainer, and Deacon West returned to the ball field. I kept on my practice outfit and went to the Library, where I met Hollie and Bakarie outside on the walkway. From there, we went to the Mansion.

I just happened to have run into Hollie and Bakarie. The bad guy had showed no interest in shooting them. Somebody followed me from campus. I now referred to the criminal as "The Killer" since Bakarie died shortly after of complications related to the assault at the swimming pool.

"Ah hah! The Killer thought he was following Aaron, and not me," I concluded. "I haven't done anything to anybody. It had to be Aaron. In his duties in the Student Ombudsman's office, he probably pissed off someone along the way."

Once per week, I checked in for an update with Roland Trotter's office concerning the incident. I rehearsed in my mind the whole puzzle, the whole pattern. "Big Bird" Trotter would surely accept my findings.

To get to the Campus Security office, I took the street west of the main campus intersection, where off to the northwest in a court stood the bronze statue of Waukeegan's founding president, under whose bronze eyes, Charles had loaned me a pistol. If you could categorize the west wing of campus as old, middle-aged, or new, the Campus Security building would be classified as middle-aged. The old buildings were single-story ones constructed with hand-made bricks of the time. They were close together with the ground between them paved with brick streets, and others were so close together that the passage way between them were narrow alleys.

The middle-aged buildings were two-story structures made of bland, factory-produced bricks, that had even rows of windows on the first and second floor, much like a two-story high school building. These monotonous buildings always had something painted white on the exterior, either window trimmings or vertical white concrete segment markings, going up from the ground to the top of the walls. And the middle-aged buildings always had flat roofs.

Now the new buildings, like the School of Engineering Complex on the right of the street, had patterned, overlaid and interspaced angles, tapered, segmented roofs, whole floor levels walled in with contemporary, dark brown tinted glass. They had off-white tile floors on the inside, and hallway passages that veered off center from the point that you thought you were going straight, and the next thing you knew, you had unknowingly turned a corner.

The Campus Security office was housed in the Physical Plant Administrative Building. A separate front entrance led you into Roland Trotter's domain. The general office had an information desk up front, with a half dozen desks and chairs scattered throughout the office. Three private offices finished out the rear section of the department.

An elderly, thin dark man wearing a black security policeman's uniform with gold-colored writing, insignia, and trimmings led me in: "Hey, Chief, Calvin Porch is here to see you."

We went through the greetings and small talk before we got down to discussing the case. Roland Trotter's office was scarcely furnished. Behind the desk where he sat were a half dozen or so certificates hanging on the wall, and three fancy plaques spaced between them. One green, five-drawer file cabinet stood against the wall behind him to the right.

It was ironic how the older retirement-age Security Guards addressed Roland Trotter as "Chief," when only a short while back, the tall, bow-legged, reddish-brown man with the neatly trimmed mustache and the long hawk nose had been no more than a student himself. Trotter had been a graduate student and

195

Dormitory Resident Manager when I arrived on campus my freshman year. Only within the past year had he been moved to the Security post. Apparently the well-intentioned Chief of Campus Security had been watching too much television in his transition into law enforcement, albeit low, almost nil crimes on campus to pursue. "Hey Chief this—Hey Chief that—Good Morning Chief—Chief, there's someone to see you—Yes, Chief, I'll take care of it—Reporting for duty, Chief." They gave him full respect.

The Chief had been given to wearing dress suits around campus along with a gray, wide brim hat, the likes of which a real sheriff might wear. Somewhere along the way, he acquired the nickname "Big Bird," after the puppet character on a children's educational TV show.

Before I got into revealing my newfound theory, he let me know that they had done a background check on Professor Mansaray concerning Bakarie and Adelaide. The girl's mother liked Bakarie just fine, so the father had to bury the hatchet and get along with him, too. They agreed to co-exist just days before the incident at the Mansion.

I revealed my hypothesis. Roland gave ear to the theory as if it were important to him. He cupped his hands on his desk with his fingers interlocking: "Yeah, Calvin, I can see how you might find a connection between y'all dressing alike and everything. And how Aaron might have some enemies because of his role as a Student Ombudsman.

"I know they are present—student government and student affairs representatives—during the times when the Administrators make decisions, but I've never heard of a retaliatory act carried out against Student Ombudsmen. It's just not done.

"Whenever students do something to get themselves in trouble, they almost always, without fail, know that they have done wrong and can't blame it on another student. They might get mad at the college for a minute or two, but they normally just go away quietly and start a new life somewhere else."

He accepted "no ifs, ands, or buts" from me. His background and experience as a Dormitory Resident Manager, the acquisition of an MBA Degree, and his part-time evening job with the Waukeegan Police Force made him an impenetrable rock to chisel away at. I could do nothing to convince him that the theory was possible.

"Even though you and Aaron dressed alike that day, and a couple of coincidences happened, that's just too weak a story to pursue." He leaned back in his chair and threw up his hands, gesturing the conclusion of the whole matter. "I'm inclined to agree with the police department downtown—that the gunman, an independent assailant, was following someone through the woods who resembled or dressed like you.

"Bakarie Seesay was just a nuisance in the way, who the gunman never even expected to run into. When he came face to face with Hollie Drummond and heard y'all speak to each other, he knew you were not the person he was pursuing.

"So the mysterious man on the run got away. And the predator shot the wrong man—you! Then he got the hell out of there, too." Big Bird Trotter summed up the matter as if he were a genius. He got up from his chair leading me toward the door.

"Don't worry about it Calvin, okay? We're working with the Waukeegan Police Department. Let us handle it. We'll get to the bottom of it. Alright, Calvin? So, let us do our job. We'll take care of it. Just keep checking back with us, alright? Okay, so I'll see you later," he dismissed me.

No sooner had I left Roland Trotter's office, I crossed paths with R.P. in the parking lot. We stood at the edge of the parking lot where the concrete curb and the front lawn of the building met. A dirt, grassless footpath ran parallel to the curb, where people had been walking to get from their cars to take a shortcut to enter the building.

"What's going on, R.P.?"

"Oh, man, somebody stole my brand new Pro Keds basketball shoes. Stole them out of my gym locker. Somebody had to see it, or either provide a lookout. They broke through the grill of the locker, not the padlock. Imagine how much noise they had to make to do that. All the bamming and banging. They probably had to do it with a crowbar."

"That's too bad, man."

"I don't even know why I came by here. All they want is a report. They never do anything," he motioned his head to the Campus Security office. "The only reason I came by was that Coach Benson said I should file it 'cause they tore up College property getting to my stuff.

"They wouldn't have even taken my report if it had just been my things, without property damage." Then he quizzed me: "What are you doing down here?"

"They all think I'm crazy. Nobody believes anything I tell 'em."

"Who are they?"

"Aaron Aldrich and Roland Trotter. I told them both about a theory; nah—a fact that I know to be true. You know the day I got shot? Well, the guy that shot me thought he was following Aaron.

"How do you figure that?"

"Me and Aaron were dressed alike. He and I both said something about it at the beginning of practice, when we were running laps around the field. He said 'Hey, I like your uniform. You got style,' and I said 'yours ain't half bad either'"

I explained it to R. P. just as I had explained it to Aaron and Roland.

"You know, at the beginning of the pre-season training when Coach Benson passes out sweat suits to all the veterans from last season—maroon to half of the team and gold to the other half. And, all the rookies and walk-ons have to wear their own stuff. Once spring training is over and Coach Benson make his cuts, then he gives us all the same gear.

"Well, you know I never wear walk-on, mixed up, colored sweat suits, not since our freshman year. Except for that day, I was running late for practice and couldn't wait to get my gold sweat suit out of the washing machine. I asked my roommate to put it in the dryer and get it out later.

"Then I threw together a mixed up blue and white outfit from my summer league team back home, and I rushed off to practice. Get this—Aaron had on the same colors, blue sweatpants, a white undershirt with blue long sleeves, and our regular Waukeegan maroon cap. I'm six-one, a couple of inches taller than Aaron, and I'm about ten or twelve pounds heavier than him.

Alfred Brady Moore

"When we bumped into each other and got knocked crazy, that would've caused the gunman to get confused. Even Deacon West had said we looked like the Doublemint Chewing Gum twins on a TV commercial laying out on the field, hurt. After Deek West drove us both up to the gym in his car for treatment, I left the gym first. That explains how I got followed to the Mansion.

"When I told Aaron the whole story, and that he should watch out because somebody was looking to kill him and might come back again, he thought I was crazy. That four-eyed dude behind those tinted lens glasses of his—he thought I was crazy. Asked me what drug I was taking, even though he know I don't take any. Told me, 'you must be tripping. Man, you tripping.' Man, that "Streak-O-Lean" joker—he don't like to be called by that name, you know—he made me mad! I know that guy thought he was following Aaron instead of me.

"So I said—knowing he don't like to be called by that name—'I said—"Streak-O-Lean," you know I'm telling you the truth. So get your head out of the sand. Maybe we can catch that dude.'"

"Porch, you're assuming that the dude didn't know either one of y'all before y'all collided on the field. Or—that he only saw y'all at the gym for the first time. Wa-ai-ait a minute!"

R.P.'s face lit up, the eyes behind his glasses moved lively. He had two books in his left hand. He repeated something I had said.

"But he don't like to be called by that name," he repeated. "When did I hear that before? He don't like

200

to be called by that name." Then he shook his right fist in the air. "That's right! That's right!"

"What's the matter?"

"Porch, you won't believe this, but just before y'all ran into each other, there was a dude standing around like a spectator, you know, behind the fence of the dug-out—a big guy with a hat on his head and ordinary clothes—a windbreaker jacket, jeans, you know. I remember him asking: "Which one of those dudes out there is Streak-O-Lean Aldrich?"

"And J.T. Moses, one of the freshman, pointed him out and said "'that's him over there, but he don't like to be called by that name.'"

"And Whump! We heard y'all's skulls crack together, and everybody on the field ran out there where y'all were."

"That means I was right, then?"

"I believe so. But you're not going to be able to convince anybody else. You know J.T. quit the team, but he's still around. He lives off campus somewhere. And, he probably wouldn't remember it if you did find him. I couldn't describe that guy that came around that day. If you add what I know to what Aaron and Roland Trotter already believe, neither one of them will think any differently now.

"And as far as the cops downtown are concerned, a campus incident don't mean shit to them. They can get more mileage out of the case by pursuing the line about one unknown dude chasing after another unknown dude, and that you and Bakarie and Hollie were messing around at the wrong place at the wrong time."

201

"I'm going to talk to Brother Aaron again," I said. "And I'll need you to go with me, R. P. Maybe he can recall something that he knows that he hadn't told me before. It's no point talking to Roland Trotter again before I talk to Aaron first."

"You're right. I'm willing to look into it. I'd like to see how this thing is going to turn out."

We agreed that we would talk to Aaron in the evening after baseball practice. At the beginning of practice, Aaron agreed to talk with me again. There were too many teammates around to talk privately during the workouts. Then, when the time came at the end of the day, R. P. got called into the coach's office, and Aaron got tired of waiting for R. P. to get free from a team trainers meeting. So he got in a car with Wiley Jakes and a few other players and they went off campus to buy some beer. I would have to wait for another time to talk to Aaron and R. P. at the same time.

On Wednesday in the cafeteria during the lunch break, Aaron pressed me for a conclusion. "Why do you keep insisting that I listen to R. P. Willingham, like he's got some kind of secret to tell me?"

"Because I know from the way you think that you'll just consider it nonsense coming from somebody else."

"I trust you. So what is it?"

"Aaron, I'm not telling you. Just wait 'til this evening."

Chapter 19
Like a Spy that Switched the Bags at the Train Station

Right after the next class that followed lunch, I walked to the old quiet road on the northwest of campus and hitchhiked a ride out to the V.A. Hospital. Promptly after the Physical Therapy session, during my review with the supervisor Belinda Ward, I volunteered to mow the lawn at her house for the upcoming Saturday.

Then, back on campus that evening when baseball practice ended, Wiley Jakes, a pitcher who was struggling with his control and his ability to throw strikes across the plate, begged me, a catcher, to stay a while longer and work with him. Although he played two other positions, he was on the verge of being taken out of the starting pitcher rotation. Coach Benson had displayed his frustration with Wiley in front of the whole team: "Hell, son! When are you going to throw two strikes in a row? We can't have that—a strike, and then a ball, every other pitch. If you can't throw strikes consistently, let me know and I'll put somebody on the mound who can. This shit's got to stop!"

So I worked with Wiley after the regular practice ended, and a second opportunity for Aaron, R. P., and me to discuss the shooting incident was lost.

On Thursday, everything about the day started out as ordinary as any other day. I returned to our room after lunch to drop off my books from the morning classes. This day I was not scheduled to go to the V.A. Hospital. I put on a sweat suit, tennis shoes, and my maroon baseball cap, and carried a textbook and note pad in my sports grip bag for an afternoon class. Of course, in the grip bag under those items, I planned to place a white folded towel on top of a pair of tennis shoes, where underneath I would lay the pistol in a brown paper sack. Mindful to rotate the towel from time to time, I took the towel out of the grip bag.

I had the door to the room locked. If Leonardo entered, I would hear him fitting his key in and turning the door handle. I had an irresistible urge to look at the gun, to admire the look, touch, and feel of the weapon with its brown handle, blue steel body, chamber, and barrel. Examining it, I turned the chamber to hear the precise click, click, click it made.

I'll go brush my teeth and take this towel and toothpaste with me, I thought to myself. It's time to rotate this towel out of the grip bag, anyway. Then I'll put another towel on top of the tennis shoes and gun. I zipped the bag closed, with the gun inside but out of the paper sack and laying on the top of the items inside. I then moved the book and note pad from the desk and lay them on my bed. I set the sports grip bag on the floor beside my bed.

"Bam Bam Bam!" someone knocked on the door. "Hey, Nardo, Porch! It's me, Cupp."

Cupp entered the room wearing a pair of khaki pants and a gray Waukeegan sweatshirt with maroon writing on it. In his hand, he carried a grip bag identical to mine—the standard, campus bookstore-issued ones common on campus. "Man, I'm glad you're here. Leonardo left some notes on his desk for a test coming up tomorrow. He said I could come by and pick them up." He went straight to my roommate's desk.

"Yeah, this is what I need. Hey Porch, I've got a table tennis tournament at four o'clock. You ought to be there."

Promptly in front of my mirror, Rec King Cupp started demonstrating how he would annihilate his opponents in a ping-pong game. Then he spun around and executed maneuvers in Leonardo's mirror.

"It's gone be good. I'm catching a ride downstairs with Ivan in a few minutes to go over to the Rec." Cupp had taken the notes—three to four pages—from off Leonardo's desk and folded them like you would a newspaper when you're swatting flies. He went through the motion of playing a table tennis match.

"I'm gone be hard to beat, today, Porch," he said sweeping the folded papers through the air as a substitute for a ping-pong paddle. "A forehand shot here, a back hand stroke there, and a chop serve every now and then.

"I've got too much firepower for them today. They gone have a hard time. It's the same as the last time— us against the foreigners. You can expect to see the same guys fighting to the end—Kojo Tarawallie from West Africa, Rajib Patel from India, and Chou Lee Su from China. Man, those dudes are hard to beat, but I got something for 'em today."

All the rooms in our dormitory had mirrors on the closet doors on both sides of the room as you entered through the door. Cupp spun around in front of both mirrors, demonstrating his skills.

"I've got to go brush my teeth," I said. "Shut the door on your way out."

I returned from brushing my teeth in the bathroom. Cupp was gone. I examined the note pad I had earlier laid on the bed. I wanted to make sure it was the one that corresponded to the textbook of the afternoon course I was going to next. On my desk against the wall on my side of the room were four note pads. Sometimes one note pad was used for more than one course; for a couple of courses, only one note pad per course was used. Certain that I had the right note pad, I placed the wire tablet back on the bed beside the textbook. Then I pulled out the built-in drawer under the bed frame and took out a clean towel to put in the grip bag.

I looked around. What's my grip bag doing over by Leonardo's wall mirror? I opened the sports grip bag.

"OH, NO!" I said out loud. "Cupp's gone off and took my bag with him."

Inside Cupp's grip bag were two table tennis paddles, a Waukeegan maroon-colored towel, and a couple of white wrist sweatbands. 'Oh, man', I thought, 'I've got to catch up with him before he finds out the gun is inside.' I'd heard Cupp say he had a ride over to the Rec with Ivan. Now I'd have to sprint over to the Recreation Center in the Student Union building.

Like a madman, I ran, books and Cupp's grip bag in hand, dodging and weaving around and through a multitude of students in my wake, across campus, a distance just over a quarter of a mile. I was gasping for breath as I entered the Rec, approaching the glass enclaved walls of the games rooms.

I saw Rusty Blair, supervisor and graduate student, standing behind the games checkout counter. Only a few students were in the games rooms. Rusty was a short young man who wore a medium-length Afro haircut, and he dressed in a white shirt and tie on a daily basis. Only a year removed from wearing sweatshirts and jeans, he was now a full-time, paid employee of the College. He was also a good friend of Cupp.

"Rusty, have you seen Cupp?"

"Yeah, I've seen him, and somebody better tell me what's going on?" He lowered his voice—"First, he comes in here and reaches inside his grip bag and pulls out a pistol, and it shocks the hell out of him and me, too. It was like he had grabbed a rattlesnake. Luckily, no one else saw it. Otherwise, I would've had to turn him in to Campus Security.

"Then he told me that the grip bag was yours, and that you must have gotten his by mistake. Then my phone rang, and on the other end is Dee Dee Pelham whispering like she's scared to death, asking me if Cupp is here. He gets on the phone, mumbles a few words, slams the phone down and swears—'I'll kill Johnny B. if he messes with Dee Dee.'"

"Where is he now?"

"How should I know? He went over to the pool room and got two of his Birmingham boys—Ted Ross and Country George Marshall—and they headed out." Ross was a skinny guy with street-life tendencies. Three years of college hadn't changed him. He was flexible for anything. Country George was a 250-pound player on the football team, normally a friendly guy, but a good friend to have around in a fight.

"Rusty, do me a favor. Don't say anything about this to anybody else. Give me some time to handle it."

"All I can promise you is—if anything bad happens, I'm going to tell what I know."

I knew that Dee Dee's home girl, Brenda from Chicago, lived off campus. I had been over there before with Cupp. Dee Dee often went over to their rented house, where they all gathered and cooked and ate and hung out. Brenda's boyfriend was from Gary, Indiana, and John "Johnny B.Good" Gooden, the basketball player, was a friend of Brenda's boyfriend. Cupp had previously mentioned this a few times to me, because he didn't like for Dee Dee to hang out too much with that bunch. Cupp hailed from a small town east of Birmingham, but he told everybody he was from Birmingham. He had a lot of friends from there, and a few of them were rough around the edges, too. This was like the old Negro League. Chicago versus Birmingham!

I rushed into the snack bar and grill down the hall from the games room and searched for someone who had a car who could take me to the supposed location where Cupp and his boys had gone. I found Ivan.

"Man, I've got a class to go to," Ivan said. "I can't be chasing after Cupp."

"Ivan, this is serious. Somebody could get killed, and Cupp and I could go to jail. Man, I need your help."

"All right! Okay, I'll do it. I don't know why I let you talk me into it. I don't even want to know about it. Just tell me where you want to go."

We headed down Old Montgomery Highway, going southwest of campus for a mile and a half, and we entered a street to the left of the main road. A dozen or so mostly white painted, wood-framed, cracker box houses aligned the street on both sides. Working class folks lived on this street. Other than college students, you would hardly find anyone home during the daytime.

I dashed out of the car. Ivan trailed behind. Raised voices—cursing and argumentative—sounded out inside. I bammed on the door. The voices inside died down. One of Cupp's buddies, Ted Ross, opened the door. "What are y'all doing here, Porch?"

"What's going on here?" I asked, walking past him. Inside the front door, furniture, tables, and lamps were turned over. "Where's Cupp?"

Dee Dee came through the hallway entrance of the next room. "I'm glad y'all showed up. Cupp's mad enough to shoot Johnny B. He's already fired one shot to scare him. When you knocked on the door, that calmed him down some."

In the next room, they had Johnny B. lying on the floor, curled up and hogtied with brown electric extension cords.

"This is what's gone happen," Cupp told the basketball player. "You and the guy you hired are going to jail. If you don't tell us where he is, you gone take the rap for the whole thing."

Johnny B. was a few years older than the rest of us, and the rugged ex-Army veteran had lived on the edge of society around small petty crimes and drugs, just one step removed from major crimes. Before the goatee-bearded student received a basketball scholarship that sent him south, the only thing that kept him off the streets was his passion for recreational basketball. He wasn't going to scare easy, but Cupp put pressure on him like a crime boss in a gangster movie.

"I ain't telling you nothing," Johnny B. said. "The only thing I'll tell the police is that you busted in the house and pistol-whipped me with that gun and shot it in the floor close to my head."

"Oh yeah? No shit. Well, I got news for you—Mr. Johnny B. Good Motherfucker. When the cops get here, I'm gone say we whipped up on you and tied you up when we found out what you did. Hey fellows, let's go in the other room right quick."

John Gooden lay on his side on the floor with his face turned toward the wall. He didn't know who else had entered the room. I hadn't spoken when I entered the room, and Ivan had stayed in the front room with Dee Dee and Brenda.

In the front room, Cupp spoke to me and Ivan.

"Look, take the gun and get the fuck out of here." He handed me my own grip bag and put the pistol in it. "The less you know right now, the better. We'll mess up this room on purpose so the police'll think we had to fight Johnny B.

"I'm going back in there and plug in that iron and threaten to burn him with it. We won't need the gun any more. Now go before somebody say they saw you here."

On the ride back to campus, Ivan and I sat silently for a while. As soon as we saw the campus greenery, the lawns, and the sprawling shade trees in the foreground of the old brick buildings, it was as if life was safe again, as if this was the real world, and that what we had just left was a surreal, slow motion dream. Now it was safe to speak.

"I wonder what happened down there?"

"Now look here, Porch. You're too damn curious. You got the gun back, and they're gone handle it as if we were never there. So settle for that."

"Ivan, turn the car around. We gotta go back."

"What?"

"I can't let Cupp take the rap for this. He could get charged with the illegal possession of a weapon."

"How can they charge him? We got the gun and have already left the scene."

"He shot a hole in the floor," I said. "Even if they cover it up, John Gooden's gone swear that they had a gun. He's gone want to take somebody down with him." When they had Gooden tied down, lying on the floor, in order to make him talk, Cupp fired a shot near Gooden's ear and the bullet went through the floor.

"This is what we're going to do. I'll tell the police I had the gun in my grip bag. You took me and Cupp out to lunch. Both of our bags were in the back seat. That's how they got switched. I had the gun because I felt my life was threatened.

"It was only today that I borrowed it. I never brought it on campus. Cupp didn't know he had the gun until he got to the Rec Center. Dee Dee calling was just a coincidence, which is true. Since I did get shot, they might understand why I might have a gun.

"But Cupp wouldn't have a leg to stand on—discharging a firearm, illegal possession, plus damage to property."

"As long as you make it clear that I didn't have nothing to do with it," Ivan said.

"Let's go. Maybe we can get back down there before the police get there. They said they were going to give us a few minutes head start before they call the police. Maybe we can get there before Cupp and them make up a bunch of lies that won't hold up."

"It's alright for you to make up a lie, but they're not supposed to, right?"

My patience was running thin with Ivan. "Man, let's go!" I said. "This ain't no time to be pissing around."

We drove up just as the two town cops got out of their car. When they got to the door, Roland Trotter came out of the house with John Gooden in handcuffs. Cupp and the gang must have called campus security first. I didn't know why, but I felt better with Roland involved than not. Cupp, Country George and Ted came out of the house. I walked over to where Roland stood talking to one of the policemen.

"Mr. Trotter, is there anything you need to talk to me about?"

"Excuse me," Roland said as he freed himself from the officer. Then he came over to speak to me privately.

"We don't need you right now, Porch. We got a full account from the guys inside. Everybody here has to go downtown to make a formal statement. You showed a lot of scruples coming back here. Not everybody would've done that.

"Your friends have told me enough that should suffice. Hopefully, none of y'all will have to go to jail.." Then he spoke in a low voice, "Go ahead and leave now. Ain't no need of giving them a chance to question you."

Later on, Cupp came by the room around eight p.m. He still had on the same clothes from earlier during the day—the khaki pants and the gray

Waukeegan sweatshirt with maroon writing on it. We had been waiting on him. By the time he and the gang reported at the Police Station, returned to sort things out, and settled down, it had taken the remaining daylight hours and a few after dark hours before it was done.

"Man, it was so confusing at first, but it started to make sense in the end," Cupp said. "Whew! Where do I start?" He sat on my bed, and I sat at my own desk in the chair that matched the desk. Leonardo sat across the room at his desk.

"Porch, I know why you got shot," Cupp announced.

"What?"

"I know why you got shot. Johnny B. hired some low life dude from Chicago named Lewis to shoot somebody else. The guy came to town the night before it happened and left town right after it happened. And he came back to town today to get his money. The dude came to the house unannounced looking for Johnny B. Johnny B.'s been living different places off campus, you know. Had been hard to find.

"Dee Dee and Brenda overheard Lewis at the house talking to Johnny B. on the phone, wherever he was. The stranger said he'd be back in a few hours to get his money. Johnny B. came by right after that and started suspecting that the girls had heard something they weren't supposed to hear.

"That's when Dee Dee managed to get in a call to Rusty Blair at the Rec, while Brenda kept Johnny B." distracted. You see, he's been hanging around campus, but he's not enrolled. He's ineligible on the basketball team, because he's expelled.

213

"You heard of the scandal on campus at the end of last semester? Where a Professor gave a lot of "A's" to athletes who let him such their dicks? Well, about a dozen of them either got suspended or expelled at the beginning of this semester. John Gooden was in that number. The Professor quietly vanished—resigned, quit, whatever."

"Here's where you fit in Porch."

"Don't put me in that. I ain't in that shit."

"No, what I mean is this—since Old Johnny B. Gooden wasn't too smart to begin with, no other college would admit him now. This was a life or death situation for him. He got desperate. He was gone fuck up the guy who got him kicked out of school. Guess who that was? Aaron Aldrich, out of the Student Ombudsman's office."

"I knew it had something to do with him," I said. "I even told him and Roland Trotter the same thing. The only person who believed me was R. P."

"Why you never told us any of this?" Leonardo asked. "All this going on right under our noses."

"It was nothing I could prove. I only figured it out a couple of days ago."

"That ain't all of it, 'Nardo. Porch's been keeping a gun for a while, too. It came in handy today, though."

"Charles Jordan's gun!" Leonardo guessed. "Porch you were acting fidgety the night I told you that Charles had run off and joined a Rock and Roll band."

"The gun is out of my hands, now. It's off campus. Now, since Rusty Blair and Roland Trotter know about it, I could get kicked out of school myself. So today I gave it to a buddy off campus to keep it until Charles

Jordan comes back around." I gave the pistol to Dwayne Norwood, but I didn't tell them.

Cupp told us the Basketball player confessed everything at the police station. The police suspected that the hired gunman left town on a Greyhound Bus, probably heading back north.

"Some kind of way, Aaron finagled a way that got Luckie, the baseball player, out of the scandal. And, Johnny B.Good heard about it. The ex-Army man was a good buddy of one of Aaron's homeboys who was also a Vietnam vet. Even though Johnny B. and Aaron were not great friends, you could see him hanging out on campus with Aaron and them. They'd hang out together and smoke a little weed every now and then.

"After Johnny B. heard that Aaron had helped somebody else, he confronted Aaron and asked him, 'how come you didn't try to help me get out of that bullshit? I thought I was your friend, man.' Aaron couldn't give him a satisfactory answer, so Johnny B. decided—I'll fix your ass. Now, I'm paraphrasing all this," Cupp reminded us. "So you'll get the gist of what Johnny B. confessed to down at the Police Station.

"So that's when Johnny B. called in that dude named Lewis, to put away Aaron Aldrich. The hit man showed up in Waukeegan late the last Friday night in February. Johnny B. was so stupid that all he gave the crook for a description of Aaron was that—he's an outfielder on the baseball team and they call him "Streak-O-Lean."

"So, that Saturday, the hit man went out on his mission. You ought to hear Dee Dee imitate that Lewis guy, the way he talked on the phone: 'I want my monn-ney. I want my muh-fuckin' money. What you mean I didn't finish the job? You said his nickname was Streak-O-Lean Aldrich? Somebody pointed him out to me on the baseball field. Calvin Porch? Who's Calvin Porch? The wrong guy? Look, whether I shot the wrong guy or not, don't matter. You didn't give me nothing to work with. You gone pay me for coming to town these two times. I'm leaving today, and I want my monn-ney. I want my muh-fuckin' monn-ney! Look, I'll be back in two to three hours. Yo' black ass better be here.'"

"What I can't understand is this," Leonardo asked. "How did you, the Rec King, a mild mannered, perfectly harmless guy, get the nerve to take on somebody like John Gooden, an old street thug that's been in the Army and fought in Vietnam and everything?"

"On my own, I probably wouldn't have. I would've thought twice. But when somebody mess with my woman, and threatens to harm her, then I don't think twice, I go after the motherfucker. And, it didn't hurt that I had the gun with me.

"Plus, big Country George Marshall and Ted Ross had my slack. George's got the strength and the weight, but it was Ted who was the real enforcer. He suggested that we walk in busting head and kicking ass first, and asking questions later. That's what we did. And he's the one who suggested that we threaten Johnny B. with the electric iron. And we did that, too. By the time the cops arrived, old Johnny B. Good was as meek as a lamb.

"But it was George that came up with the idea that we needed some legal representation before we talked to the police. So we called Roland Trotter to stand in with us during the questioning. In fact, we called him before calling the cops. Campus Security radioed him and found out he was already in the area. That's how he got there so fast.

"So yeah, Porch, y'all would've helped by coming back to the scene so we could get our lie straight. But the best help came from Roland Trotter. He advised us to keep it simple—don't talk about the gun, just stick to the point that we physically subdued John Gooden. Campus Security was after Johnny B. for selling drugs anyway. Roland talked to the police and we didn't have to say anything about the gun."

Around twelve-thirty in the afternoon the next day, I found Luckie in the Cafeteria. He sat among a group of students, talking and eating and grinning like all was well with the world. I spotted him from a distance because he wore the team maroon-colored cap. During the season, Coach Benson let us wear our practice caps around campus during the daytime.

"I told you why we got to go," I said quietly, not wanting the others at the table to know what I was talking about. "Aaron is in his office every day from twelve-thirty to one. Come on, let's go."

"Look, I haven't even finished my dessert."

"Let's go, Luckie. You got me into this mess."

We found Aaron sitting in the outer office of the campus newspaper office, wearing a green and white tie-dyed dashiki shirt. When he saw us come in, he got up from his seat where he had been talking to two staffers—a young man and a young woman. He led us into a smaller office in the back of the general office.

217

I started the discussion: "From his confession at the Police Station, John Gooden said he overheard you talking about it to somebody else, Luckie."

"Damn. If I could've just kept my mouth shut, none of this would've happened."

"If you had earned your grades like the rest of us, none of this would've happened," I said.

"It's hard for more than one person to keep a secret, anyway," Aaron said. "It's my fault. I was trying to help you, Brother," he said to Luckie. "I really love Waukeegan College, and I was trying to insure us some pride in the school by making sure you were given a shot at playing professional Baseball. I wonder if it was worth it."

"It wasn't worth it," I said. "Bakarie Seesay lost his life. Me getting shot and inconvenienced don't mean anything compared to that." The hit man John Gooden hired, shoved Bakarie into the swimming pool at the Mansion. After he was revived, Bakarie developed respiratory problems and died of pneumonia a few days later. "Man, I'm sorry," Luckie said. "I'm going to have to make it now. Ain't no turning back."

"Luckie, you're gonna have to learn how to live your life so that nobody has to clean up your mess for you," Aaron advised.

"I know. I've done some stupid things in the past, but from now on, I'm going to change that. I'm going to do better."

"Now, its down to what you're going to do, Aaron," I said. "I told Cupp last night to get with the few people that know about it and see if they can't keep a lid on it until you do something official, to quieten things down."

"Official? There's nothing much I can do right now, is it? What do we have, another six or seven weeks before school is out? It's bound to come out sooner or later anyhow." Then he stood up, sighed and took a deep breath and let it out. It was as if a resolution had come.

"Oh, man, what are we talking about? Keeping up an appearance? Saving face? The best way for me to quiet things down is to keep a low profile for the rest of the semester. Effective today, I'm resigning from the Student Ombudsman's office, and from my position as a columnist on the newspaper staff.

"I'm walking out of here the same time y'all are. I'll bring my written resignation by here later this afternoon. From here on out, I'm just going to go to my classes, and get off campus when classes are over. I might even quit the baseball team. I'll deal with that part on a day-to-day basis. We might as well get out of here, right now. Let's go."

Aaron told the few people in the outer office of the staff room that he would see them later. Then the three of us—all seniors—walked out of the office. Aaron had shown a sense of decisiveness and maturity. Each of us had survived an ordeal that we would remember for a long time. We now moved in the realm of the adult world. Our innocent, carefree days were gone forever.

Chapter 20
Sneaking Around

On Saturday morning, I walked down the main road that passed through campus and trailed from east to southwest of campus. One thing that growing up on the outskirts of a small town—actually in the country—did for me was that it gave me the survival skills of knowing that I could walk a few miles if I had to. City folks used to riding everywhere in cars or on buses, sometimes complain about the slightest thing to do with walking.

The distance I walked to get to Belinda Ward's house was just under two miles. I didn't tell her how I was going to get there, only that I would be there.

When I left the V.A. Hospital on Wednesday, I regretted that I had volunteered to mow her lawn. Why did I do that? It had been weeks since I had a free Saturday to do absolutely nothing. Before I got shot, I had baseball practice every Saturday since the semester began. After getting shot, I spent the next few Saturdays trying to catch up on simple things—getting my laundry done, writing letters home, studying borrowed notes from friends for the classes I missed, and working on the individual exercises and calisthenics assigned to me by the staff supervisor at the V.A. Hospital. Though I was now back with the team, the baseball team had no game scheduled for this Saturday.

I knew the real reason for offering to cut Miss Ward's grass. I liked her and was just happy to be around her. It had not even been decided if Belinda

Ward was going to pay me or not, broke student that I am, and employed, working professional that she is.

The past Wednesday had been a typical day for my rehabilitation exercises at the V.A. Hospital. But I had a lot on my mind at the time. That ordeal about the shooting at the Mansion and my unproven theory that I had been the victim of a mistaken identity had consumed my thoughts. To go with that, after refusing to tell his dad that he loaned me the gun, Charles Jordan's running away from home, added to my woes. The puzzle hadn't been completed at that time. It was a day later before Cupp stumbled upon the case and solved it. The workout on the gym equipment, sitting in the hot water pool, and then talking to Miss Ward did me a lot of good.

The Therapeutic Treatment Center at the V.A. Hospital was far more superior than anything local that I could've gotten on my own. I would've had to drop out of school for the whole semester and spend a lot of money to receive the same care. The Hospital department and staff had the wherewithal to develop an individual program, supervise it, and monitor it. They had various types of exercise machines, weight lifting equipment, isotonic and isometric equipment, heated whirlpools, gymnastic apparatus, a basketball and racquetball court, a cold-water swimming pool, and a warm-water swimming pool.

Some of the military veterans being helped at the Center were wheelchair bound, some were paraplegics, and others were amputees. This group all wore blue khaki clothes to and from the facility. The men that were physically able to work alone, dressed in ordinary gym clothes—shorts, T-shirts, sweat suits, tennis shoes, etc.

Dressed in all white—shirts, pants, socks, and shoes—the supervisors and technical assistants stood by their patients to insure safety and to see that their patients followed individualized programs developed by the Director.

I was left to work on my own, once the technical assistants showed me how to use each apparatus or piece of equipment. On completion of my regimen, I ended the session with an update and review with Belinda Ward. I remembered why I was receiving this therapeutic treatment in the first place. Without it, I risked a future of limited motion and minor atrophy in my left upper leg, thigh, and shoulder.

Belinda Ward's office stood on a corner of a hallway that faced a second intersecting hallway by virtue of having glass-framed upper walls on two sides of the room. The glass-framed walls started just below the mid-height of the room, and ran all the way up to the ceiling. She was a cocoa brown-skinned woman about five feet seven inches tall, and was well proportioned. She wore her hair about the length of a medium-sized Afro, but it was straightened and cropped above her ears, and she combed it down-and-around on the sides and back. Like the other supervisors and program assistants, she dressed in all white. She wore a short-sleeved jacket-cut blouse that hung below her belt line, but not covering her fine posterior. After three weeks of rehabilitation treatment, I still felt like an infatuated teenager when I came by Miss Ward's office.

"So, how did we do today?"

"It went well, Miss Ward. I can tell it's doing some good."

"I'm glad to hear that. According to your chart here, it looks like you'll be finished by next week, a little ahead of schedule," she said and smiled.

I had just recently turned twenty-two years old, and from her previous comments on her years in college and professional tenure, I figured she was somewhere between twenty-six and twenty-eight years old. Sometimes I would ask her questions about her profession, which college she attended, where she received her graduate training, and how she ended up at the Veterans Administration Hospital in Waukeegan, Alabama.

I liked her a lot and wished to tell her so. But how was I going to bring it up and what kind of response would I get? Good-looking women like her could pick and choose among successful men already in the working world. Here I was a mere student, no job, and nothing to offer. I didn't even have a car.

"Miss Ward?"

"Yes?" she looked at me in a way that I took to be a special look. A smile and a twinkle in the eyes came from her.

"Have you ever wanted something so bad and you were close to getting it, and it slipped out of your reach?"

"I suppose. It depends on what you're talking about."

I went into a long discourse about how I had worked hard over the past three years on the baseball team to improve my game; how I had been a walk-on athlete and had never been on great terms with Coach

Benson. And just when it looked like I might be competing for the starting catcher's position, the opportunity was lost when I got shot.

"In so many words, he was telling me that I should just quit, being that I am a senior and all. I didn't think he had to tell me that while I was laying in a hospital bed. It was a month ago, but it seems like it was yesterday."

"I've known Coach Benson for a while," Miss Ward said. "He's come across as a good guy, as far as I've known him. He's sent several athletes over here in the past to rehabilitate from injuries, just like he did you."

Then she added: "I didn't know he told you that while you were in the hospital." She looked incredulous.

"Yes he did. Told me—'You are not going to start when you get back, and we may be over half-way through the season by the time you are able to help us. You are going to have to work yourself up from the second string or even the third string position.'"

"Maybe the coach had a reason to tell you at that time to keep you from getting your hopes too high. He can't be all that bad. He referred you here when he could've let you drop classes or receive incomplete grades and be forced to pay for a lot of the services we provide here for free."

"I guess you're right, but it sure didn't make me feel good about it at the time. Anyway," I said, "I've told you about something that I wished would happen that's not going to happen, so why not tell me something you looked forward to that never happened."

"Must I?"

"Sure. Why not?"

"I don't talk about it much, but when I was in high school, the student body elected me Miss Senior, and when it was time to go compete with other schools at the State Capitol, the administrators said I couldn't go.

"Later, I learned that the senior counselor, who was the advisor, had said that I was too dark, that I wasn't light-skinned enough. Imagine that—coming from a Black woman, who was even darker than I am. I can still remember her name—Mrs. Oberton."

"That's pretty bad."

"And I was a cute little girl, too. I didn't find out the real reason until a year after I graduated."

"What did you do about it?"

"I cried for a while. And I hated Mrs. Oberton for a while. Then I came to realize that she shouldn't be the one to define my life or my future. The trip to the Capitol didn't take away from the fact that I was elected queen.

"I just prayed and asked the Lord to forgive her and to give me strength to carry on. If it wasn't for my faith in God, I'd probably still be wasting my time hating a woman who's probably dead by now, anyway."

The she changed the subject: "You know, I forgot to call my neighbor. Excuse me, please. Oh, you can stay, don't leave," she said, motioning for me to stay. After two phone calls, she told me that the elderly man who mowed her lawn regularly was called out of town for a family matter, and the backup guy she used infrequently had said he would be tied up for two weeks before he could work her into his schedule.

"Oh, well, it's supposed to rain anyway for the next couple of days," Miss Ward reasoned. "I can go another three to five days without getting the grass cut, but I can't go two weeks. I'll just have to make other arrangements. Good-bye.

"Now, who could I get?" she spoke to no one in particular.

"Miss Ward, I'll cut your grass for you."

"I wouldn't want to inconvenience you. Plus, you've got your rehabilitation to consider."

"Oh, I'm fine. You said so yourself that this last week was just a formality, that I could end the program right now if I really had to."

"Alright then. How about Saturday?"

"Okay."

Then Saturday morning came and the springtime breeze cooled the air even though the sun was out. The grass and the leaves on the trees were turning green, and the brown of winter vanishing.

Belinda Ward lived in a small bungalow-type brick house about one and three-fourth miles southwest of campus. It was on a quiet street off Old Montgomery Road. This was an older neighborhood where each house had a big yard, set off far from the street with ample space between neighboring houses on either side.

In an earlier conversation, she had told me that she leased the house and had no present interest in buying it because she could be transferred on short notice on her job, even though she had been at the V.A. Hospital for three years. She shared the house with a niece, a recent Waukeegan graduate who worked and boarded out of town as a substitute teacher but returned every other weekend to stay with her. I had seen her niece on campus before, but didn't know her personally. She was out of town this Saturday.

I could've gotten a friend on campus to drive me by, but this walk gave me a chance to exercise the old legs.

I suspected the lawnmower hadn't been used in awhile—probably not since the Fall. I checked the oil and put some gas in it. After I had been working for a half-hour, she brought out a glass of lemonade. I turned off the lawnmower as she approached.

"I thought you might like something cold and refreshing," she said.

"Thank you." I drank the lemonade slowly as I watched her walk back across the lawn to the house. "She's fine as hell," I said to myself. I wondered what it would be like to make love to her. I watched her physique. The clothes she wore were ordinary enough, but I could tell she took extra care to make sure they fit her well. The orange and white-checkered designed blouse fit her close, with the calculated taste that it was a fraction of an inch of being considered too tight. In case she wore it out in public or to a picnic, no one could say she was showing off her stuff.

The jeans had that same calculated fit that outlined her thighs and her behind excellently, just short of being too tight. It was definitely springtime. Belinda had on brown sandals that showed her red-polished, manicured toenails. I had heard girls say—it's a fine line between classy and tacky. Miss Ward was definitely classy. She's got it.

Back to work, I told myself. Perish the thought. Think of something else. Keep the lines straight when I mow the lawn. Get the job done. I'm here to cut the grass.

She came back outside when I was finishing the job in the backyard. "After you put the lawnmower away, come around to the patio entrance. I'll be in the kitchen."

I came in through the sliding glass patio doors.

"You can wash your hands in the bathroom," she said. "Don't worry about the twin set of towels. You can use them. They're just there for show. I've got sandwiches and cokes on the table for lunch."

The lunch was scrumptious. She showed me great hospitality. The ham and cheese sandwiches, potato chips, and the soft drinks poured in a glass half filled with ice, hit the spot. As I finished the meal and had nothing left but the soft drink in my hand, she, sitting on the other side of the table, reached under the table, touched my thigh, and squeezed twice with her fingers and nails.

"Go take a shower and meet me in the bedroom," she whispered.

"Yeah?"

"Yeah. Come on." Belinda stood up. She came around to where I stood and pressed up to me and initiated a long, wet, deep kiss. I felt myself awakening; the arousal was immediate.

"Hum-mm, you're getting hard," she said. "I can feel you. Come on, let's go."

I came into the bedroom with a blue towel wrapped around my waist. She had the light dimmed, but I could still see everything in the room. The bed spread and the covers were let back on the side where she sat wearing a peach-colored, see-through negligee, waiting for me. The nipples of her thinly veiled breasts stood out as if they were awaiting a feather-soft stroke.

"Come here, baby," she said.

I sat beside her, beholding the gorgeous body of this woman whose smile, touch, smell, and kisses gave me the feeling that this was as good a loving as I could get. While I reached to unveil the negligee and all that was visible in sight, she unwrapped the towel from around my waist, and we gently caressed each other's body. This continued as we moved under the covers in more exploration amid deep kisses and easy and gentle stroking.

She had told me to take my time. When I entered her, she was ripe and warm. The rhythmic cooing, breathing, and humming brought us together as one, and I thought I can't get any closer to another human being than this.

Belinda awakened first. She got fully dressed but lay on the bed beside me, her head resting on a pillow. I turned and looked into her smiling face. Her eyes were set on me.

"Hi, baby, how you feeling?"

"Good. How long have I been sleeping?"

"About twenty minutes. I've been out of bed for about ten minutes myself. I was just thinking about how beautiful it was and how good it felt—especially the second time."

"It was good to me, too. You took good care of me. I feel like I was well-fed."

"Literally and figuratively," she told me. "Glad I could help you out."

She had gone out of the room as I got dressed. When I entered the den, I heard a popular song on her

229

stereo—"Killing Me Softly With His Song," by Roberta Flack. Belinda was sitting on the carpeted floor with her legs crossed, looking through a stack of record album jackets for a particular record. I sat down beside her. She pointed out some of her favorite albums and singers. I nodded, commenting approval on a few of them.

"I'm just curious," I said. "Why did you do it? You know, take me in—give me some—let me make love to you?"

"I just felt like it," she said matter of factly. "Here, put this one on." She gave me a record to play on the stereo.

"There was no plan to do it, no forethought. I just felt like the time was right. There were no constraints. I'm a woman. You're a man, albeit a young one. We were both here in the privacy of my home.

"And no, I don't do this with just any man. So don't go around thinking I'm easy. 'Cause I'm not easy. It might not happen again. Who knows? But it could. Just be sweet, Calvin. You might get some more."

"I won't ask any more questions," I said, raising my hands palms out as if swearing off on a promise. I reached down and asked her to dance. We danced to an old Dells song, "Oh What A Night." I held her in my arms. Now she was as fully clothed as before, but now with her bare feet on the carpet, without the sandals.

She leaned against my chest, "You know, one thing I haven't mentioned to you?"

"No."

"I felt a sense of tenderness towards you that day when you told me about your personal struggle and passion to be a good Baseball player. And, you showed compassion and concern for me when I told you of the time that I was elected a queen and was told I was too dark skinned to go on a trip that I was entitled to go on."

"Yeah, I remember that."

"I haven't told many people that story. And, the few people I did mention it to, took it as a light thing. But, Calvin, you understood it and recognized that it was important to me. So, I felt there was a deep understanding between us. Does that make sense to you?"

"Yes. You still are a queen, Miss Belinda."

She drove me back to campus in her car. I asked her to let me out near the entrance to campus, down near the bookstore, and I'd walk to the dorm from there.

"You know how people can talk," I said in defense of her putting me out there, instead of in front of my dormitory.

"Does it matter?" She gave a conspiratorial smile and a wink of an eye that conveyed the meaning—"Yeah, I know what you mean."

"Not really," I said. "It's just nobody's business but ours."

"That's fine. Then this is good. She parked the car on the street to let me out. "I'll see you Monday afternoon."

"Okay. Bye."

Now it was the beginning of the second week of April. On Monday, I went to classes until midday, to the V.A. Hospital between two-thirty and four p.m., and was back on the ball field by five p.m. Even though all I did at practice was run laps, catch batting practice, and warm-up pitchers, Coach Benson told me I was progressing well and could expect to play in the two games coming up later in the week.

As was customary with the guys on the team, during the evenings after practice, whatever serious endeavor you had to do, such as study or go see a girl, didn't take place until you had spent at least thirty minutes hanging out in the Rec Center.

I told three teammates I was going to the Library to work on an assignment that I was behind on. Out of their sight, I put in a fifteen-minute appearance in the section of the Library designated for browsing through newspapers and magazines. Having shaken off the guys, I called Belinda Ward from the telephone booth in the common hallway in the lobby and told her to meet me in ten minutes about two blocks off campus across the street from a laundry mat. I left the Library with the notebook and textbook that I had carried as a pretense.

Everything was fine at her house. After small talk and refreshments, our lovemaking took on the joy of two lovers at a party who felt like they had sneaked off into the night and stole a moment of bliss away from the party crowd.

Someone rang the doorbell. She whispered that she wasn't going to answer the door, as most of the lights were dimmed or off anyway. We stayed in the bedroom. Whoever it was at the door waited about a minute and rang the doorbell again. Then there was silence. We heard a car drive off.

About a half hour later, she dropped me off at the same street curbside as the time she brought me back to campus on Saturday. This time, I went back to the Library and killed another half hour before going back to the dormitory.

The next day after lunch, I returned to my room to drop off books from the morning classes and to pick up my books for the afternoon classes. In our dormitory, student mailboxes were located at the front office facing out to the lobby and main entrance. A wall facing the twin glass front doors contained square cubbyhole boxes that were like miniature strongboxes, each with a small combination dial and clear glass front that opened up with hinged doors just like a strongbox safe.

I checked my mailbox. A note in it had a short message on it: "Call Miss Ward at the V.A. Hospital as soon as possible."

I immediately called her from the phone booth in the lobby, closing the accordion-type door behind me.

"Hello, Miss Ward, this is Calvin."

"Oh, Hi Calvin, how are you?"

"I'm fine. How about yourself?"

"I'm doing alright. Listen, hold on while I close my door."

I imagined her closing the door to her office, a room enclosed with glass walls on two sides that intersected a corner of two hallways. I imagined her wearing a two-piece white pantsuit like she always did. "Listen," she talked softly, almost in a whisper. "I just want to prompt you on a situation that happened after I dropped you off last night.

"John Benson called me last night asking me questions like he had some kind of a right to know my business."

233

"Coach Benson?"

"Yes. That was him at my door last night while you were there. For some reason, he doubled back later as we pulled out of my driveway. He followed us and saw me let you out on the street."

"What was he doing over there?"

"That's a long story. He thinks he can talk to me any kind of way."

"I don't understand. What's he got to do—?"

"I didn't tell you before, but Coach Benson and I went together for a few months. About six months ago, I ended it. You see, he was separated from his wife at the time, and they were going through a divorce. They later reconciled and called off the divorce." Then silence.

"Are you there? Are you still there?"

Momentarily, I was silent and speechless. "I—I didn't know." Now I sensed that I had a rival, an enemy.

"I know you didn't know. We kept it quiet. It's very easy for a Coach to hide an affair, with their hours varying so much. I'm just going to fill you in on a few details," she went on.

"First, no matter what he says to you, you're not to admit that we are lovers, that we had sex. Even if he lies to you and tell you that I admitted it to him, which I haven't."

"I don't understand," I said. "If what y'all had going ended months ago, why is he coming 'round now?"

"The reason I'm telling you this is because I don't want him taking it out on you, out of jealousy or spite. You see, Calvin, you're far along now that you don't need him in order for you to graduate. All he can do is put you off the team. But even that would put him in jeopardy of folks finding out, even his wife.

"What you don't see right now, darling, is that when you graduate and apply for jobs, they are going to ask you for references—from instructors, professors, department heads, and from individuals who head up extracurricular activities. You're going to need a good reference from Coach Benson."

"I hadn't thought about that."

"You see what I'm talking about now, don't you?" she advised. "But you know, not only that, but I've got a personal reason for John not to know anything about us. It's none of his business.

"He had the nerve to tell me that due to the age of his children and the fact that his wife stands to gain some property as an heir, that he couldn't afford to divorce her for another two to three years. But in the meantime, why don't we keep what we have going under cover. That was six months ago. That's when I dropped his ass.

"So Calvin, when he talks to you, you just go on as if you didn't know any of this."

"That's what I'll do. It'll make things simpler and give me less to think about."

"I told him I invited you over to look at my collection of old record albums. He wanted to know why I didn't come to the door when he knocked and rang the doorbell, that I was there because my car was outside.

"I told him I don't answer my door for anyone after dark unless I'm expecting someone to come by. He said, 'Don't give me that. That's bullshit. I know you were fucking him. I'm not stupid. You know you were fucking him, weren't you?'

"You don't have any right to ask me anything— who comes to my house whether it's a man, woman, or child or whether or not I fucked Calvin Porch." Her voice had an edge to it, as if she was still angry with Coach Benson.

She apologized. "You'll have to excuse my French, darling, but I was pissed off." She mimicked Coach Benson's voice: 'I sent Porch out there to the V.A. Hospital for y'all to get him well, not for you to let him fuck you. I came by that night to see how come you and I couldn't get back together again. Now I know.'

"John Benson, you and I have nothing more to talk about. I've got to go. I said bye and hung up the phone."

Her voice returned to normal and that was reassuring, giving me the feeling that I could hold up under Coach's interrogation.

"Anyway, darling, I know you'll handle this little situation well. Everything will go smoothly. Just remember to admit nothing, under any circumstances."

"Yeah, sure, I'll take care of it," I said, trying to sound like I had more confidence that I actually had.

She ended by telling me that we should cool off our relationship until after this thing passes over. Who knows how long, she admitted. Maybe a couple of weeks or so. We'll see. After concluding the telephone conversation, I was immediately more concerned about the uncertainty of the cooling off period than I was about the upcoming ordeal with Coach Benson.

Later in the afternoon, the baseball team practice began as routine as usual. Sooner or later, I knew Coach Benson was going to call me to the side.

Chapter 21
In the Dog House Now

By now, the team had played nine games. About a fourth of the season had passed, and Coach Benson had only a few days ago promised me that he would find opportunities in the next two games to gradually work me into the game plan.

The field was prepped for the season, the green grass neatly cut on the level outfield grounds and on the infield inside of the base path. The pitcher's mound had red soil piled up and tapered off even on all sides, and the infield base path had the same red dirt topping. The outfield fence, from left to center field, had honeysuckle vines hanging off the top. Nobody had bothered to trim the vines off. The wooded area beyond the fence was on the property of the owners of that notorious Mansion site less than a half-mile away—property that I wanted to forget about.

I did stretching exercises standing beside Aaron.

"Your new glasses fit you pretty good, got a lot of style."

"Thanks to you, Porch. But, I could've done without the headaches though," Aaron said, referring to our collision on the field weeks ago just before I got shot. I hadn't commented on his eyeglasses before, even though he had been wearing them for over a month.

"Looks like you're coming along pretty good. Two weeks ago, you were walking a little one-sided, like Chester on the Gunsmoke TV show."

"I wasn't that bad, was I?"

Luckie was standing nearby playing catch with another player. He scooped up a "one bouncer" ball out of the grass and in a quick flip, released the ball to throw it to a teammate on the field. He heard us talking. Then he spoke out: "Yeah Porch, we thought we were going to have to put you out of your miseries, just like they do horses in the Wild West."

"Please, no more talk about being shot," I begged. "I'm just glad I was able to work-out at the V.A. Hospital."

"Yeah, it's a good thing Coach Benson has connections with their Physical Therapy Department," Luckie said.

"You're right," I acknowledged. I thought to myself, I wonder how good those connections are now. Sooner or later, I was going to have my little pow-wow with Coach Benson concerning Belinda Ward.

"You know, I feel like this gone be the year," Luckie said, "when all of us seniors will be on the field at the same time, Porch. Me, you, Aaron, Deacon West, and Wiley, if he gets his pitching arm right."

"I hope so," Aaron wished. "It's about time. Me and Porch have been back-ups for the past couple of years. Every time it looks like we may get a chance, Coach bring in these hotshot freshmen and he has to play 'em, 'cause he promised them the world when he recruited them out of high school."

He was not finished. He needed to have his full say. "Half of these guys he's brought in have washed out—completely bombed out. Hell, he could've given me and you scholarships by now, Porch."

"I told Coach Benson at the beginning of the season that I felt that I should be starting some games this year," I added. "At least give me equal time on the field in real games, not in practice only. He said he would give me opportunities to play. Then I got shot.

"And now I'm in a come-back situation. Anyway, no matter what happens now, I'm never going to go up into his face and beg him to put me in a game. He knows what I can do."

"Don't y'all worry about it," Luckie assured us. "I went to him as Captain of the team at the beginning of the season, and I told him that all the seniors are good enough to start, whether they are on scholarship or not. I'm just going to have to remind him again."

Nehemiah Luckie was a Pro prospect and had been scouted by Major League teams the previous season. This year, he began the season with outstanding statistics. All he had to do was coast through the season and wait on the Major League Baseball draft to see which team would choose him. Luckie's performance over the last season and a half had brought attention throughout our conference, and it had boosted Coach Benson's reputation as a good coach and recruiter. More than once, the speedy left-handed athlete with the low, tight-cut Afro, complained that he wished he had more power. He stopped complaining when a Pro scout reminded him that most of the better players made it to the big Leagues with their batting averages, not with home runs. Most teams could always use a fast, left-handed batter as a leadoff man. Luckie fit the bill. That was why Aaron, as a friend, willingly helped Luckie get out of that scandalous mess toward the end of last semester. Aaron thought he was helping to bring pride to the school. So far, the cost had been gun shot wounds to me and death to Bakarie.

Just when it seemed that no discussion would take place between me and Coach Benson, a messenger appeared. Practice was over. The last of the team members were drying themselves off after taking showers. There were always a few athletes in the locker room who got dressed without taking showers, and vacated the locker room within minutes of putting away their practice gear. I had dried myself off and got dressed except for my socks and tennis shoes. I sat on the bench next to my locker putting on my socks.

R. P. came in exchanging banter with the two players whose lockers were nearest to the door that led out of the locker room. Ripperton Patrick Willingham was a skinny, dark-skinned kid who had come to Waukeegan on a basketball scholarship. When it was determined that his skills were not good enough to get him past his freshman year, in order to keep his athletic scholarship, he opted to become a trainer for the baseball team and to assist other trainers for other sports when he was available. Sometimes, an athletic trainer is called a team manager. Other times, he may be called a "Water Boy." At birth, R. P.'s mother had named him Ripperton in honor of the doctor who delivered him. He wore eyeglasses and was a good score keeper and bookkeeper, and he wore his cap backwards while on the sidelines during games. R. P. claimed he couldn't concentrate unless the cap was on backwards. "You're just superstitious," I once told him.

After R. P. finished talking to the other ball players, he came over to me, as if it were an afterthought: "Oh yeah, Porch. Coach Benson wants to see you before you leave."

All the coaches had their offices in the Toland Hall building. Like a small town municipal complex, this three-story, brick building contained the gymnasium court on the first level and a wrap-around balcony enclosing three sides above the first floor. The administrators occupied the office on the northern, front entrance. The Athletic Department used the offices on the south end of the basketball court, adjacent to and behind the maroon-curtained, theater stage.

I marched up the concrete steps to Coach Benson's office and passed through "The War Room," a large, empty general office room that sometimes was occupied with tables and chairs, film projectors, and field diagrams, where athletic teams held meetings or watched game films. The door to the Coach's office was open. I saw the brown-complexioned man talking on the telephone. He motioned for me to come in, and he kept talking on the phone as if that conversation was much more important than for whatever reason he had summoned me. I heard the plop and creek of my own footsteps on the hardwood floor. Ordinarily, I probably wouldn't have heard the sound, but I was scared speechless. That must've intensified my ability to hear. In the past when I got nervous, scared or was under pressure about something, I would involuntarily start stuttering. Please don't let me stutter. Don't let me blink or hesitate, I repeated to myself. I wasn't in a situation where I was going to be honest, so I knew it wouldn't help if I prayed to God. I knew I was going to tell at least two lies, if not more.

John Benson was a man who acted older than he was. About the same age as Belinda Ward, somewhere between twenty-six and twenty-eight, he often addressed us in such a manner as "Hey, son; Look, son; Alright, son; Son, what's wrong with you?" If he was angry with you, he might say, "Hell, son; Shit, son; Damn, son; can't you get this right for a change?" He was an old-fashioned coach that taught us to say "yes, sir" and "no, sir" and to take off our hats in a building.

About six feet, two-inches tall, Coach Benson had kept himself in good physical shape over the years. He loved to show us his college yearbook, which had shown a youthful version of him as a versatile football player—at quarterback, split end, and at corner back on defense. He had the height and the weight, about two hundred and ten pounds, to play any number of sports in addition to football. At Waukeegan College, he was an assistant football coach, but was the head coach of the baseball team, although he hadn't played that sport since high school.

Not a bad looking man, the varnish brown-skinned coach wore a low-cut Afro hair style without side burns, and he had a mustache that was neatly trimmed and cut like an officer in the military.

I rehearsed in my mind what Belinda Ward had told me: "No matter what he says, admit nothing."

Coach Benson hung up the phone. "Close the door," he said.

I sat in the chair across from the metal desk where he sat. Behind him, mounted on the wall, was a newspaper clipping in a picture frame, showing a previous team celebrating a championship, each player with an arm raised and index finger pointing as if to say "We're number one." On an end table in the right corner of the room stood a collection of football and baseball trophies.

"How's the shoulder? How's the hip coming along?"

"Fine. Real good."

"You know why I called you in here, don't you?"

"No, sir, Coach."

"Well, I'm glad that you're about where you should be right now. I had high hopes for you, Porch. At the beginning of the season, I had envisioned you sharing playing time at your position. But that's changed now. You know why?"

"I can't see why, now that I'm back in shape."

"To cut through the bullshit, Porch, I'm going to tell you why. You're out there screwing around with Belinda Ward, and I'm disappointed in you. What makes you think you can go behind my back and start going with her?"

"Coach, I'm not going with her. I just talked to her at the end of my physical therapy each day. And, I went to her house once."

"Don't expect me to believe that shit. Hell, I go out of my way to help you out after you got shot. And this is what you repay me with? You're not on a scholarship and you're not that good a player to begin with. I could've left your ass in a sling.

"If I hadn't arranged with the V.A. Hospital to help you, your ass would've had to withdraw from school this semester and pay a lot of money at an independent center."

"I know that Coach, and I thank you."

244

"You're ungrateful, Porch, you know that? I do all this for you and you end up going with my woman."

"Coach, I didn't know you went with Miss Ward. You're married," I acted surprised. "Why do you need to go with her?"

"Nev' mind that. Whether I go with her or not is none of your damn business. I was separated from my wife a few months ago," he volunteered. "Was gone get a divorce, but we worked things out—my wife and I. Then that fell apart again.

"So the other night I went by to start things up again with Belinda, and I knocked on the door and found everything quiet at her house, 'cause y'all was back there fucking, wasn't you?"

"Coach, I went over there to look at her collection of jazz records." I was not going to say anything more than I had to.

"Bullshit. Answer me. Did you fuck her?"

"No, Coach. I only went over there to look at her albums, to listen to them and read the stuff about the musicians on the back of the album covers. That's one of my hobbies, listening to music and reading up on musicians from their album jackets."

"You don't have to lie to me. I already got the truth out of Belinda Ward."

Don't go for that, I thought to myself. She had said he might try that. 'No matter what he says to you, you are not to admit that we are lovers, that we had sex. Even if he lies to you and tells you that I admitted it to him, which I haven't.'

"Coach, I didn't have sex with Miss Ward," I denied it for the second time.

"Tell you what. Ain't no need of us talking about this any more. I'm going to deal with this man to man. You're on the team, and I'm the coach. I can't kick your ass off the team or make you quit—that's up to you. But I can give you pure hell along the way.

"Porch, you're not going to play one inning for the rest of the season. Not one game. I'm going to bury your ass so far down on the depth chart, you won't even see the light of day. You're going to be so far down on the bench, you won't even be able to hear me call out your name.

"If you want to keep coming to practice, that's up to you. I'll even let you dress out for games, but that's as far as it goes."

"Coach, I'm not quitting."

He dismissed me by looking down on his desk at a note pad and waving his left hand bye-bye across the air with fingers spread and palm outward, "That's up to you," he concluded.

His whole action hinted—goodbye; get the hell out of here. I don't even want to see your face.

"I'm not quitting," I said, as I turned and opened the door to leave. "I'm going to stay on the team." By then, even in my own ears, my own words had withered away weakly, like dying leaves on a vine. Timbuktu was awaiting me. Or should I say Siberia? An exile and banishment was going to be my lot. A doghouse at the far corner of the team bench had my name on it.

During the following week after the Coach—the "Field General"—had declared a "Cold War" against me the "foot soldier," we played two home games. Both of them had been close games to the end, with the scores low, with limited substitution, involving only a few pitchers, pinch hitters, and fielders. So I couldn't be certain whether Coach was implementing his silent battle or not. Then it happened!

Towards the middle of April, we played a doubleheader set of games in Tallahassee, Florida, where we thoroughly dominated that team in both games. Apart from two starting pitchers that were kept on their rotation schedule for future games, Coach Benson played every player on the team except me. To add insult to injury, he put in a reserved player at the catcher's position—my specialty—who had gone two weeks without even practicing at the position.

Now it was for sure. Teammates kept coming up to me asking why hadn't Coach Benson put me in the game. "Hey, that's up to him," I tried to say with a straight face. Down in my heart, I felt hurt, humiliated, like a fool. Here I was a senior, not even on scholarship. I had come to college on a student loan. I didn't need this. Why not just quit, walk away?

"Man, you must really be on his shit list," Luckie said. "I went to Coach Benson over a week ago to tell him you were ready, that you should be starting some games. All he told me was, 'Everybody's gone play when I need 'em to.' Luckie shook his head, "I can't figure it out."

"I think he's trying to run you off," Deacon West said. "I've seen it before, in high school and in college, too. My cousin let them run him off the football team. They put so much shit on you that you just throw up your hands and quit.

247

"It don't have to be anything big either. They can do it to you just because they don't like the way you comb your hair."

"I'm not going to quit. I'm going to hang on," I said. It took everything I had inside to hold my head up under this scrutiny. I told no one on the team the real reason why Coach Benson and I had a falling out, nor did I tell my roommate. The only person I told the whole story to was Dwayne Norwood, a friend who lived off campus. I made Dwayne swear to tell no one else.

"Damn, Man! This is some heavy shit," he said. "I wished you hadn't even told me this. You're going to have to be careful, I mean real careful."

The next day out on the field, Coach Benson called the whole team over to the bleachers behind the home plate screen. He had us sit down on the benches. Then he reviewed the latest statistics from the conference. The report showed how many games we had to win to place in the regional playoffs and how many we had to complete to be eligible to qualify. We couldn't have any forfeits, or any more rainouts.

Sometimes, when a small college baseball team is going nowhere, it is very easy toward the end of the season to forfeit a game just because it might be inconvenient to the team or coaching staff. Things come up—exams, tests, science labs, field trips, etc.— that might weigh against traveling to another school for a game. A rained out, cancelled game at a far away college, often never got rescheduled. But now we needed every game to be played, and a certain amount of them won.

Since half of the remaining games were away games, Coach Benson informed us that he would have to trim down the travel roster to make two costly trips that the Athletic Department hardly had enough money in the budget to cover the baseball team, since we hadn't gone this far before in the season, where a few rained out games could not be allowed.

Waukeegan, like many small college baseball teams, operated on a limited budget. Only eight of our players were on baseball scholarships; three were on football scholarships; all the rest of us were walk-ons.

"We've got a brutal schedule out of town, where we have to play three games in two days," Coach Benson said. "I've pared it down two or three different ways, and this is what we're going with. For this trip, we're going with only fourteen players instead of the normal twenty-two. These are the names of the players who are going."

He pointed out that our general liability insurance covered only university vehicles, so no personal cars were allowed for team trips.

This road trip to Nashville, Tennessee would include eight position players, one of which must be able to pitch if needed; three pure pitchers, one of which must be versatile in another position; one utility infielder; one utility outfielder; and one back-up catcher with sure hands. All of a sudden, my value to the team increased. I had good, sure hands.

I didn't hit better, nor throw out base runners as good as the starting catcher, but I could catch wild pitches, trap balls in the dirt, and call a game—signal to the pitcher the best pitch to throw to a batter—better than the starting catcher. Overall, we were about even.

Even Coach Benson, bearing a grudge against me, had the wisdom to know that it was good to have me on the field late in the game when opponents had base runners in scoring position, and a runner could score by a mere wild pitch.

When it was time to travel, we had to use a station wagon and a sedan car because the track team had taken the limousine van. On the morning of the trip to Nashville, we met out in front of the gym at five a.m.

Coach Benson was superstitious about the number thirteen. Wiley Jakes found out about it first. One of the key utility players failed to show up. Coach Benson had planned the trip on a tight schedule. We needed to leave within a half hour to keep on schedule. We had already waited over thirty minutes for everyone to show up. As it were, we should arrive at the first college by mid-afternoon, play two games before dark, travel across town to another college after the game, bunk down at the second college for the night; play one game the next day, and hop in the cars and head back to Alabama, and be back in our own beds by midnight of the second night. We needed to get that double-header in against that weak team the first day. The player in question lived off campus with his parents in the rural, outskirts of town.

"Why not go by the dorm and wake up another player to go with us?" Deacon West, the co-captain asked.

"By the time we did that, we would've lost about an hour and a half all together," Coach Benson said. "Besides, the next best player needed for the trip lives out in the sticks, too. We can't wait any longer. We might have to travel without stopping to eat. Hey, Wiley Jakes," he called out. "Come here."

Wiley is a dark-skinned athlete with a receding hairline. He's even-tempered and mild-mannered. He reminded me of the Olympic star Jesse Owens.

They went up near the front of the light blue station wagon by the hood. Coach Benson propped one foot up on the car's bumper and talked privately to the senior pitcher. After that, Coach said, "Load up, let's go."

He drove the light blue station wagon with the college name written on the sides, and Wiley drove the plain, unmarked gray car. Thirteen players and one coach took to the road. Later on, after we stopped to eat, we trickled out of the restaurant while Coach Benson made arrangements with the manager to pay for the food.

Standing out on the parking lot by the cars, Wiley spoke out: "Man, I can't believe what Coach Benson told me. He said: 'Take your uniforms and all your game equipment, but you can't dress out. You're not gonna play unless somebody gets hurt or we need an emergency player. If it comes up that you get to play, then the player you replace is gone have to put on his street clothes.'"

Wiley had pitched a complete game in the last game played, and he was not scheduled to pitch again until after the road trip. He was useful for the trip because he could play a couple of positions in addition to pitching.

"He wasn't joking," Wiley said. "He told me all this with a straight face. Can you believe it? A college educated man, teaching and coaching on the college level, and he's superstitious about the number thirteen."

"It's kinda inconsistent," ex-Army Sergeant Deacon West said. "He claims to be a God-fearing man. If you're a Christian and believe in the Bible, you shouldn't have anything to do with stuff like that."

So Coach figured out how he would deal with that character called *"Thirteen,"* that superstitious nemesis that had just raised its ugly head. In his mind, he must have figured that he had twelve players and a car driver named Wiley. To those who believed it, thirteen was an unlucky number. Coach Benson must've thought it prudent to eliminate an ominous pre-existing cloud that hovered over the road trip. *Sufficient unto the day is the evil thereof.*

"That ain't nothing," Luckie added. "I got kinfolks down in Mobile, Alabama, and Louisiana, too. They got all kinds of voodoo and root workers down there. But they go to church every Sunday."

"I just can't see it," Deacon West said.

"Oh, yeah, they believe in God alright. You see, they just feel like they gotta have a little something extra to go with it—like a dip of snuff for your nerves, or a rabbit's foot tied 'round your neck for good luck. Just a little something extra, that's all. Can't take no chances."

"Luckie, you're crazy," Aaron said.

"I ain't lying. I even tried it myself," Luckie revealed. "When I was in high school, there was this girl that I liked, and I kept asking her to go to a dance with me. And she kept telling me no.

"So I went to see an old lady that lived on this dirt road, way outside of town. I heard that she could work some shit on somebody—both good or bad, depending on what you wanted done. And it only cost you three dollars. Well, let me tell you what happened.

"She gave me this handkerchief, you see. Then she told me, next time you see this girl, don't say a word to her. Just go up to her and drop this handkerchief in front of her. Then pick it up."

"You're lying, Luckie."

"I ain't lying, Porch. I did just what the old lady said do. And just like this—Bam!" he snapped his fingers. "The girl said, 'what time do you want me to be ready for the dance?'"

Those of us standing around Luckie all broke out laughing. Deek West pointed out: "That was just a coincidence. The girl had already made up her mind to go with you."

"All I know is that it worked. I'm not saying that I wouldn't ever do it again. Shoot, man, you never know."

"I can't help it," Wiley worried. "I feel like this bullshit that Coach came up with just made me look like the butt of a joke."

"Don't feel bad about it," I said. "You didn't have anything to do with the stuff that caused this. Coach Benson could've left your name off the travel team to begin with. Then, you would've been at home with no chance to play at all."

"You're right. I shouldn't be complaining. Who knows? I might get a chance to save the day."

As luck would have it, or misfortune if you look at it that way, the starting catcher, Austin McCoy, got hit in the throat, right in the Adam's apple by a foul-tipped ball in the fifth inning of the game. Though a Baseball catcher wears protective armor—chest protector, mask and helmet, athletic cup, and shin guards—there are certain areas on a player's body that cannot be protected from a foul tip.

A foul tip occurs when a batter swings the bat at a pitched ball and the bat barely touches the ball as it crosses home plate. In less than a second, in the twinkling of an eye, the ball is deflected in such a way upward, downward, or to the side of its intended path that the catcher cannot catch the ball. If he's lucky, the ball gets blanketed in the chest protector, absorbed with a "thump" sound. Sometimes you get your clock rattled when a foul-tipped ball hits your facemask squarely in front of your nose. Foul tips have a way of pelting you on your arms, the fingers of your ungloved throwing hand, your thighs, your toes, and, on rare occasions, your neck under the facemask.

A couple of players helped the hurt catcher over to the team bench. Whatever question Coach Benson asked him, Austin's voice sounded like the raspy squawk of a Disney cartoon character. The stocky-built athlete in a gray flannel road uniform was slumped over on a wooden bench, holding his neck, one hand over the other, talking like Donald Duck.

"I tell you what," Coach Benson said. "Go ahead and take off your stuff. Drink some water. See if that'll help." Then he looked around. "Porch! Where's Porch?"

"I'm right here, Coach."

"Put on the equipment, Porch. You're going in."

The superstitious Coach had the injured catcher put on his street clothes and had Wiley, the car driver, dress out to play.

In the two-game set played that day, we won both games—the first at 4-to-3, and the second game at 6-to-3. In the first game—after drawing a walk in the eighth inning—I advanced to third base. From there, I scampered home, sliding head first in the dirt. Dirt got in my mouth, gritty between my teeth, and all over my face, the gray uniform, and the maroon cap. I scored the tying run after the opposing pitcher had thrown a wild pitch that the catcher had to run to the backstop screen to fetch.

Converted car-driver-turned-ballplayer Wiley Jakes hit a double in the top of the ninth inning that allowed Luckie on second base to score the go-ahead run. All we had to do was hold off the opponents for the bottom of the ninth inning, which we did.

At the beginning of the second game, Austin felt better physically, but his voice was still raspy and hoarse. A catcher needed his voice to call out plays and alignments to the fielders. Coach Benson sighed and reluctantly gave out the command: "Alright Porch. Keep on the equipment. You're going to start this one."

After the game, he came over to the bench while I was taking off the Catcher's equipment. Out of earshot of the rest of the players, he told me: "You played good today, but that don't change anything between me and you."

The next day, still in Nashville across town, we lost to the State College by the score of 5-to-1. Tired, weary and glad to get out of Tennessee, we felt satisfied winning two out of three games.

Though he would let me enter games as a late inning substitute, Coach Benson never let me start

255

another game the rest of the season. Other than basic greetings when around teammates and discussions of game strategy on the field, we never talked to each other. Our last true conversation took place the day he promised me that I would never play again. All is fair in love and war.

Chapter 22
Kiss Me and Smile for Me

By the end of April, a month had passed since Charles had fallen in with that traveling Blues Band. When I returned from the Nashville trip, I found a post card placed on my desk.. Across the room, I saw an identical post card on Leonardo's desk. Charles had put the same wording verbatim on each one of ours, except that he put a note in parentheses at the bottom of mine that was not on my roommate's—"(You know exactly what I mean, Porch.)"

The post cards showed a sprawling view of a city with two freeways crossing, one going east and west, and the other emerging from the south, among green tree lines and fading into the stair-stepped skyscrapers on the fringe just north of the east-west freeway. Down in the right quarter below the plane of the east-west freeway passage, stood a metallic silver, perfectly round sports stadium. Scripted below the picture was written: "Come grow with us. Atlanta, Georgia, a city on the move."

> *Hey Dude,*
>
> *What's happening? Everything's going well. I get to announce the band when they come out, and do a comedy routine when they're on a break. Other times, I play drums and sing background vocals. We are home-based in New Orleans. When we get back off the road, I'll call you. We play the smaller clubs. We have crossed paths*

with James Brown, The Staple Singers,
and B.B. King.

I'll leave you with this motto: Don't
show your cards until you're ready to
play. Stick to your guns, and don't rat
on your friends. (You know exactly what
I mean, Porch.)

Bye—C. J. Jordan

Two nights later, I got a phone call around 10:30 p.m. Someone from out in the hall yelled out: "Telephone call for Calvin Porch! Calvin Porch, come to the phone!" There was a bam-bam knock on the door and the young man that brought the message had vanished by the time I came to the door. I walked down the hall of the second floor to the phone booth in the lobby. I closed the door of the booth and spoke into the receiver. "Hello, this is Calvin."

"I told you I was gone call you. You didn't believe me, did you? Porch, this is Charles."

"Hey, Charles. How you doing?"

"I'm alright, man. I thought you'd never get to the phone. I'm on a pay phone, long distance, you know. I'm in New Orleans."

"I got your post card. Thanks."

"Yeah, I had to put the message in a hint," Charles said. "I know if I had written only to you, Leonardo would've wanted to know what it was about. And Cupp hanging around y'all's room all the time—he would've wanted to know what was going on, too."

"You got that right."

"So, about that gun, Porch. Like I told you before, you're gonna have to keep it a secret that you got it. I

258

can still kick myself for letting you talk me into loaning it to you."

"I haven't done anything stupid, yet. It's just good to know it's nearby in case I need it. But let me tell you—Leonardo and Cupp already know about the gun."

"What?"

I told him how Cupp had used the pistol to nab John Gooden, and that the gun is now off campus for safe keeping in the hands of Dwayne Norwood.

"But what happened to the hit man?"

"It turned out the gunman, a guy named Lewis Todd, was arrested on a Greyhound bus at the Memphis bus station a day later. The police handcuffed him and marched him off, when he broke and ran out into traffic and got run over by an eighteen-wheeler transfer truck and died on the scene."

"Oh, man. That's sad. What a bad way to go. But better him than you. You know, I had to go through some changes with my dad to keep him from knowing what I did with that pistol."

"Yeah, I heard."

"What did you hear?"

"It came from Nadine Fuller."

"I might've guessed it. Nadine and her mama—they both talk too damn much, but they're good neighbors, though. Since she told you—"

"She actually told Leonardo, and he told me."

"Same thing. But it was a lucky break that I got to go on the road. The argument with my dad over that gun was actually a blessing in disguise. You gotta take your chances sometimes."

"I hate it that you didn't stay around to graduate. I feel guilty, like it's my fault that you're not graduating two weeks from now."

"Aw—don't worry about that. I would've needed another semester anyway. I'm thinking about taking some courses at Xavier later on, if I can get on with a local house band that plays only at one club. Enough about that—what is Millie Yates up to?" Charles and Millie were among the less than two-dozen white students on campus.

"She's going with Professor Kinisky now. He teaches freshman English.

"Yeah, I know Frank Kinisky. Skinny white guy, always badly dressed and wearing a neck tie with tennis shoes and blue jeans with a sports coat."

"That's him."

"Hmm-mm-mm! That Millie's a fine young thing though. I knew she wouldn't be available long. Whatever happened with you and Maureen Ezell?"

"We sorta drifted apart at the beginning of the semester when she pledged into a sorority."

"Y'all were a cute couple, Porch. But you know something Porch? Don't get mad at me, but I think she fell in love with Sidney Poitier and not you. Last semester when we were in that play, *A Raisin in the Sun*, I could see she was mesmerized by your acting, by the words you said as a character.

"She'd be looking at you lovingly, with tenderness, completely absorbed in the moment. I'm not lying. Millie and I both talked about it. She noticed it, too. That's why actors and actresses fall in love all the time. Look at the movie stars.

"I'm in entertainment, and I see it all the time, Porch. All the time. Actors, singers, and musicians are more powerful at their craft on the stage than they are in their real, everyday lives. And the stage life is what's appealing to women.

"You ever hear of this famous white comedian, an ugly guy always talking 'bout he don't get no respect? Hey, even me, I get more play from the women for being a background singer than from being a stand-up comedian."

"Well, it was good · while it lasted," I acknowledged. "I fell for Maureen for about the same reason she fell for me. She's engaged now. With all the stuff that's happened with me lately, that seems like it was a long time ago.

"Look, Charles—where are you staying? What's your phone number? How are your gigs going?"

"Well, since you asked. I quit the band yesterday. Got in a dispute over money. I felt I should've gotten a raise, and they didn't feel like I had earned the money I *was* getting. And to go with that, the road manager insulted me. So I said—fuck this shit. I quit.

"So now, I'm staying at a Catholic Student Hostel in uptown New Orleans. It's a glorified bunk-bed situation with not much privacy. I can't complain. It's about the cheapest, cleanest, well-kept place you can stay for the money you pay.

"To get in, I finagled them into thinking that I was a transfer student to Xavier University, and because the college messed up my paperwork, I had to come down here on short notice without much money to straighten things out.

261

"I showed them my Waukeegan I.D. card and some orientation material from Xavier, and that was enough to get me in. I could probably go a month before they catch on. They got this Italian priest temporarily as the desk clerk. He's only been in the states for a short time.

"Fellow named Father Giacomelli. He's still mixing his English with his Italian. His first day here was my first day here. So, I'm in like Flynn."

"But how are you making it financially?"

"I'm still living off the money I made with the band. I've got a couple of irons in the fire with two different clubs, but it's going to be a week or two before something definite comes up. I'll be alright.

"I've got a stage name now—Dr. C. J. Nightingale. I use it when I introduce the Band or when I'm doing a stand-up comedy routine."

"How did that come to be?"

"I was thinking about how all the great entertainers had stage names—Muddy Waters, Howlin' Wolf, B.B. King, Chubby Checker, Dr. Jive, Professor Long Hair, Wolf Man Jack, Redd Foxx, Moms Mabley, Pigmeat Markham, Bobby Blue Bland, Night Train this and that, Cool Pappa so and so, Sweet Daddy this and that, Nighthawk this and that, Midnight so and so.

"So I came up with one for me, you know. Dr. C.J. Nightingale."

"It sounds like you got it together," I said. "Man, I'm glad you called, though. I was beginning to worry about you."

"Well, don't worry any longer. I'm going to make it out here. I'll be passing through Waukeegan before you graduate. You can give me back the gun then. Tell everybody I said hello. Gotta go. I'll keep in touch. Bye."

Charles had been a military brat. His dad was a non-commissioned officer in the U.S. Air Force who retired in Alabama in order to obtain a job at the V.A. Hospital in Waukeegan, where he worked in the administrative office. The family had lived and traveled around in the states and a couple of countries in Europe. Accustomed to dealing with racially integrated conditions, the military nomad had no qualms with settling the family down in the predominantly Black town of Waukeegan.

Wherever they lived in the past, young Charles listened to rhythm and blues radio stations. He stayed up late at night, quietly in the dark, slowly turning his dial to whatever R&B radio station he could get. While in high school, some of his schoolboy chums introduced him to "party albums" or "Blue Comedy" albums by Pigmeat Markham, Redd Foxx, Buddy Hackett, Moms Mabley, and cleaner albums by Bill Cosby, Dick Gregory, and others. After spending over three and a half years in college, he was now pursuing a dream that most folks only talked about doing.

By the month of May, the number increased among the lovebirds, couples, and "items" on campus. Cupp and Dee Dee talked about getting married. Leonardo dated Dee Dee's home girl Brenda who worked in Sister DuMaine's office. Hollie hung out with Luckie for a while, and then started dating Dwayne Norwood. Millie Yates and Dr. Frank Kinisky, the white couple, walked around campus holding hands like two teenagers. Kojo paired up with Adelaide. Maureen got engaged to a student named Eric, and I approached graduation day without a woman I could call my own.

Graduation day on the campus main lawn upheld a rich tradition. The ceremony was held in this outdoor setting every Spring. The Fall and Winter graduations took place indoors at the Toland Hall gymnasium building. This same plot of land, the green lawn, situated like a large town square, had its highest point on the south, terraced and bordered by a boulevard that ran east and west above it, and the lawn rolled gradually downhill, approximately eighty yards toward the north. The green turf was approximately thirty-five yards wide.

Every student that lived on campus daily crossed the sidewalks that intersected the green lawn square. The Student Union-Cafeteria building towered on the southeast. Evergreen trees and hedges stood inside and along the border made by the boulevard above on the south. A contrast existed among the designs of the women's dormitories that faced inward to the square on the east, west and north; some had the more modern, flat rectangular designs, others with old brick character of accumulated years, designed with the old cathedral and church steeple fronts. About three-fourths of the way down the lawn in the center of the grounds stood the old fountain, concreted at the top with the water surface of the pool a foot below the top ledge. This was another favorite resting and meeting place, only second in use to "The Breeze Station." Stout, tall oak trees stood on the edges of the lawn between the sidewalks of the four borders and the buildings.

Army-green metal folding chairs were lined up facing south to the wooden platform stage built on top of the fountain. The day's speaker at the podium would stand approximately six feet above the ground level.

Twenty minutes before it was time for us to assemble and march to our seats, I escorted my parents and young brother to their seats on the lawn. My mother, Francine Porch, wore her best blue dress, matching shoes and purse, and a red hat with a small brim. My dad, the stately A. J. Porch, wore a dark gray suit and a gray dress hat. My twelve-year old brother, Nathaniel, wore a white shirt, dark necktie, black pants, and shoes.

"Mama, can I go with Calvin?"

"No, child. He's got to go line up to march in."

"Make us proud, now," Dad said.

"I will," I answered. I was dressed in a navy blue suit, a white shirt, and a blue and white striped necktie, and I carried my black gown folded across my left forearm as I walked off. All the candidates for graduation wore black caps and gowns. I held the graduation cap in my left hand and strided away with my right hand free to greet or shake hands with other students.

I headed down the street that ran the length of a city block from the lawn to the point of assembly near the traffic roundabout, just in front of the old President's statue. This street going to the statue was lined with trees on both sides, and cars were parallel parked on both sides. Many of the students were doing the same thing I had just finished doing—getting the parents and guests "situated" for the ceremony.

I saw Maureen dressed in a white dress, standing beside a white Buick car parked on the opposite side of the street. She had just waved off a goodbye, rather a "See you later" signal to a middle-aged couple and another woman that resembled the woman with the man. I nodded and greeted them, "How you doing?" as they passed me.

"Oh, Calvin. Calvin. Come here. I want to talk to you."

"Hi, how you doing? Are those your parents?" I nodded in the direction of the three people.

"Yes, my mom, dad and aunt. I'm glad I got to see you before the day is over."

"You're looking good, Maureen."

"Calvin, come sit with me a minute. This is my parents' car."

We sat in the backseat of the car. "Do you realize this is the last time we may ever see each other again?" she asked, not waiting for an answer. "We take so much for granted that we forget the importance of somebody until it's too late. I regret that I didn't spend more time with you to get to know you better."

"I wished it, too, Maureen. But here we are now, kinda on our own course, you know—the point of no return. I wonder though—if you hadn't seen me right now, when would you have taken the time to tell me this?" I still harbored feelings of hurt and abandonment, even though four and a half months had passed, and I still cared for her.

"You're right. I had that coming. Being selfish, not considering other people's feelings or their time. If I hadn't seen you just now, I would've thought about it later when reflecting how these last two semesters went. I would've thought about you, and I would've been sorry I didn't tell you."

"We make choices, don't we?"

Maureen, sitting in the car in her white dress, looked down at her left finger. "I'm engaged now. Eric gave me this ring a few weeks ago."

"I heard."

"I've met his parents. We've made all these plans and stuff, and now I feel like I'm not ready. I care for him, but I feel like I've been swept away at a pace that's just too much for me. This whole semester passed in a flash."

"I don't know what to tell you," I said. "Where's Eric, now? Have you talked to him about it?"

"No, I haven't. He's in Birmingham. Got a summer intern job. He starts on Monday. He left Thursday afternoon right after his last final exam. In order for Eric to work with the company, he had to be present for orientation on Friday.

"He told me he'd try to make it back today, but I told him not to worry about it. I can see him later. I won't be alone. My folks are here."

"And your Sorority Sisters?"

"Them, too."

Eric was an Engineering Major and he had completed five years of college and was scheduled to graduate in December. The summer internship was a curriculum requirement, plus it put some money in his pockets to get through the next semester. The courses remaining for the fall semester were mainly mop-up courses to get out of his way before embarking upon a lucrative career.

"We're planning to get married in December, a day after he graduates."

"Where will you be until then?"

"Oh, I'll be teaching elementary school in Meridian, Mississippi. You know I told you once that my grandmother grew up on an Indian reservation over there—near Philadelphia, Mississippi. While I'm there, I'll do some research on my Indian relatives.

"We live less than thirty-five miles from the Mississippi state line, so I'll stay at home for a while. Eric and I will see each other on the weekends, somewhere between West Alabama and Waukeegan."

"It sounds like you've got it all planned out."

"Well, it's a plan. And what are you going to do, Calvin?"

"I'm going into the Peace Corps."

"You're kidding!"

"No. Going to West Africa. I'm leaving around the end of August or the first of September. It's not definite about which country I'll go to, but it will be an English speaking country. I'll know by next week. So I'll be a teacher, just like you."

"That's wonderful, Calvin. You'll have all kinds of experiences and wonderful stories to tell. Oh, I'm jealous. Let's keep in touch. Promise me you'll write to me. And I'll write to you."

"What about your fiancé?"

"That has nothing to do with corresponding with a friend. Just say you will."

"Alright, I will," I conceded. We wrote down each other's parents' address. I got out of the car and put on my black gown. "We'd better go. They're lining up," I said, looking down the street at the gathering place.

Maureen got out of her parent's car and closed the door. She put on her gown, too. "Calvin, do something for me—Kiss me before you go. Hold me. Just hold me. Just for a moment."

I wrapped my arms around her and held her and kissed her. For a moment, it was like old times. Then reality brought me back to the present. Two of Maureen's sorority sisters walked up and startled us. They both had on their caps and gowns. Shirley was the one who first told me that Maureen liked me. I had seen the other graduate named Joyce around on campus but didn't know her personally. Joyce was a cute, short, mahogany complexioned woman given to wearing a large Afro. Today the hair was cut low so she could get the graduation cap on her head.

"Well, well! What have we here?" Joyce said teasingly. "Miss 'Engaged-to-be married' getting all the gusto she can?"

"Girl, be quiet," Shirley admonished. "Just hush! Hey Maureen, Hey Calvin," she greeted us in a tone volunteering to restore normalcy to a potentially embarrassing scene for one or both of us who were embraced in a more than salutatory kiss.

"Hi, Shirley," I said. "How you doing?" I greeted Joyce.

"I know you're going to give me a hug, too," Shirley said.

I gave her a short "wish you well—good luck to you" hug. I didn't hug Joyce. "Listen, Maureen, I'll see y'all later. I'm going on ahead." I put the cap on my head and walked in a fast pace to find my place among the group that was assembling down by the President's statue. The three women followed close behind me. I heard Shirley say something to Maureen: "Typical Maureen. You always let the good ones get away."

During the commencement speech, I sat among the soon-to-be graduates out on the lawn. The speaker, a white man in an honorary black cap and gown, spoke in a dull, boring, monotone. Someone thought it was a good idea to invite this speaker because he had been an astronaut. Maybe it would motivate us to shoot for the stars, to set high goals and achieve them. It wasn't working.

The best motivational speech I could think of came from a fellow sitting right out there with us on the lawn, waiting to graduate—Wesley "Deacon West" Knuckles. Deacon West had the astronaut beat by a mile. Deek West performed his speech in a huddle, with the players standing in a tight circle, with one hand each joining all other hands stacked in the center of the huddle, just before the team charged on to the field.

Out of respect for a player on the team who really was a preacher, we called Knuckles "Deacon" instead of "Reverend." 'Why not let Deek get up there and do his thing and let us go home?' I thought to myself. Classic Deacon West:

"Repeat after me," Deek started out. "Calvin Coolidge once said –

> *Nothing in the world can take the place of persistence. Talent will not; nothing is more common than unsuccessful men with talent. Genius will not; unrewarded genius is almost a proverb. Education will not; the world is full of educated derelicts. Persistence*

and   determination   alone   are
omnipotent.

"But the slogan press on," Deacon West preached, "has solved, and always will solve, the problems of mankind. All for one—one for all! God for us all! Yea-eah!" Then we charged out to victory—most of the time. Brer Deek could take this simple pep talk and make me feel like I could run through a brick wall.

The astronaut standing at the podium in his black cap and gown on the platform that was built upon the fountain went on and on, providing nothing memorable to hold on to. I reflected on the recent conversation I had with Maureen. From the recesses of my mind, an old Peter, Paul, and Mary song took over the occasion, and the refrain of the song wouldn't leave my head. Leaving On A Jet Plane. Silently, I hummed the song over and over again, and in a day-dreamy state of mind, it drowned out anything the speaker said. That was graduation day on the second Sunday in the month of May, during the days of the early 70's.

271

Chapter 23
A Charge to Keep … To Serve the Present Age

On the first Saturday in September, the humid, muggy temperature reached the high 80's. The football team had been on campus three weeks and the Marching Band a week before the fall semester started. I had left the game immediately after the half-time show and quietly walked across the center of campus to view a half dozen buildings and landmarks, knowing I might not ever return this way again.

I parked my borrowed car in the parking lot that was close to the middle of campus. At the entrance to the lot stood a small, green-painted, cinder block building with sliding glass counter windows that served as a campus information booth for visitors, and a parking attendant's booth for daily use. When I walked back to the parking lot, I encountered Roland "Big Bird" Trotter, Chief of Campus Security, standing in front of the booth giving instructions to a uniformed security guard.

"Calvin Porch! Man, come over here," he called out. He wore a gray and white pinstriped dress shirt, black necktie, black trousers and shoes. Gone was the classic gray dress hat that he usually wore. Instead he sported the college-colored, maroon baseball-type cap with the "W" logo on the front.

"I'm glad to see you. How you doing?" He seemed genuinely glad to see me.

How could he forget me? Roland had taken a lot of credit for solving that case on 'Who Shot Calvin Porch.' As the case had unfolded, he convinced the cops downtown that the Campus Security force had been on the tail of John "Johnny B. Good" Gooden from the start, which they had; but not for plotting the shooting, but for suspicion of selling marijuana and other drugs. Plus, Roland had a part-time job moonlighting with the police department as a way to get seriously involved with the law enforcement profession.

"I'm doing alright, Roland."

"What are you doing these days? You working yet?"

"Yeah. I've got a teaching job." I didn't mention that it was in West Africa and that I hadn't yet reported to the Peace Corps. He must have assumed it was in Alabama since most of Waukeegan's graduates were from Alabama.

"Good. Good. I always knew you would make something of yourself. Don't forget to come by and see us sometimes when you're on campus."

"I will. So Roland, do you still work part-time with the police department?"

"Oh, yeah, sure. I enjoy police work. It's exciting and it's always a challenge. In fact, I'm taking some law enforcement courses right now. Some day I hope to get into it full time, when the time is right."

"That's good to know," I said. "You never know when you might need the law on your side." I was getting ready to go and then I thought about another thing I wanted to find out. "You know, I didn't see Coach Benson on the field today. Is he still coaching here, or has he moved to another school?"

"Oh, man, I thought you knew. Coach Benson got hurt in a car accident—a head-on collision—about two months ago. Broke his jaw and had both legs amputated."

"I'm sorry to hear that."

"Yeah. He's not paralyzed, or anything. But, he's still in a wheelchair until the healing is complete. They're going to outfit him with some artificial legs in the future, something like the legs of a doll. John Benson is one lucky man to still be alive after all that."

"Where is he now?"

"Oh, he's still living in the house that the college provided him. His wife left him. Took the kids and went back to her hometown. From what I heard, his marriage was on the rocks anyway. He went out, had too much to drink, and decided to call on an old girlfriend—some lady that used to work at the V.A. Hospital.

"She turned him away, and he had the accident less than a quarter of a mile from her house. You might know the street." He told me the exact location. It was just down the street from Belinda Ward's house.

"The noise of the collision was so loud that the woman he went to see heard it and was the one who called for help. When it all boiled down, the wife left him and the girlfriend transferred to another job out of state.

"You ever heard that blues song, 'Nobody Loves Me But My Mother And She Might Be Jiving Me, Too?' Well, his mother moved in temporarily to look after him until he can get on his feet again. What am I talking about? He don't have any more feet? Until he can get himself situated.

"But overall, he's going to be alright. You ought to go see him, Porch. I'm sure he'll be glad to talk to one of his players."

"I think I will. I've got time to go. Yeah, I will."

I had time to visit Coach. I had accomplished two of the three goals I set at the beginning of the day. The first task had been to stay at the game long enough to witness the Music Department's tribute to a deceased friend. The second goal was simply to view for posterity's sake a few buildings and campus landmarks. Last on my list of things to do, was to dispose of that pistol that was tucked away in my car. With those three things out of the way, I could put Waukeegan in the past and move forward with my life.

Coach Benson lived in the area of town near the main road going east off of campus. Going east of campus, I passed the old Mansion to my right and took a right turn on the second street to the right. Two blocks down the oak tree-lined street stood among similar houses, a white, wood-framed house with a high roof and a wrap-around porch with railing running the length on two sides of the house. It was a well-built home from around the turn of the century, the kind made of wood so hard you had to put two coats of paint on it to make it look good.

I greeted Mother Benson. She let me in. I waited in the front room. Straight ahead in line from the center of the house to the right walls, was the dining room, followed by the kitchen. The bedrooms and bathrooms aligned the walls on the left side of the house. Coach Benson wheeled himself out of the second bedroom. He looked the same except for sitting in the wheelchair. The broken jaw was not evident, but I

275

noticed that when Coach said certain words, he talked out of the side of his mouth. To see him sitting in the chair, and not looking at his legs for height, he looked normal. The low-cut Afro hairstyle and neatly trimmed mustache were still in tact.

"Hey, Porch, come on in. Glad to see you, man. How have you been?" He showed a demeanor towards me that I hadn't seen since the time before he found out about my affair with Belinda Ward. Now he was "glad-handing" and cordial. He acted like all was forgotten. Mother Benson left us alone and went into another room.

"Come on back here," Coach Benson motioned to the dining room table. "Can I get you anything?"

"No, thank you. I'm fine."

"Did you go to the game?"

"Yeah, I was there for a while."

"The football team's not doing too well this year, huh? I wish I was able to contribute, but what can you do?" Coach threw his hands up in the air in that coded salute that conveyed—I don't know; what can I say; what can I do?

"I don't know what brought you by, but I'm glad you came."

"I was talking to Roland Trotter and he told me about your accident."

"Oh, this? Don't worry about it. I'm doing fine. I guess he filled you in on all the details."

"Yeah."

"Good. That means I won't have to go into it again. You know, that now seems like it was another time, another life, a phase I went though. I'm not like that anymore. I learned some lessons. I hurt a lot of people—even a tall, skinny baseball player named Calvin Porch."

"Don't worry about it, Coach. I'm alright. Just forget about it."

"I want to apologize to you, son. In my heart of hearts, I know I did you wrong. I kept you in the doghouse. Didn't let you play as much as I should have. Didn't let you get the recognition you deserved."

"It was just a game, Coach. I was hurt by it at the time, but now it's all in the past. I accept your apology."

"Thank you. You showed a lot of character. You hung in there. You took everything I put in front of you. You and I both know you could've folded your tent and walked away, but you stayed on the team. You never spread the news on campus about our dispute over Belinda Ward, when you could've made me look bad if you wanted to.

"You had the decency to keep it just between me and you. I'm not sure I would've done the same thing, had I been in your shoes. You're a better man than I am, Porch. I can't blame you for anything that happened with Belinda. If it hadn't been you, it would've been someone else."

"I'd rather just forget about it, Coach."

"I'm just trying to make amends to the people I've hurt or caused trouble for along the way. You see, I didn't just arrive at this automatically," he confessed. "This whole thing was about using people to advance myself. Using athletes to put me in good standings. Using Belinda Ward to have my cake and eat it, too. Using my estranged wife because she might inherit some property. Running around on my wife with other women.

"But, you know it was the Lord that cut me down to my knees. You know, before the accident, I thought I was a fairly religious guy. But I know now that I was only playing with God, trying to make deals. 'I'll do this, if you do that. You do this for me, and I'll do that for you.' No, no, no, no, no! You can't be making no deals with God!"

It seemed that it was important for him to talk. I thought to myself, "Why is he telling me all of this? What is it leading up to?"

"I've never been too big on testifying," Coach Benson said. "But when I was laying in that hospital bed, in pain, my legs gone, and my jaw broken, I kept asking—Why, Lord? Why me, Lord? Why now? Why not somebody else, Lord? Why me?

"I finally went into a deep sleep. When I woke up, I remembered a voice had whispered an answer to me—'My grace is sufficient for you.' I wasn't sure if I was dreaming or not. I opened my eyes in that dimly lit room, looked around, felt myself, and knew that I was awake.

"Then the voice spoke to me again, 'My grace is sufficient for you. Get up, go home and heal. Then prepare yourself for a greater calling.' So, from that point on, I started to look at myself in a positive light. I've been blessed."

"That's good, Coach. I'm glad to hear that." I was glad to know that he was not bitter or depressed.

"Although my wife has taken the children and gone, there's still a chance we may get back together again. Time will tell. And the college hasn't released me or let me go. So I'll still have a job after I've healed, but it's no guarantee as to what kind of job they'll give me. But that's a blessing in disguise.

"Since they've promised me continued employment, I'm going to take advantage of that benefit and go on a leave of absence. I'm going to Atlanta, Georgia to enter the Seminary to study to make myself approved. I'm going into the ministry. I've been called to preach."

"Man! That's really something, Coach. I never would've thought you would decide to do that. But I can see why you would."

"It wasn't my decision. God decided for me. I know it's not going to be easy. It's going to be hard sometimes. But while I'm recovering, I'm going to relax and get strong. I'll get some artificial legs, eventually. If I don't, that'll be alright, too.

"Right now, I'm just going to relax and take it easy, like you do on a Sunday morning, when you got no worries and no cares. Just take it easy—easy like Sunday morning."

My baseball coach sitting in the wheelchair with gray pants legs folded on the area above the knees of the amputated legs was a man under the age of thirty, and he talked like a man older and wiser than he was before. When I told him of my upcoming job in the Peace Corps, he had nothing but praise for me, saying that I had made a true independent decision and was willing to take a challenge. "I hope my coaching had some influence upon you."

"It did."

When I got up to leave, he reminded me: "Live right in the beginning, son. That way you won't have to worry about something happening to you later on."

"I'll do my best." I gave the Coach a final handshake and said goodbye.

Chapter 24
Easy Like Sunday Morning

The road out of town to the Interstate Highway had been one that I traveled many times before. Most memorable was that gloomy day I rode with Neville and Adelaide over to County General Hospital to see Bakarie. There was a small airfield and three hangars on the right side of the road, a motel on the left, and just before I approached the entry lane to the Interstate Highway, I saw two gas stations—one on the right and one on the left side of the road.

These buildings seemed to mark the time in history, to recall to memory the time of day, mood and state of mind we were in that day. We had few words to say to one another that day, as we passed this place. It was only the view out of the windows of the car that had provided me with a moment of distraction.

Now, today on my way out of town, I parked the borrowed car in a vacant lot in front of a vacant building next to the gas station on the right. A footpath led between the two buildings through a thicket of green trees and overgrowth to a river bank less than sixty yards away. The ground along the riverbank had been cleared by local citizens who liked to fish from the banks. With high school and college football games underway this weekend, not many fishermen were on the river.

I'd planned how I would conceal the pistol. Before I left town, I purchased a hamburger, French fries, and a soft drink at a fast food restaurant. I asked the cashier to give me a larger bag for my order. Then I waited until I was down at the river before I ate any of the food. The wonders of a brown paper sack. Inside the bag, I positioned the unloaded gun with the barrel pointing up to the open end of the bag. The French fries and the hamburger remained in the bag, too.

Down by the river, I'd nibble on the French fries until I was out of sight of any bystanders. Then I'd hurl the gun into the river and that would be it. I thought about returning the gun to its rightful owner, but felt it was better to do it this way out of respect for the dead.

I came upon an elderly man, who wore a green baseball-type Army fatigue cap, a gray-and-white plaid shirt, khaki pants, and Army boots. "The man was probably an Army veteran like my dad," I said to myself. Beside the man were a boy and girl in jeans, T-shirts and tennis shoes. They were twins, nine or ten years old.

I greeted the man, "How's the fishing? Are they biting today?"

"Aw-naw, they ain't doing nothing. Just a nibble every now and then."

"Look, Granddaddy. Corretta's got her line tied up in a limb," the boy said.

"I can't get it loose, Granddaddy."

"Hold on now," Granddaddy advised the girl. "Looks like we gone have to break the line to save the pole. Here, let me take it."

"She don't know how to fish anyhow," the boy said.

"I do, too," Corretta said.

"Y'all just calm down. Correy, here, take my keys. I want you to run back up to the car, look in the trunk, and bring the extra fishing line back with you. You'll see it on a spool just as you open the trunk. I don't know why I didn't bring it down here in the first place. Now loan your sister your pole while you're gone."

"You better not mess mine up," Correy warned his sister.

"I'm not going to mess up your little old fishing pole."

I walked around a curve along the riverbank until a thicket of trees separated me from Granddaddy and the twins. There was no one in sight. The river was not a wide river, perhaps only forty yards across from one side to the other. A dark, algae green body of water, it flowed slow and steady. An occasional island of stone jutted out of the water, that parted the water in splashes and rippling waves in a dozen or so places.

I looked out into the river as if I was addressing a headstone in a cemetery. Well, here we are, Junior," I said in a low voice. "I missed the funeral, but the Marching Band gave you a good send-off today. They even played one of your favorite songs. They gave tribute to you for being their half-time announcer last Fall.

"Incidentally, I didn't know they called you Junior at home. You know how it is with nicknames, hobbies, and favorite songs? Sometimes you only learn these things about someone when they're gone.

"I was really hoping that one day you'd really make it, but that didn't happen. You almost made it though. So, now I'm going to throw this gun out into the river, and give you a salute, a good salute like they taught us in ROTC class our freshman year. I was going to return it to the "rightful owner"—your dad— but I'm doing this in tribute to you."

I hurled the gun far out into the water, and gave a military salute. "See you later Junior, Mr. Bo Jangles, Dr. C. J. Nightingale, my brother—Charles Jordan."

I sighed. A moment of relief came across my chest. I knew this was the last ritual required to put the Waukeegan experience behind me. I turned to leave and saw Correy, the little boy, facing me from the clearing near the trees by the curve along the riverbank. The boy turned and ran. I wondered how much of this did he see. Anyway, it's all done now.

The demise of Charles Jordan. It was Leonardo who finally got in touch with me in time for the tribute. When it all happened in the middle of August, I had been out of town visiting relatives when Leonardo tried to reach me for the funeral. He had gone to summer school. His girlfriend, Brenda, was working at her desk in Sister DuMaine's office when the call came in. A Catholic priest named Father Giacomelli managed an International Student Hostel in New Orleans, Louisiana. He found a Waukeegan I.D. card among Charles' possessions, when the police came by. A previous acquaintance of Sister DuMaine from the past, the priest promptly called and informed her that a Waukeegan student had died.

Charles had been mugged and killed near a wharf in a warehouse district in uptown New Orleans in a place, where after dark, local thugs lay in wait to rob Merchant Seamen. He had simply gone for a walk in the wrong neighborhood. A few people on campus heard the news even before Charles' own family heard it.

To get to my car from the riverbank, I had to pass by the old fisherman and his grandchildren. I would play it cool, since the boy had seen me throw the gun away. I still had the brown paper bag with me. The only thing in it now was the soft drink cup and lid and the paper wrapping from the sandwich and French fries. I spoke to the man again, "Any luck? Caught anything yet?"

"Oh, yeah. We got a few. Looks like my granddaughter's doing better than the rest of us."

"Granddaddy, that man threw a gun in the river," Correy said. "I saw him."

"Aw, child, come on. Don't worry about it. Let' get back to fishing. Whatever it was, it was his own business. We came here to fish. If you don't get busy, me and your sister gone catch them all."

"That's right," Corretta said.

"Uh-uh, no you're not. I'm going to catch some, too." The boy dropped the issue of what he saw and pursued the challenge of outdoing his sister.

"These kids nowadays," the elderly fisherman declared. "You got to spend time with them to teach them about life—when to talk, when to listen, when to be quiet, when to take it easy."

"I see what you mean."

"You look like a smart fellow. Tell me why you think I'm out here? Certainly not for the fish."

"To spend time with your grandchildren."

"I'm just here to teach them that life is simple. Enjoy the simple things in life. The best things in life are free. You have to learn how to take it easy, you know—easy like Sunday morning."

"Maybe that's what I need to do."

"It couldn't hurt you."

"I'll see you later. Y'all take it easy."

285

"See? Now you're learning," the fisherman said. "That's what I'm talking 'bout. Take it easy—easy like Sunday morning."

I got in my car, drove northeast on the Interstate Highway, where tall pine trees stood in the median space between the oncoming and outgoing lanes, and along the sides of the expressway beyond the shoulders of the pavement. I heard that "saying" twice today about taking it easy—once from Coach Benson and then again from the fisherman. Was there something to it? I was sure I would try it sometimes. I was going to a place where I heard that things were slow. I would have plenty of time to take it easy there.

About the Author

Alfred Brady Moore is a native of Phenix City, Alabama. After he graduated from Tuskegee University, he joined the Peace Corps and served as a teacher in West Africa.

Al once held a job at a small town newspaper. He also completed a correspondence course in creative writing. *Goodbye to Yesterday* is his first novel. An earlier draft of the manuscript was evaluated at the Harriette Austin Writer's Conference in Athens, GA.

Al lives in an Atlanta suburb with his wife, Connie. They have three children and are grandparents.

You can write to him at P.O. Box 2455, Stone Mountain, GA., 30086 or email.

ABTMoore@msn.com.

Printed in the United States
1138600001B/49-51